I0825344

Human World
Avall
Fearnan Ogh

First Published January 2015
Paperback ISBN: 978-0-9875635-6-9
Hardcover ISBN: 978-0-6487080-8-7

THE MEMORY'S WAKE TRILOGY

Book One - Memory's Wake

Book Two - Hope's Reign

Book Three - Providence Unveiled

www.memoryswake.com

PROVIDENCE UNVEILED

SELINA A FENECH

CHAPTER ONE

Memory laughed a strong, high-pitched laugh that made her sides ache. The surrounding cloud of dust was chalky on her tongue and the last small pieces of falling tiles and roof shingles clattered onto the debris that surrounded her and her friends. Eloryn, Roen, and Clara sat sprawled where they had tumbled out of the tower that had collapsed around them. Will was right beside Memory, close enough for her to feel his warmth and hear him still panting from their wild escape. They were all powdered with dirt, but safe and mostly uninjured. Memory was sure one of her fingers was broken. Everything was such a blur, she wasn't sure if it happened during the tower collapse, or earlier when she and Will hit the mattresses after their fall. But

she was grateful for it. Grateful that was all they'd suffered, and that she was still alive. Will held her other hand.

Memory couldn't stop laughing.

Eloryn sighed. "It's not a joke. You are now the Queen of Avall."

Memory paused long enough to take a breath. "That's even funnier," she wheezed, and started laughing again. "I thought I was the crazy, irresponsible one, and then you go and make me queen!"

Memory wiped tears from her bottom eyelids and tried to breathe between her giggling. It didn't help. Trying to stop only made it worse and her whole body shook with uncontained laughter.

Roen grinned roguishly. "I have to admit, it is rather funny."

A chuckle burst from Eloryn as though she had been holding it in and was no longer able to contain it.

Small at first, her laughter built until it matched Memory's. She moved forward and wrapped her sister in a tight hug. Memory put one arm around her, the other hand still entwined with Will's.

They laughed together there in each other's arms, and Memory whispered, "What the hell happened? I'm really queen? What am I going to do?"

Eloryn whispered back, "You'll manage. You'll be great. I know you can do this."

"I'll try."

"I'll be there for you. Anything you need, anything I can do. You're my sister, and I love you."

Memory pressed her face into her twin's shoulder. "Can you fix my busted finger?"

"Of course." Eloryn tightened her hug. "I like your new hair color."

"Want me to do yours? You'd rock a fading pink."

Eloryn kissed Memory on the cheek. "Don't ever leave me."

They separated and stood up, smiling at each other. Will, Roen and Clara also stood by Memory, holding her hands and her shoulders, supporting her.

My family.

Memory still felt shaky and overwhelmed. In the last fifteen minutes of her life she'd tried to kill herself, had someone else try to kill her friends, then had everyone almost all die again from the fall of the destroyed tower. Her emotions were so high strung and confused she could barely think. She drew deep breaths, letting herself accept the support of her friends, accept that they were there for her now, and for whatever lay ahead.

I will manage. I will be great. For them.

Shocked servants and guards appeared at the end of the hall, gawking at the destruction. The entire north wing tower was now a pile of rubble, and the wall it had been attached to was all but gone, opening the corridor to the cold winds of night outside.

Memory felt guilty for having a part in knocking down one of the palace's towers. Not a great move for her first day as queen.

Acknowledging the arriving servants, Clara said, "I'll inform the staff to begin organizing the cleanup and bring help."

"Thank you. I think we're all okay though. Just make sure no one was injured outside," Memory said.

Clara nodded and took a step away, then with a puppy dog expression, turned back and gave Memory a firm hug. Then she hurried down the hall to speak with the other staff.

Roen moved in next and held Memory.

Memory giggled at the tag team. "I'm okay, really. Only current risk is being cuddled to death."

Roen let go and looked insulted. "Do I need a near death experience to embrace you now? Being queen is already going to your head."

Memory laughed again, then stopped abruptly. "Hang on. I'm the queen. That means Hope got what she-"

Swirling winds and gray smoke filled the room, interrupting Memory. Sparks of gold swam within the Veil mist like fireflies as it opened up in a round portal. The sound of distant rain dripping on bells came with a flood of warmth, and a crowd stood before them.

A crowd of fae royalty. The Seelie Queen, Aine, and her human consort Lugh were flanked by a dozen fairy knights. Each guard wore armor of woven silver with embedded mother of pearl and held a fairy gold spear twice his or her height. Behind the unearthly beauty of the queen and her companion, stood a group of sprites, including Mina, and Yvainne, the princess of the sprites with whom Eloryn had once made a bargain. Standing all together, the sheer beauty of them made tears well up in Memory's eyes. Pearlescent skin was contrasted with tangles of silky hair and the pretty tatters of their cobweb and feather dresses. Aine's dress was more whole, full of draping translucent folds that teased at the shape of her body, leading a viewer's eyes up to her face. Her long auburn hair that Memory had once seen trail on the ground behind her was bundled into a tall and intricately woven mass atop her head, stuck through with glass flowers and silver twigs. Her skin had a warm shimmer, like

diamonds drenched in honey, but her expression was far from warm.

Aine's gaze swept across the rubble and settled on Memory's face. Her lips were stretched thin and eyebrows lowered. "So, the fickle humans have changed their ruler yet again."

Memory looked to Eloryn, who gave her an encouraging nod in return.

Memory lifted her chin. *Time to start being queen.* She curtseyed to Aine. "I only just found out myself. News travels fast."

"We have watchers for anything we consider important, or dangerous."

Yvainne and Mina stood proudly behind their queen. *They've still been keeping tabs on me after all.* Memory wondered just how much she'd been watched, and what they might know. Mina stared Memory down with her usual glare. With the malicious creature Hope now confirmed as being a fae, standing in front of this group of them made Memory's paranoia tie itself in anxious knots. *Hope could be Mina, or Yvainne, or Aine. Any of them.*

Memory calmed the shiver chasing up her spine and curtseyed a second time for good measure, then pointed with her thumb at the ruined building around them. "Your Majesty, you can probably see that this isn't the best time for a chat. Can we do the ruler meet and greet a bit later on if there's no urgent issue?"

Aine's eyes narrowed. "We take issue with you."

Mist from the torn Veil spilled into the corridor again, and a second group emerged from it. A raspy male voice hissed, "As do we."

The Unseelie King, Finvarra, and his daughter Nyneve became clear as the smoke faded, their own darkly armored guards following.

Memory noticed down the hallway a troop of palace guards led by Peirs rushing to the scene, and held up a hand to halt them. She turned back to the newly arrived fae royalty with what she hoped was a brave face.

Nyneve wore her usual shades of mourning, her hair even blacker, impossibly black, not a highlight showing in the nebulous masses swirling around her silver skin. Her father's gnarled body was clothed in a maroon color darker than night. Between them they presented a front of imposing darkness. Nyneve stood a step behind her father, head bowed slightly, as the black eyed king growled at Aine like a feral dog. "Trying to slip in and make decisions without us? We must have our say as well."

Memory cleared her throat. "Inside voices, please. I'd already noticed that the fae aren't very keen on me. You guys have always known I'm full up on magic. What's changed?"

Aine said, "Now you are monarch of the humans. We can't allow such power to be in the hands of a ruler. There must be restrictions."

Restrictions? Memory shook her head. "You let Thayl go about his business."

"You compare a candle to a forest fire," Aine said.

Finvarra's needle-like teeth ground against each other, scraping like chalk on a blackboard. "She's unnatural, stealing away the life of the earth, hoarding it within her. Restrictions aren't enough. She should not be allowed to be queen. She should not be allowed to exist."

By her side, Will took a step forward, and Memory matched him, blocking his way. She said, "*She* is right here and doesn't appreciate threats to her existence. I am queen and you should treat me with some respect."

Nyneve raised a silver hand and put it on her father's shoulder. It seemed to calm him and he muttered what might have been an apology.

"Whatever magic is inside me, it's not there by my choice." Memory knew it had been given to her by Providence, whom she was sure was a fae. But now didn't seem the best time to be making wild accusations. There were still too many questions. *If I'm going to be queen, I need to be smarter, better. I need some answers first.* "There's not much I can do about it. It's in me now, part of me, for better or worse."

Aine tilted her head in a supplicating motion, but the slight sneer on her lips made the motion a lie. "We ask that you give an oath never to use your stolen magic again. For the safety of our worlds."

Eloryn spoke up. "Is that really necessary? Never before has a human ruler had such a restriction placed on them."

Nyneve added her voice, deep and concerned. "It does seem a great imposition."

"Never before has there been a human like her. We won't accept her as queen without it," Aine said. "Agreed, Winter King?"

Finvarra grumbled. Memory could see Nyneve's hand squeeze his shoulder.

"Father, no," she whispered.

Finvarra shook her hand from him. "No? It is barely enough as it is. It is agreed, this girl should use none of her stolen power."

Never use magic again? Memory wondered if that was even possible. One emotional slip up could change everything. She was more in control now but the risk was there. It would also mean she'd be stuck with purple hair for good, unless Eloryn could behest hair color as well. She whispered to Eloryn beside her, "Out of curiosity, what's the penalty for breaking a fairy oath?"

Eloryn replied in hushed tones, "Tantamount to a violation of the Pact, punishable by Branding and death."

"Serious like a pinky promise. Gotcha."

Memory addressed Aine and Finvarra again. "What if I don't agree? What if I think you should trust me to rule fairly despite the magic inside me?"

"Just as we trusted your double to rule?" Aine walked up to Eloryn and stared down at her from at least three feet taller. "Maellan girl, we requested that you be the human ruler. We wanted you, not your volatile sister. You made an oath to rule with the sprite princess, Yvainne. You may not have technically broken your oath, as you did rule - briefly, barely - but we will be less inclined to trust you or your twin to persevere in her promises now."

Eloryn looked at her feet. "I'm sorry, Your Majesty. I did not intend to dishonor my oath."

"And yet you did, the moment ruling became difficult for you."

Something changed in Eloryn's expression. "Had I not ended my rule then, you may have found a new human ruler that would please you far less than my sister."

Aine turned her back and walked away, striding around the room. "You mortal creatures with your in-fighting displease us. We want stability for Avall, for all our peoples."

Finvarra spat into the debris. "Don't pretend you have a care

for our kind. You prefer the human vermin over the unseelie fae, when we are your other halves, the dark to your light. We are your balance. You don't care that they treat us as monsters. You would not care if we were hunted clean from the world, when it is those parasites that should be removed!" He clawed a hand through the air toward Memory and her friends.

Aine rolled her eyes at his dramatics and addressed Memory. "Agreeing to the oath offers us some stability. A show of faith to allow our peoples to work together. Denying it can only lead to chaos for all."

Finvarra grinned and his all black eyes twinkled. "We welcome chaos. We are born of chaos."

"All right, enough! I'll make your oath," Memory said. "I agree. It *is* time for the fighting to stop. Between all of us."

"Mem, are you sure?" Eloryn said.

Memory looked to her friends, and found them all staring back at her. She nodded to Roen and Will. "It's not so bad. Some of the best people I know don't use magic."

Aine smiled and the simple expression seemed to light her from inside. "Then we make the oath. You shall not use the magic within you again from this moment forth."

"Not quite. I don't always have complete control over all this," Memory said, swirling a pointing finger at her chest. "I can't be held accountable if a bit spills out here or there against my will. But I do swear I will not knowingly cast any behests with my magic."

Aine paused, assessing her, and then placed a hand over Memory's heart. "Agreed. This is our binding deal."

All the fae around her chanted, "The deal is binding."

Finvarra's ragged lips curled around his teeth. "And when

you break this deal, I will relish enforcing the penalty."

Aine stared him down. "You will take no action. My hand bound the deal, my hand will enforce the penalty when the deal is broken."

"Guys. It's *if*. *If* the deal is broken. A little confidence, please." Memory tried not to feel shaken. She had as little confidence in her ability to keep the oath as they did. *Girls with impulse control issues shouldn't be agreeing to binding oaths.*

Aine simply nodded, and the creeping mist in the corridor began to build again. Mina, who had been giving Memory all kinds of filthy looks, turned to Will and flicked her chin up. Will looked toward Memory, unsure.

When Will didn't leave Memory's side, Mina stamped a foot on the ground. "Here, boy. Now."

Aine and Lugh, Finvarra and Nyneve, and the host of seelie and unseelie guards all turned their attention to Will, and Memory could see a defiant look in his eyes. He took a step forward and something tugged Memory's arm.

Will's hand was still around hers. It had never left it, not since they'd escaped the tower, as though they'd been fused together. He turned back to look at her, frowning deeply.

"It's okay. Go. You know where to find me," she said, offering him a supportive smile. Memory didn't like the idea of Will going anywhere with Mina. She didn't like the idea of letting go of his hand. But she could tell he needed to go. No matter how Memory felt about Mina, it was clear Will didn't want to make a scene in front of fairy royalty.

Will's hand slipped slowly from hers, fingertips trailing along her palm. Memory put her hand into her other one, so it didn't feel so empty.

Will stood beside Mina, and the seelie fae faded into the Veil, taking him with them. Finvarra turned his back on Memory and was simply gone. Nyneve gave Memory a sympathetic nod before following her father.

Memory waved goodbye to the empty space. "Good talk. No, no, thank *you*."

Eloryn and Roen remained with her.

Memory smiled at them wryly. "Onwards to our next crisis?"

CHAPTER TWO

"You did? And then he did that? Really? Wow. Just, wow."

Eloryn filled Memory in about the reason for her abdication while they rushed back toward the Round Room. She covered the horrible things Hayes had done, and saw something dark cross Memory's features when she explained it was Hayes who set off the bomb that killed Waylan, and sent the bounty hunters after Roen, all as part of his long campaign of manipulation.

"Hayes is all locked up, right? Lucky bastard. He'll be safer there." Memory scowled.

The forced marriage, and Eloryn's contract to ruin Hayes's plans came next. "Abdicating was the best solution I could see. It passed power to you, including power over Hayes's militia

thanks to the pre-nuptial contract, and stripped all power and options from him."

Eloryn glanced at Roen, walking on the other side of Memory. She wanted to reach out and touch him. She knew, regardless of Hayes, she would have given up her throne for Roen. Her heart was not in ruling. Her heart was his. Her lips still tingled from their kiss. It felt like weeks ago, but her confrontation with Hayes had happened barely half an hour before. They were already encountering the aftermath of her abdication as they walked. Pages and guards ran about, spreading the news, dealing with the changes to rulership in the palace. Between that and the collapsed tower, the castle was a chaotic hum of activity.

"Hayes really was one skeezy bastard." Memory put a hand on Eloryn's shoulder. "Can I get away with an I Told You So? Just a teeny one?"

"I think you could get away with a quite large one," Eloryn said.

Memory grinned. "Nah, I'll skip it. Sounds like you kicked his ass. I wish I'd been there to see it. And join in the kicking of said ass."

The Round Room came within sight, and was still filled with the remaining Wizards' Council, milling about, shouting at each other and arguing.

Memory slowed her pace. "We can't let them know I'm not allowed to use magic anymore. We can't let anyone know. It could be exploited too easily."

Roen nodded. "It's a secret worth keeping."

"Have your parents left yet? Can you go and check? Bring them back if you have to. And can you send after Erec and Peirs,

too?" Memory asked him.

"Of course," Roen said. His gaze turned to meet Eloryn's and his lips curled into a tiny smile. She blushed, remembering what the curves of those lips felt like pressed against hers. With a nod, he hurried off back the way they'd come.

Memory stared at Eloryn with a toothy grin.

"What? Stop that. You're being dreadfully creepy," Eloryn said.

Memory tilted her head down, making her grin even more lecherous. "You and Roen, huh?"

"Me and Roen?" The innocent tone Eloryn aimed for was spoiled by a catch in her voice.

"She plays it coy! There's no fooling me, I saw you guys all smoochy before. It's about bloody time. I'm so happy for you both." Memory grabbed Eloryn in a quick hug.

Eloryn let out a deep breath and closed her eyes. Part of her had been worried about what Memory would think and feel about her relationship with Roen, that it would somehow hurt Memory. But her sister seemed truly happy, and that filled Eloryn with warmth.

Memory pulled back and looked down the hall at the room of squabbling old men. "Okay, it's wizard wrangling time."

Memory continued into the Round Room and Eloryn walked at her side. Returning to face these men felt surreal after she'd just abandoned her title and destroyed the plans and credibility of their leader in front of them all. But she had to be there for Memory.

The two of them made their entrance.

Their arrival was barely noticed by the wizards. Their discussions were heated, and the small statures of the twins were lost in the room full of men.

"Shame I don't have a cattle prod on me. Could be handy right now," Memory muttered. She took Eloryn's hand for balance then climbed up onto a chair then up again onto the long table in the center of the room. She put her finger and thumb between her lips and let loose a piercing whistle. The Council silenced and all attention turned to her, skepticism clear on all faces.

"My sister tells me she's abdicated," Memory said. Her voice started out rocky, but grew in strength as she continued. "And now I have to stand in front of all of you and make you somehow believe in me as a leader. That's going to be hard, because I don't even believe in myself as a leader. And from what I've heard of Hayes's actions, I imagine you'll be struggling to have faith in any leader right now."

A grumble of agreement came from a few of the gray-haired men.

"But someone needs to rule this land and make things right. We owe it to the people to get our acts together and stop seeking revenge or grabbing for power or generally squabbling like idiots. I'm just a kid; I haven't been trained for this, not enough. One day I hope I can be the ruler Avall deserves, but right now I need all of you to step up. I need you all to do your job, and I want to be able to trust you to do it. But I'm not going to trust you blindly. I will be watching you all closely and if you intend to betray my trust, remember this- were you scared of Thayl? Well, he stole his magic from me, and only ever had a fraction of my power. Be scared of *me*."

Silence filled the room as Memory let those words sink in. "And if that's not enough, I think you also know what my

sister is capable of. What do you all say? Are you ready to work together, work with me, to start making things right?"

Eloryn smiled up at her sister, filled with pride. Memory spoke forcefully, passionately, and without pretense. Memory was everything she was not when it came to ruling. *I made the right decision.*

"What are we to do?" Bors asked, more to the men around him than to Memory. He still seemed panicked by nearly meeting death at Hayes's behest. "Hayes went too far, too far, but he was our leader."

"We did not always have a leader." Madoc, the oldest of the Council, pushed his way to the front. His raspy voice made the white whiskers around his mouth quiver. "The Council is meant to be a body of equals. It was only during Thayl's rule that Hayes took control of us. We don't need a leader."

"You have to admit, having someone with overriding authority did expedite many decisions," a wizard behind Eloryn said.

She turned to face the crowd. "And where did that blind faith in him lead us? He even killed one of your own for challenging his authority."

Memory addressed the group again from her position on the table. "Whether or not you want a leader for the Council, and who that leader is, can be something you decide for yourselves. But for now, Bedevere will be the point of contact between me and the Council."

Bedevere, who had remained quiet through the bickering, nodded solemnly to Memory. The rest of the Council exploded again into turmoil. "Him? With his foolish notions of the other world and its artefacts?"

Memory's mouth set firmly and she raised her voice. "I've got my memories back now and can tell you his *notions* of the other world are correct. It did not become Hell."

Her statement only fueled the voices in the room, and wizards argued, demanding more information, or disputing her claims.

"All you know how to do is argue!" Memory grunted. "You've all been hidden away from the world too long. Consider this my first order for you all. It's time you did some real work in the real world." Memory waved her arms, pointing out wizards and sectioning off groups. "I need men to head to the city, to reopen my shelter and fix any damage Hayes's militia might have done. The militia itself needs bringing under control and there's also the matter of clearing up a tower that collapsed in the Northern wing. There is work to be done now. Prove yourselves as the great wizards I know you must be."

The crowd grew quiet. Madoc moved to the front, bowed to Memory and said, "Yes, Your Majesty."

By his side, Lambeth and Bors did the same. Soon the whole Council followed, bowing, then leaving to carry out their assigned tasks. Bedevere stepped in front of Memory and bowed low for a long moment.

"Bedevere, stay with me, please. We've got more to do," she said.

Eloryn reached up for her sister's hand and helped her down from the table. Memory's hand shook violently between Eloryn's fingers.

Memory's bottom lip pulled to the side and her eyebrows wrinkled. "Did I do okay?"

"Better than okay," Eloryn said.

"Ugh, that was hard! I put on my best grown up voice but felt like I just sounded ridonkadonk. They're going to think I'm an idiot."

Ridonkadonk? Eloryn smiled inwardly. Her sister often surprised her with strange new words. Eloryn saw the uncertainty in her sister, but only grew more confident that Memory was the natural ruler she never was. "The message will come through regardless of the words you use. Just be yourself, be sincere and open, as you always are, and people will respect you."

Memory seemed about to say something more, but was interrupted by Isabeth.

"Oh my dears, my dears!" she cried, as she rushed toward Memory and Eloryn with her arms outstretched. She gathered them both into an embrace, then looked over their damaged and dusty appearance with a scolding gaze. "Can't leave you two alone for a moment, can we?"

Roen and his father followed her in. Roen seemed out of breath and a flush of red highlighted his cheekbones that made him all the more beautiful. He smiled. "Duke and Duchess Faerbaird, as requested."

As Memory greeted them properly, Eloryn stepped across to Roen and took his hand. He gave her a small questioning look, and she smiled back in return.

It only took a moment before Isabeth, and then Brannon, noticed the pair. Isabeth put both hands to her mouth as though she were about to cry, then grabbed her son and Eloryn into her arms.

Memory sighed and put her fists on her hips. "Here I am, queen now, and look at my sister still hogging all the attention."

CHAPTER THREE

Memory stared at the group before her. People she trusted. Memory and Eloryn caught everyone up on what had happened with Hayes while they waited for Erec and Peirs to arrive, and for Bedevere to create a Veil door to bring Lanval in. Memory already regretted giving up her magic. The traditional Veil door behest was pages long, and Bedevere's droning of the words quickly became tedious when Memory knew how fast she could open one.

She turned her back on his progress so she could address the others. They had seated themselves along the temporary table in the Round Room and all faced her where she stood. She cleared her throat. "The very first thing we need to do is establish some proper leadership in Avall, the government Hayes neglected to set up. I know I'm queen and Maellan blood and whatever, but I'm only seventeen for chrissakes. It's time for some adults to be doing the adult things. But how am I supposed to choose who makes up that government? Who do I trust? As Lory pointed out, I don't know one Avall noble from another. But you do," Memory said, acknowledging Isabeth and Brannon. "Between you and Lanval, you know the bloodlines, the individuals, the who, what and where. I trust you to make the right decisions. Bedevere will have the Council start Veil-dooring people in ASAP, nobles from each region, heck, even non-nobles as far as I'm concerned as long as they can do the job. I'm so sorry to hold you back from returning to your home, but could you do this for me?"

Isabeth looked to her husband. "We will do our best, although you know we've been removed from politics for many years. Still, in just the short time we've returned to court, it has been very easy to judge the character of those around us based on how they treat our return. Lanval has been well connected both within Thayl's circles and without, and will be valuable indeed in making these decisions. You are right to ask for him."

Memory nodded firmly and smiled at Erec and Peirs who waited at the entrance. She waved them in.

Peirs had a sly half grin on his face, stretching the sandy freckled skin, as he kneeled in front of Memory. "Your Majesty. The position suits you well. As does the new hair color."

"Quit it." Memory swung a foot playfully at him. "Can I make a no kneeling rule?"

Peirs remained kneeling and became solemn. "You are worth kneeling for even if it means breaking the rules. You will be a fine queen."

A swell of pride and worry clogged Memory's throat. She had so much to live up to. "Just a title so far. Speaking of titles, I want you back as captain of the guard. I need you, Erec, and the people you trust out there removing Hayes's loyalists from positions of power in the military. Right away, please. We need everyone to know things have changed before any more damage is done."

Peirs stood and he and his brother bowed and turned to leave. Memory grabbed him by the arm. "Any news of Maeve and the kids? How are they doing?"

Peirs shook his head. "I lost contact with them when they were found by the militia and forced to move again."

Memory frowned, but patted Peirs on the shoulder and let him leave. She turned back to the others. Beside her on the table was a small tray of her favorite foods. Memory knew they were from Clara, but hadn't even noticed her come in and leave them there. Her stomach grumbled. She smiled inside at how Clara mothered her and predicted her needs. Bedevere continued to read his behest and Isabeth and Brannon were already writing notes on who they wanted to see as candidates for the government.

Eloryn had a pained look on her face. "There's one more thing we will be required to do."

"What?" Memory asked. Her brain was starting to get fuzzy. She was too tired and had already put so much effort into trying to do things right and get everything under control. What had she missed?

"There will need to be a public announcement about the change in rule."

Memory winced. "But do we really have to? There's enough confusion and disrespect going around because of our age and how we came back, and now we go and play swapsies for who is queen. Can't we just, you know?" Memory mimed picking up a mat and sweeping under it. "I'll just pretend like I'm you and nothing has changed. No one will have to know, right?"

Eloryn fought a smile. "I somehow think people would notice, even if we change your hair again. There will be no harm from this announcement. The people of Avall love you. You are their hero. When they think of me, they think only of my connection to Hayes and everything he did. When they think of you they think of the person who defeated Thayl, who has shown such courage, compassion and ingenuity in helping the homeless and fighting for equality."

Memory groaned. "Fine. Okay. I'll make an announcement. Just enough with the compliments. And I'm not all that popular. I haven't been making any friends amongst the noble crowd with my efforts."

Roen leaned back in his chair and shrugged. "Some of your efforts challenge their traditions. But a tradition is only that until you don't do it anymore. People will learn, and grow, and it will be for the better."

The full impact of being who she was started settling on Memory. She had that power now, to make great changes to this world. She desperately wanted to use that power well, and realized how many plans and dreams she had to improve the land for the people she now ruled. A smile spread slowly on her lips. "Maybe it is time to break some traditions."

A faint glow of morning light had begun to show through the glass ceiling of the Round Room by the time Memory had

reestablished enough stability to leave affairs in her advisors' hands.

Eloryn and Roen walked Memory back to her room, arms linked and shuffling along together. Clara had returned as well. Memory wasn't sure when. She blinked often, trying to keep her eyes open. Exhaustion had set in, aching in her temples and burning her muscles where adrenaline had been keeping her going since the tower collapse. Since she'd tried to take her own life. It all seemed like a distant dream.

Memory wanted to go to the Ivy Room, or what was left of it, to try and find Will, to see if he'd come back yet.

When she explained where she wanted to go, Eloryn just shook her head.

"He will come to you when he can," she said.

Will he? Memory still wasn't sure what their relationship was, or of how Will felt about her. He'd said he loved her, loved her so much he chased her off a balcony. *How could he? How could anyone love me that much?* Doubt settled like an uneasy sickness in her, its voice sounding like the voice of Hope. Not just the dark manipulations of the creature that had pretended to be her, but the voice of her past self, a self that was now part of her again. With her memories returned, Memory knew she used to be the kind of person who had no love for herself, and no concept that anyone could love her. Even she could see how much she had changed since coming to Avall, but the old, painful feelings remained. She was too tired then to process the discord of her past memories conflicting with her new identity. It wasn't long ago that her affection for herself was so low she'd almost ended her life, but the spark of life remained, and she could feel it now wanting to grow. She didn't want to doubt any more that anyone could love her. She wanted to allow herself to be loved and accept that she could be loved.

Memory's heart rushed and she bit her lip hard at the thought that overwhelmed her. *I don't just want anyone to love me. I want Will to love me.*

Eloryn and Roen had escorted Memory all the way to her bedroom before she blinked her vision clear again and saw where she was. Clara turned the bed down for her, fluffing the pillows more than a few times each as though she'd become stuck in some sort of loop.

Memory shook her head and her vision and speech blurred. "Can't sleep yet. Still have talking about to do, about Provi-Hope."

Roen locked Memory's bedroom bi-fold doors into their fully open position. Yawning, he undid his top shirt button and slumped down into an armchair in the adjoining sitting room. "You can't even talk straight anymore. You need to rest. Don't you think we've done enough for one day?"

Eloryn picked up a purple velvet cushion from the lounge and curled up in an armchair beside Roen's, cuddling the cushion under her chin like a teddy bear. "We'll be right here."

Memory was about to tell them to go back to their rooms and sleep themselves, but knew exactly why her friends were here, and why they weren't giving her any privacy.

I tried to kill myself. The thought now felt surreal to Memory. She ached when wondering how it made her friends feel, to have almost lost her that way.

She smiled at how protective they were. If they weren't a reason to keep living, she didn't know what was. So many of the negative thoughts she'd been having had been whispered to her by Hope, and now she knew that Hope was just an imposter, everything seemed different, and better. Sunrise had broken fully and the new day looked glorious through Memory's bedroom window. She kept smiling as her head hit the pillow and she instantly passed out.

When her eyelids rolled open again it was still daylight. Memory felt disoriented, with no idea how much time had passed. She was groggy, and so hungry it could have been a week later. At the end of her bed, Will sat cross-legged, staring through the diamond glass of the closed balcony windows.

He came back. Memory's heart back-flipped.

Will had found a shirt somewhere, warm grey with a wide poet's collar, but his feet were still bare. Memory moved to sit up and he turned to her. His eyebrows were low over his light blue eyes, his dark hair a wild mess the way she liked it.

He put a finger to his lips. Memory looked behind him. The doors between her bedroom and sitting room were still open, and she saw Roen and Eloryn, heads bowed, both fast asleep in their chairs.

"As much as I feel like I did, I'm guessing I haven't slept for a century. What time is it? What day is it?" Memory whispered. She sat up on her pillow, leaning against the headboard while she stretched her arms up and arched her back.

"Afternoon. Same day." Will's voice was also hushed. Even in a murmur it was a beautiful voice, always deep and strong, reminding Memory of how he used to sing when he was a boy. With all her past returned to her, the man that sat in front of her was now also so much the boy she used to know. Always ready to hide his fear to show off for her, take up her dares and challenges, and get into trouble with her. She'd been unkind to him back then, in the way a big sister would be to a weakly younger brother. The way he used to look up to her, idolize her, made Memory blush now. She felt their roles had been reversed. Will was her constant point of reference, always patient and loyal. She wanted to be like him; be with him.

Will shifted uncomfortably and Memory realized she'd been staring at him for way too long.

"I'm sorry I left with Mina," he said.

"I'm sorry I tried to kill myself. Boom. I win the Sorry Game."

Will's smile was more of a frown.

"Too soon? Yeah, you're right. Sorry… and that's a Sorry Game DOUBLE VICTORY!" Memory whispered a crackling sound like applauding crowds.

Will gave her a patient look.

Memory gave him a cheesy grin in return. "Fine. Moving right along. What happened with Mina? I wasn't a big fan of her jealous girlfae act," Memory said.

"It's not as simple as that."

Swallowing away her embarrassment, Memory asked, "Do you… love her?"

Will remained quiet for some time, too long for the answer to be a clear no. "She saved my life, just like you did. But Mina doesn't do things selflessly."

Memory remembered the time he meant about her, when

she'd saved him from a bad fight with some bullies. "I didn't really save your life, you know. I probably just saved a few baby teeth."

Will shrugged. "Either way, from then on, I was yours."

Memory blushed so hard all over she felt ready to self-combust. The recollection of that day was so clear to Memory now. She hadn't thought anything of the kid back then. Being honest with herself, she wasn't sure if she'd stepped in to help Will or just because she wanted to get into a fight. When she'd chased the bullies off, young Will had looked up at her with those startling blue eyes, wide and grateful, like she was a hero. He really did think she'd saved his life, and even at that age he had these romantic and childish notions of repaying that debt. He became her shadow. He had been hers, from that moment on.

Memory looked at Will now, grown and having lived and suffered through so much. She didn't know how she could ever repay Will, or live up to that. Maybe the only way was to become the hero he saw in her.

"Do you remember when Mr. Hindmarsh came out and found us together after the fight, after the others had run off?" Memory had a chuckle in her voice as she spoke. "He totally thought I was the one that whaled on you. When you denied it, he thought you were just embarrassed about getting thrashed by a girl."

Will smiled and dropped his head bashfully. "You saved me, and got detention for it." Looking up at her, his eyes searched her face. "You really have it back? All your memories?"

Memory tapped the side of her head. "Every last one. It's massively screwed up. It's not like just remembering a

life normally. It's like I just watched my whole life again on fast forward. I can even remember being a baby in hospital, recovering from the cut on my chest from the ritual. So vividly. I can remember… All sorts of things." Memory put a hand to her chest, running her thumb over the ugly bumps of the old scar. "But I'm whole now. I feel like all of me again, the good and the bad. The only thing I need to do now is keep adding good into my life to balance the contents out a bit."

"I hope I can help add to the good," Will said.

"You already have."

The way Will smiled then filled Memory with happiness even more.

The entrance door opened and Clara walked in, balancing a silver tray full of food.

Clara placed the tray down on a table in the living room, and the sound of jostling plates piled in hamburgers woke Roen and Eloryn. Memory didn't ever remember discussing breakfast burgers with the chef, but there they were, neat little buns with bacon and eggs and a thick, chunky ketchup. She wondered whether it was the chef or Clara who'd been experimenting. Memory's hunger returned and she smiled at Clara gratefully.

Memory threw her legs out of bed, and caught a foot on the covers as she tried to stand up. Before she could wobble or fall, Will caught her wrist to balance her.

He let go quickly. "Sorry."

Memory reached out and squeezed his hand. "It's okay. Don't worry, it's all about breaking rules these days. Those rules were Hope's rules, anyway. Consider them gone."

Taking quick stock of her appearance, Memory realized she was still in her old broken heart t-shirt and long skirt she'd

changed into the day before. It felt like so long ago. She knew she probably stank, and was still covered in any dust that didn't rub off in bed, but she needed to talk things out with her friends and didn't want to take time out for a bath first. She also wanted to eat. Now.

She wandered into the living room. "Thanks for reading my mind, Clara."

"Well, I know it's well into the afternoon, but I thought you would all be in need of some comforting breakfast foods," Clara said, with a neat curtsey. She'd been somewhat more proper and formal since their ordeal, and Memory worried she'd offended her somehow. "I've also seen to re-assigning the queen's guard from Eloryn to yourself. Erec and his finest men are already outside."

Memory groaned and rolled her eyes in a wide dramatic loop. "You of all people should know I don't want guards trailing around behind me all the time."

Clara raised her chin, looking more at the ceiling than at Memory. "You will simply have to tolerate it as best you can, Majesty. Who knows what threats there are to you out there? Dylan is still unaccounted for. That Hope creature is who knows what or where. We can't have you wandering around unprotected. We can't have you—"

Clara's voice broke, and she turned away, but not fast enough to hide the tear on her cheek.

Memory dashed across the room and drew Clara into a tight hug. "I'm so sorry. You're right. I'll keep the guard. I won't let anything happen to me, okay?"

Clara sniffled. "You'd better not."

Roen stood up and stretched. "Indeed. I, for one, expect a

written apology, and perhaps some form of ritualistic dance of penance."

Eloryn smirked at him from her chair then addressed Memory seriously. "You did give us all a fright. We only want for you to be happy and well. And to know you can talk to us, if you need to, about anything."

Memory tried to think of something absurd to talk to Eloryn about then and there, but knew it wasn't the time to be flippant. She paused a moment, gathering together how she really felt, right then in time, how she felt about what she'd almost done, and how she felt about the future.

"There's still a lot of pain inside me," she said. "Enough that I know it's going at be hard at times to keep going. But I'm not planning on doing anything rash. I know now that I'm whole. I'm not missing my memories. I'm not missing any part of my soul. This is me. It's all I have to work with and for the first time in my life I want to work. I have so much in my life now to be grateful for. When I first got my old life back, I forgot all the good in my new life. It's my turn now to work hard and be better."

Memory looked around at all her friends. The pride she saw so clearly from them was everything she needed to stay strong. "So, let's eat already!"

Memory picked up a burger and handed it to Will before taking one for herself. She took a seat on the floor between Eloryn and Roen's armchairs. Clara began tidying the room, which was still in disarray after the fight between Will and Dylan, and Memory's magical tremors. Memory scolded Clara until she came and joined the picnic on the floor. They each chewed their food silently for a while, until a thought that had been plaguing

Memory had to be voiced.

"Lory, is the Maellan family cursed at all? Have there ever been any mentions of a curse?" she asked.

"Not that I've heard of or read in my studies. Why?"

"It's just that I've seen our family tree, and it seems to me that all Maellan die young. A lot of them before they even have children, which is why we're pretty much the last of them, right? I mean, isn't that a bit weird?"

"It's true. I know some of the deaths have seemed suspicious, but there's never been evidence to prove more than simple ill-fate, I'm afraid. It's been that way since Arthur's time, maybe even before, but since Arthur was a commoner there is no record of our family tree before him."

"But what if there was something, or someone, out there, taking out some wicked huge grudge on all Maellan?"

"Only a fae could live long enough to be the sole cause. Which I admit isn't unlikely. There were many fae who were in opposition to the Pact, especially in opposition to Arthur when he pushed to include Branding into the agreement."

Memory nodded, her theories confirmed. "Providence. Providence was a fae, and I also think Providence was Hope. It was like everything she told me, everything she encouraged me to do was to punish me. She told me to be with Roen, which almost ruined our friendships. It was like she knew Dylan was using me and encouraged it to happen. She told me all the time that everyone hated me, and did everything she could to prove it."

Eloryn reached out for Memory's hand. "She was just trying to separate us, drive you against us so you had nothing left but her."

Memory took her twin's hand. "I think it was more than that. She wanted things from me, wanted me to do things, horrible things. She…" Memory winced at her sister, but it had to be said. Everyone had to know the full story. "She wanted me to kill you so I could become queen."

"Queen, like you are now?" Roen asked. "Is that going to be a problem?"

"I don't know. Maybe she just wanted to screw with my life as much as possible. Maybe she's been doing it to all Maellan all this time."

"Providence's magic, and Hope's magic, is a very old form of magic," Eloryn said. "All fae have natural traits that seem like magic- their glamour, strength, and travelling through the Veil. But they don't have behests like humans do. Only a few fae have learned human magic. Nyneve is most famous for it, having learned the runes from Myrddin, who was her lover. But she's gone on to teach other unseelie fae."

"Like her father? If anyone was capable of this kind of cruelty, I'd put money on him. He's got them crazy eyes." Memory wriggled her eyebrows and jiggled her eyelids. "Nyneve has always seemed pretty tame to me. A bit emo, but I can't exactly talk."

"Working out what Providence wanted is the key." Roen finished his burger and leaned forward in his chair. "She may have used Maellan blood in her rituals, but it was Thayl she wanted something from."

Memory shook her head. "Yes and no. Whatever she wanted from Thayl, she wanted it bad. Their deal was that she would help him kill all the Wizards' Council, and then he would somehow repay his debt to her. But he never got his side of the bargain while there were members of the Council still alive, so she never got what she wanted in return. I think she was still trying to help him get rid of the last of the wizards. Remember those banshees in the wagon? They said they were hunting for wizards for their master, and the Council said that other unseelie fae were also hunting for them."

Memory stared down at the woven rug she sat on, seeing a small spray of blood there from Will and Dylan's fight. She shivered. "Hope first showed up right after Thayl died. She kept pushing me to become queen through any means possible. Kept saying she would help me if I owed her. That's what makes me think Hope and Providence are the same. The one thing they both were pushing for was to get a human ruler, with iron magic, into their debt. Providence needed Thayl for something but when he died she turned to me as a backup. Whether or not that has anything to do with all Maellan or not is unknown, but I can't help feeling it does. It's a crazy idea, but I just keep going back to it like it's a bad boyfriend."

Clara had turned white. "The more powerful fae can glamour themselves to look however they wish, so Providence could be anyone."

"Do we think she'll try again?" Roen asked. "In a different form, or maybe a different target?"

"No idea," Memory said. "I'm just a hunter lost in the wilds of speculation. But we have some leads. Some creepy, gangly fae attacked Dylan and me out in town one night. It was one of the ones stealing people, and it sounded like he was connected to Providence. I've already got Peirs keeping a watch out for any more of them."

Will frowned, and Memory wasn't sure if it was at the

mention of her being attacked, or of her being out with Dylan. "I could ask Mina. Fairies gossip," he said, simply.

Memory nodded reluctantly and got to her feet. "Any lead is worth looking into. There may be fairy intel that could help that humans aren't hearing. And speaking of our fluttery friends, I want all of us to start carrying iron, just in case."

"We can't," Eloryn said. "Even if we had your knife, that's all the iron there is."

"Oh, dear sister, have I got a surprise for you." Memory reached down and helped Eloryn up. "We've got somewhere to go. I want my knife back, especially now I can't use magic. I want it for protection and don't care what anyone thinks."

Roen stood quickly as well. "Mem, you still look tired. How about I take Eloryn? I know the way."

Memory pouted, wanting to give Eloryn the big reveal herself, but even the idea of walking all the way down into the cavernous depths and back left her feeling exhausted. "Fine. I absolutely trust you are doing this to let me rest and not to take my sister off into a dark and isolated area."

Roen just shrugged. "It appears that my deception skills are getting sloppy through misuse."

Eloryn blushed from head to toe.

CHAPTER FOUR

In the old servant runs, Roen smirked as he pushed a section of stone wall and it swung open to reveal a long tunnel, winding off into the darkness.

Cool air that tasted of mossy stone met Eloryn's tongue as she caught her breath. She thought she knew everything there was to know about Caermaellan castle. She was clearly mistaken. "I can't believe you and Memory kept this secret from me. This is of tremendous historical and societal importance. We should have been trying to discover where all the iron down there originated."

Roen shrugged, causing a lock of caramel brown hair to fall in front of his eyes. He pushed it away. "I bade Memory tell

you. I think she was too worried about Hayes taking control of it at the time."

Eloryn sighed. "I suppose she was right there. What a fool I was."

Roen put his hand against Eloryn's cheek. "Do not think that. You are trusting and kind in the most beautiful way. If others misuse that, it is their offence, not yours."

Eloryn shivered as Roen turned away and lit the oil lamp he carried.

Roen had retrieved a lamp from his room while he explained to Eloryn where they were going. She understood why the lamp was required. She wouldn't be able to summon a wisp with a behest around so much iron. The living energy of the fae creature would refuse the behest. But she could still magically enhance the flame of the oil lamp, and they travelled down the ancient stone stairs in brightly lit comfort. Dripping water in the distance kept a steady rhythm and the temperature dropped as they descended. The carved tunnel was narrow and steps slippery from a slick coating of mud, and Eloryn kept bumping against Roen as he walked beside her. The warmth of his body seemed contagious, and whenever she felt it, a flush of warmth spread through her as well. Roen slowed to help her down a steep section where a step had crumbled away and she brushed against him with half her body.

Roen let out a breathy groan. "Are you trying to drive me crazy on purpose?"

His tone was playful, but Eloryn could only blush and shake her head. "I'm sorry."

Roen frowned. "Don't be. I'm sorry. It's not proper for me to voice my desires so. It's just… to have you so near, knowing

you feel for me how I do for you, it's all I can do not to take you and hold you and do all sorts of delicious things with you." Roen bit his bottom lip and his smile returned.

Eloryn didn't think she could blush any harder, but she did. Her body turned to fire just wondering what delicious things Roen could mean. She didn't know what they were, but she knew she wanted them, and wanted him. She also couldn't help but wonder whether there had been other women in the past that he'd done such things with.

"You know I've never…" Eloryn began, but choked up. When her words returned, they came at rambling speed. "My first kiss was yours, and I know little else of love apart from the simple romance in fairytales and one archaic text book on anatomy and reproduction. I fear that love may be an area in which you are more knowledgeable than I."

"Whatever experiences I've had, they weren't of love. You are my first experience of love." Roen took both her hands in one of his, and the warm light of the lamp he held beside them seemed to make them glow. "I don't expect you to act at all outside of your comfort, or of society's standards. I would never think to pressure you further. I simply want you to understand how desirable I find you. How strong, and brave, and kind you are."

Eloryn wanted Roen to kiss her then. She wanted it with every nerve in her body. But he only stood and looked at her with an expression that filled her with love. He was being so patient, so gentle with her. She knew he would wait for her as long as needed, and it was up to her to take the next step.

Her voice seemed very small when she asked, "May I try something?"

Roen tilted his head, confused, but nodded.

Pushing herself up on her tippy-toes, Eloryn very slowly placed her lips against Roen's, a soft brush against his skin. Her eyelids fluttered and she lowered herself back down, smiling widely. Light headed with emotions and pride, her foot slipped on the step and she wobbled backwards.

Roen caught her around the waist with one arm and the lamp clattered against the wall beside them. They gasped together, as though the movement had sucked the air from both their bodies, and time slowed as the sound of the lamp hitting stone echoed through the stairwell. Then Eloryn brought her mouth to Roen's again, her fingers running up his neck. His arm tightened around her, bringing her chest toward his, pressing them together. Their footing slipped again and they stumbled together down the stairs, ricocheting from one wall to the other, trying to stay on their feet, tangled in each other's arms, unwilling to let go. Eloryn's lips burned delightfully every time they met Roen's. Her hands sought his golden hair, his shoulders and muscles on his chest. Desire left her head spinning and when the stairs finally flattened onto a pebbly floor she felt just as dizzy. The two remained entwined, stumbling, gasping, until the both of them tumbled into the icy water of the underground lake.

Will had waited while Memory cleaned herself up and changed into the rust-red gown she often wore, the first dress he'd ever seen her wear. When she returned, she put her head down on a cushion on the floor beside him. She said she'd just rest her eyes for a moment while they waited for Roen and Eloryn, then promptly fell asleep. Clara cleared up the food and left, and Will remained sitting beside Memory.

A strand of her purple hair fell across her face and Will reached over to push it back behind her ear, then hesitated.

First rule - No touching.

He took a deep breath, then allowed his fingers to meet her flesh. The old rules were no more. Her skin was soft and warm as he brushed the hair off her cheek. His Hope had changed so much, and he knew shedding the old rules meant she had grown so much stronger. He was happy for her, but there were other rules he still lived by that left a deep sadness in him.

Memory said it was time to start breaking rules, and he agreed. No matter his situation with the fae, Memory was more important. He would no longer sneak in what time he could with her. He would outright defy Mina if he had to. Only, he didn't know how effective that would be. Denying Mina something only made her want it more. He considered keeping away from her amongst the iron in the secret cavern, but he wanted to be with Memory, not hiding underground. And he couldn't explain to Memory either. Not now, not yet. Memory had enough to deal with right now. And despite how he felt about his relationship to Mina, he still felt an obligation toward her. She had saved his life.

When he first arrived in Avall as a small boy, Will didn't know how long it had been before he first met Mina. He only

knew he was starving to death and lost in an endless forest. He'd eaten berries despite knowing they could be poisonous. He'd even eaten grubs and insects he found, desperate for any sustenance. But it wasn't enough. He'd never been a strong child and he quickly grew weak, too weak to keep going. He had curled up on the leafy forest floor, unable to do anything but cling to the last scraps of life.

When Mina first appeared, he thought he had died and Mina was an angel. She was so beautiful his face ran with tears and his weak body crumpled at the sight.

"Little boy," she said, and the jingle of tiny bells seemed to carry after her words. "Are you hungry?"

Will tried to speak but couldn't. He barely managed to nod.

The beautiful creature reached out her cupped hands and a plump and luscious fruit appeared cradled there. Shaped like a pear and twice as large, it was a soft pink with a purple blush on one side. "Take it," she said, smiling.

He did without hesitation, biting in. Juice ran down his chin and strength, hunger and desire burst inside him. He tore into the fruit, consuming the whole thing in seconds. When he was done, the woman held another one for him, and giggled.

"My sweet pet," she sang, and twirled around him, dancing as he ate. She had delicate, tattered wings which trailed a stream of glittery light behind them.

Will ate and ate. Mina sang and smiled. He thought he'd received a miracle. He thought he was saved. He had no idea what had just happened. His life had become the property of the fairy before him.

"My little boy. Who saved you when you were too lost and hungry to survive?"

"You did," he said, grinning a juicy grin at his savior.

"Who will show you wonders greater than you could ever imagine?"

Will knew of fairies and magic from storybooks. He knew now what the woman before him was. "You."

"Who is the most beautiful thing you've ever seen?"

"You are." He knew it was true.

"Who do you love above all else, even your short mortal life?"

He hesitated, and Mina scowled. A deep fear of realization and regret filled him then. He was so far from home, so far from anything he knew, so far from the only family he had left, the one girl he would wait for forever. He would do whatever he had to do to stay alive and stay strong while he waited.

"You. I will love you."

The fairy smiled again, and Will swore a promise to himself that no matter what wonders he was shown, no matter where this creature took him, he would never forget Hope.

Beside him, Memory shuddered in her sleep and her eyes snapped open. Back in the group home she often had nightmares. She would always deny it, but Will knew it from the haunted look in her eyes. He had his own nightmares, of being trapped under rubble, so he knew that look well. He wondered which of many terrors tormented her dreams then. But when she looked up at him, she smiled. He smiled back down at her.

Roen and Eloryn returned then, looking as wet as they looked embarrassed.

"You two miss a step?" Memory said. She sat up, leaning against Will's shoulder.

Roen looked at Eloryn and chuckled. Eloryn looked

mortified and excused herself to change into a dry gown in her room next door.

Memory grinned at Will. "Cough-cold-shower-cough."

Roen sat down and emptied his pockets onto the ground between the three of them. He handed Memory her flick knife and took a small dagger for himself as well.

"We tried to pick small things that we can always carry with us, concealed. El already has the arrowhead with her," he said. That left two items, a small hooked tool and a large button, one for Will and one for Clara.

Will shook his head. "I can't take one. Not if I'm trying to get info from Mina."

"I'll keep it for you for later." Memory nodded and picked up the hooked tool, slipping it into her bodice with her knife.

She picked up the button as well.

Clara rushed in through the door then.

Memory flicked the button across to her. "Good timing, this one's for you."

Clara caught it in almost a daze and clasped it in her hands. She frowned deeply. "There's news," she stuttered. "News from Hayes. He's still demanding to marry Eloryn."

Memory and Roen frowned at each other and got to their feet. The doorway between Memory and Eloryn's chambers clicked closed and Eloryn stood there, neatly dressed in a simple lace gown, her face almost as white as the fabric.

CHAPTER FIVE

"What do you mean he has the legal right? He's a scum-sucking criminal!" Memory paced up and down the long table in the Round Room.

Bedevere's expression remained stoic. "It is also legally within your rights to have Hayes executed for those crimes of treason, which would solve the matter."

Memory cringed visibly. "No more death. I don't want that to be the way I deal with problems. When something tough comes up, it's not right, just snuffing out a life so the issue disappears. We'll find another way."

Eloryn nodded, backing up her sister. It felt important that she support Memory's decisions as queen, since it was her actions that made Memory queen. And her actions that brought her now to this ordeal. Eloryn sat still in the center seat, with Roen on one side and Bedevere, Lanval and Roen's parents seated around them. She put her hands on the table and it felt so flimsy. She really had to get to work on repairing the table that belonged in this room, the true round table that had been there since Arthur's time. Memory would be able to pace much more effectively around the circle it formed than up and down this straight edge.

Curious, the things one ponders of at times like these. Eloryn wondered if she was in shock, or simply in denial. As soon as Clara shared the news, Eloryn realized what a fool she'd been. Her contract of marriage with Hayes had foiled his plans to become king, and had revealed the crimes he'd committed. She thought she'd won then. She didn't consider that the contract still stood, or that he would take advantage of that. She should have known better. Hayes was the type to take any advantage he could.

He looked far too pleased with himself as he was marched into the meeting by the bailiff and two other guards. Eloryn recognized the shackles as the same that Thayl had used, that block magic on the wearer.

Roen's hand rested on the table beside her and she moved hers closer, so that their little fingers touched, seeking that smallest comfort. He locked gazes with hers and she took strength from him.

Hayes stood before the group and smiled at Eloryn in a way that crinkled his hooked nose. The spite within the expression made Eloryn's stomach churn.

He bowed a shallow and mocking bow. "My dear soon-to-be wife."

Eloryn stared back at him, keeping her voice and gaze level. "You are doing this only to punish me. Why must you be so cruel?"

"Oh, not only to punish you. It's your little trick that has turned to bite you. You may not let me be king, but I can still hope that your wild sister never bears an heir, and that one of our many, many children will come to rule."

Memory choked. "I just threw up in my mouth a little."

She stood right beside Hayes, although he completely ignored her. All his attention and venom was focused on Eloryn. Something wild and desperate filled him now, something darker than the simple greed he had within him before. Eloryn wished she never had to take an action again that would create such an enemy to her. The feeling that this man could have so much hatred for her left her drained to her core.

"Despite the brain bleaching I now need, the fact is, Hayes, that you'll be in jail," Memory said. "How can you make her be your wife while you're in jail?"

Hayes replied, but continued to look at Eloryn. "It doesn't matter where I am, or what I am. King or prisoner, Eloryn will be my wife. She is legally and magically bound by contract, and I intend to follow through."

Memory put her palms to her forehead as if she was trying to contain herself. "Gah! I hate you so much right now if someone doesn't get you out of this room I'm going to pull your eyeballs out and vomit in the empty sockets."

Half the room stared open mouthed at Memory as the guards led Hayes away, but Hayes just glared at Eloryn the whole way out.

Memory pulled a chair out across from Eloryn and flopped into it. "I'm sorry, I guess that wasn't very queenly of me."

"Are you all right?" Eloryn asked.

"Am I all right? How are you not a living emotional explosion right now?"

Eloryn took a deep breath. She didn't know the answer. She just knew she had to believe they would find a solution, and believe that nobody could force her away from Roen. "I guess I'm simply putting all my energy into not vomiting in someone's eye sockets, which is a horrendous concept, by the way."

Roen laughed, but it was short and sharp with anger. "Although if anyone were to deserve it right now, Hayes would have my vote."

"Good luck to Hayes, thinking he's going to get a wife and family while he's in prison forever," Memory said.

Eloryn stared at the table again. "But he will. I must marry him, even if the wedding takes place in his cell. And a wife has certain duties under law."

Memory paused for a second, clearly trying to add up the meaning. "Women have to have babies as a legal duty? Hell no, not in my kingdom they don't. Bedevere, do I have a legal advisor? If I do or don't, bring me one. We're going to find a way out of this. Including starting right now, we're going to change the laws about what 'duties' women have in this land."

"Oh. My. God. That's it. I'm done. I quit being queen," Memory said. She dropped her forehead onto the stack of paperwork on the desk in front of her and pretended to drool incoherently.

"You never did like homework," Will said with a sly grin. "Made me do it for you half the time."

Memory let out a groan that went for as long as she could force breath out. Rubbing her eyes with one hand, she flicked through the stack of unfinished documents and compared it to what she'd completed so far. Her first day of paperwork as queen was not proving very productive.

The monarch's office was a dark room, filled with timber furniture in rich chocolate tones and a desk bigger than what Memory thought a dining table should be. Going in there that morning had seemed fun, exploring all the quill pens, ink pots, shifting rulers and other gadgets around the desk. The room made her feel important, like a proper queen. Then the paperwork began.

At least the chair was comfortable, and she rocked back in it and stuck her tongue out at Will where he sat cross-legged on a sideboard. He was reading a copy of Shakespeare's complete works, which they were both amused to find on the shelves. It seemed the fae imported all sorts of things back when they still travelled between the worlds.

"Can I help?" Will offered.

Memory sighed and picked up her next piece of parchment. It was velvety and thicker than the modern paper she remembered. "Nah, I'm okay. I need to get through this. It's part of my job now. And to be honest all I'm really doing so far is sorting things into stuff I know what I want to do about but

not how to do it, stuff I can sign and be done with, and things I'm completely clueless about."

There was a knock on the door and Memory pumped a fist into the air and whispered, "Distraction! Yes!"

"Do come in," she said formally.

Peirs opened the door and remained standing in the threshold. He was out of his guard uniform and wore a simple fawn colored suit that matched his graying sandy-blonde hair. He held his cap in his hands against his chest and weariness accentuated the fine wrinkles across his face.

"Your Majesty," he said. "I've been doing as you instructed, undoing the wrongs Hayes committed. While undergoing this task, I've been visiting a number of prisons Hayes established for the masses he deemed to be wrongdoers, troublemakers, or undesirables. At one such prison I have found someone I thought you might like to see."

Peirs extended his arm, and from behind the door Clara stepped out, bringing with her a young girl with wiry red hair. The child's eyes were full circles, wide with awe and fear, and although she was clean, in fresh clothes and with an additional blanket around her shoulders, Memory could see the girl was even skinner than she had been when under Maeve's care at the orphanage. Skinnier and shaking like a leaf.

Memory got to her feet, a deep frown aching her forehead. In a few steps she was around her desk and kneeling in front of the girl to look her eye to eye.

"Hey, Isa," she said softly. "Where's your sister?"

Isa shook her head.

"Do you know where Maeve and the others are?"

Isa's lips pulled in and she shook her head again.

Memory stood back up and gave Peirs a questioning look.

He leaned toward her and whispered so the girl couldn't here. "After we got her out of the prison, while we got her fed and cleaned up, she said she saw Maeve and the others get taken by gaunts. She was the only one left. Apparently she was trying to find you when she got caught by Hayes's militia."

How dare they? She's just a child. Memory felt the fires in her chest roaring. She closed her eyes and took a deep breath. "Clara, can you find Isa a room in the guest wing below my chambers, and a handmaiden to look after her?"

"Already sorted," Clara replied, her eyes watery and lips tight.

Memory bent back down to the girl. "We're going to find your sister and the others, and bring everyone back here, I promise. Won't it be fun, living in the palace together?"

Isa made no movement to respond.

"I was a bit scared of getting lost when I first started working here," Clara said, smiling at Isa. "But don't worry, I'll draw you a map, and soon you'll be running all over like you own the place." Clara scooped the girl up, and carried her away on her hip.

Memory waved to them, then headed out of her office as well, beckoning Peirs and Will to follow her. Will jumped silently from the cupboard he'd been perched on and walked at her side.

"Have you had any luck tracking those fae critters who work for Providence?" Memory asked as she took long strides down the polished marble hall.

Peirs shook his head. "We've checked through all known unseelie fae territories in Caermaellan, and even seelie ones, but found nothing. We've spotted gaunts trying to take people a few times, but haven't been able to follow them. As soon as they've noticed us they leave their victim and flee, or worse, turn and fight to the death, the crazed beasts. They seem to have no fear for being Branded, and are blatantly showing more hatred toward humans."

"I'd like to blatantly show my hatred right back again," Memory muttered. "Have things always been this bad?"

Peirs's grin was wry, stretching the skin on his cheeks. "Not like this, but there has always been tension between the unseelie fae and humans. They are monsters, and they see us as inferior animals. That's why the Pact was made to include Branding, to protect each side from the other. In the old times, we used to be free to hunt the monsters for sport. I figure that's the only reason the unseelie fae went along with the Pact because they were so under threat. But many in the unseelie court have outright stated they didn't want the Pact as it was, that humans should have been made subservient to the fae."

Subservient to the unseelie fae? Memory could just imagine the kind of horrors that would involve. Still, having seen a fae creature suffer the fate of a Branding, she was pretty sure it fell under the category of horror as well.

Peirs slowed his stride, and Memory turned to see why. He still held his cap clutched against his chest. "Your Majesty, it is my fault the children have been taken. I should have stayed to protect them."

"Shoulda, woulda, coulda, nonsense. This isn't your fault. This is the fault of the damned vampires."

Peirs raised an eyebrow. "There really is no such thing as vampires."

"Color me unconvinced." Memory started walking again and Peirs and Will matched her step.

"This is new, what we've been seeing, and targeted solely on Caermaellan," Peirs said. "Some unseelie fae, like trolls, have been known to eat humans, but never drain their blood in the way we've seen in the bodies we've found. It's almost medical precision. No teeth."

"But we know it's those rotted dark fae though," Memory said. "How were they able to take everyone without being Branded?"

Will spoke up then, although his voice was quiet. "Fae tricks. Lost children are easy targets. They're easy to seduce and trap with promises of riches or happiness, a home, or even a simple bite of food."

Peirs nodded. "And when they make the wrong deal, they lose any protection from the Pact."

Vampires or not, Memory knew she had to find and stop the fae doing this, and find out what their connection to Providence was. No matter what, Providence had taken enough blood.

Memory took the stairs up and headed into the Round Room. She found the room a mess, with piles of splintered wood in small stacks all over the marble floor. Eloryn sat amongst them, sorting the pieces out, holding them to her ear and whispering to them in turn. She'd managed to recreate almost a quarter of the round table from the shattered and charred timber that remained after the explosion. A makeshift desk sat in the corner, out of the way, where Roen, Roen's father and a mousey legal advisory sat bleary eyed. They looked over contracts and searched through legal precedents to find a way to prevent Eloryn's marriage to Hayes. Eloryn looked particularly worn. Memory was sure she hadn't slept for days.

Memory worried about her sister, how she'd become so

focused on repairing the round table, but Eloryn had said it helped her to think, and to relax, and that it was her way of trying to find a solution.

"How is it going?" Memory asked.

Roen looked up from the desk, his eyes red rimmed with grey smudges beneath. "Going splendidly if we want to amend the marriage contract for requiring a dowry or we wish to allow the husband's family to inspect the bride before the wedding to approve of her or her virginal status. The more I look at the laws in detail, the more I'm beginning to agree with your sentiment, Mem."

"That Avall kind of sucks for women? Yep, worked that one out back in etiquette class."

Eloryn placed a finger length splinter of wood against the restored section of table and spoke a few words. The wood crackled softly as it melded and blended back together. "We'll find a way. We can fix this."

"I'm glad you're still feeling positive, sis, because I need to break up your team. I need Roen for something else. I want Roen to find the place the gaunts are taking people and draining their blood. We think they have Maeve and the kids."

Everyone around the room stopped their work and looked at Memory.

"I know you probably want to be here, finding a way to stop Hayes's crazy demands, but I need you out there. You've got mad ninja skills like no one else I know. Finding Providence's blood drinkers is important."

Roen looked at Eloryn for a long moment, then turned back to Memory. He nodded, his jaw tight. "I know. I'll do it."

Brannon stood up from the table and put his hand on Roen's

shoulder, the look of pride on his face overwhelming.

Roen gave a small bashful chuckle. "To be honest it will be good to get out onto the streets again. The best luck to ever strike me has been when I've been working. Maybe I will find some luck again to help us here as well. Different ways of dealing with problems work for different people."

Eloryn rose from the floor and scattered a stack of splintered wood when she rushed over to Roen and held him tight. "Don't worry, I'll find a solution to this before you get back."

Peirs bowed to Memory. "Let me accompany him. I need to help. I need to right this."

"Of course," Memory said. "I'd go too, but there's more I need to do here."

Will, who had been standing to one side during the conversation stepped forward. "Do you want me to look too?"

"Yes, if you can. But somewhere else. I need you talking with the fae to find out what they know. There has to be some gossip to be had, and Mina strikes me as the kind of girl to gossip."

Will flinched ever so slightly, making his icy blue eyes flash. "I will go to her."

He turned to leave, and Memory caught him by his hand. "Come back soon, 'kay?"

Will turned away, his expression hidden behind tangled hair. "I'll try."

CHAPTER SIX

Eloryn walked slowly through the halls of the castle toward Thayl's old quarters. She had grown so used to hearing many sets of footsteps walking with her wherever she went, that now she was without her guards she felt very alone. She knew there was only one person she truly missed, and made a silent wish that Roen would stay safe and return to her soon.

Her sister had summoned her, and when Eloryn reached the entrance to what had been Thayl's chambers, she nodded to the guards that used to be hers waiting outside, then stepped in to see Memory.

Eloryn gasped. "Mem, you look… Stunning."

Memory grinned bashfully and tugged at the short skirt

of the new outfit she wore. "Not bad, right? This was Clara's newest mission. I gave her my old clothes and asked her to work with the seamstresses to come up with something that was more me. I kind of just wanted some new pants, but I think they saw the little skirt-belt-thing on my jeans and rolled with it."

Eloryn smiled. The outfit was traditional enough not to cause a scandal, but at the same time very much suited her sister. Fitted pants in grape purple had lace cuffs around Memory's ankles, and around her waist a full bustle hung from the back with a shorter frill of skirt at the front. The seamstress had incorporated pink lace onto the front of the tight bodice, in a cascading collar reminiscent of the heart design on Memory's shirt from the other world. A black, ruffled shrug jacket kept the whole ensemble modest and practical.

Memory had also taken to wearing most of her old piercings again, except the one in her lip, and over the top of lace gloves, she wore the collection of bracelets, buckles and cuffs that she had worn the day Eloryn first met her.

Eloryn hid her smile and stuck her nose into the air. "First hamburgers, now this. You'll have everyone wanting fashion like yours."

Memory laughed. "Just wait until I introduce Avall to coffee."

Smiling back, Eloryn ran her finger over a layer of dust on the desk beside her. "So, where do we start?"

"I guess I'll have to import some coffee beans or trees from the other world somehow…"

"I meant with your search plan, here, now," Eloryn said.

"I was honestly hoping you'd walk in and be all bam, solved the mystery with superhuman senses of observation and

deduction, Sherlock Holmes style." Memory turned on the spot, looking around the room. "But you didn't. So I guess we just poke around."

"You really do think far too much of me," Eloryn said.

The rooms had barely been touched since Thayl was deposed. Eloryn knew the Council had been through once, looking for clues to Thayl's powers, but left quickly when they found no magical documents. His chambers consisted of a single large room that served as bedroom, lounge and office, unlike the royal chambers Memory and Eloryn now occupied which had a separate bedroom and sitting room each. The room hadn't been on the cleaners' rounds for a while, and grime had settled across all surfaces. Thayl's old clothes, worn during his imprisonment, still lay on the floor in front of an open wardrobe.

Eloryn frowned at the bed, which was small, a single bed only. As though Thayl had never even imagined sharing his bed with another person again after Loredanna died.

Eloryn made her way to the bedside table and began flicking through the books stacked there, searching for a journal or some other clue.

Memory followed, and bent down next to the bed, feeling around its base for anything hidden. She glanced at Eloryn a few times as she did so. "How are you hanging in there, with that whole nasty forced marriage business?"

Eloryn paused for a moment, then continued to flick through the copy of *Troilus and Criseyde*, although she doubted it would be of much relevance to their search. "Hayes has set a date for the wedding, a week from today, to be held in his cell."

"He's being a right asshat about this, isn't he? I'm starting to rethink my position of anti-killing."

"Don't. I do not want his death on my hands or yours. We will find a solution. Anything broken can be fixed. Changing the laws about a woman's rights in marriage will help me a little, but unfortunately I will still be married, just with more rights." Eloryn closed the book and a puff of dust blew into her face, stinging eyes that already felt raw. She blinked them clear. "It would almost be funny if not so horrible. We fought Hayes for wanting to arrange marriages for us, and now I've locked myself into an arranged marriage with him."

"If it weren't for this damn fairy oath, I would whoosh him away to the rest of the world for you." Memory winced as she reached her arm full length under the bed, fumbling around.

"I would still be bound by contract to marry him, regardless of his location. And without your magic we are unable to get to the other world anyway, regardless of what miraculous wonders it may hold, be it coffee or a solution to my problem."

Memory stopped searching and sat on the side of the bed, looking up at Eloryn. "What if you do go through with the marriage, and then get a divorce right after? Would that satisfy the contract?"

"A divorce?"

Her sister explained the concept to her. Apparently it was more common in her world than marriages that lasted.

"Happily ever afters aren't really a thing where I come from," Memory said.

"That would be a very big change for Avall in order to solve my problem."

"Meh, it should be allowed anyway. Even in the rest of the world I'm pretty sure divorce becoming legal was always because of some king or another wanting to do it themselves."

Eloryn nodded, a small spark of hope lighting in her then extinguishing just as fast. "It may be a solution, but it's not the sort of law change we could rush through. Nor are the other changes regarding women's rights. I will still be married to Hayes for some time."

"And any amount of time is too much time, I know." Memory leant back on her elbows, staring around the room as though it held answers. She pointed at the wall behind Eloryn.

"That's Thayl's sister," she said. "I saw her once before, in a dream."

Eloryn turned and looked at the large portrait on the wall. The girl looked about twelve years old and her rose red lips were highlighted by her pale skin and thick, ebony hair. She smiled like she'd just seen a rainbow for the first time.

Eloryn's heart sank like a sack of stones into black water. Memory had explained what happened to the child at just sixteen years of age. She'd been lost to sacrifice in Providence's dark ritual.

"She was so pretty," Memory said, looking as grim as Eloryn felt. "I can almost see some of her in you. In us, I guess."

"We do not know for sure she is family," Eloryn said.

Memory opened her mouth but Eloryn spoke first. "If you want to know, if you truly feel the need to know for sure, there are magical ways we could use to discover whether Thayl was our father. But I don't feel the need. Since learning the rumor about Loredanna not consummating her marriage, I see more and more a resemblance to Thayl in our features. I know he was special to our mother, and I know he was to you, too, in a way. Knowing all I know now, I don't hate the thought of him being our father. But nor do I wish to embrace it. Alward was my father in all ways that mattered, and I cannot forget that it was Thayl who killed him."

Memory had turned away so Eloryn couldn't see her face. "I thought I was a fool for wanting a father figure in my life so desperately that I turned to Thayl. You had Alward, who sounds like he rocked the father role. I had no one. Either of the men who could have been our father is just as tragic really, Thayl or Edmund. I think I also prefer not to know for sure. I know Thayl made mistakes, but at least I knew him, for a while. It would hurt too much for both of us, I think, to know for sure he was our father, or to know he wasn't. Maybe sometimes it's best to just leave things at maybe."

With a shake of her head, Memory stood up and ran her hands around the gilt frame holding the life-sized portrait of Thayl's sister. "Help me lift this down."

Eloryn took hold of the other side, and together they hefted the thick framed canvas from the wall.

Eloryn looked at the space on the wall the painting came from. "Nothing behind the painting."

Memory pried the backing board off the frame and then pouted. "Nothing, damn it. People always hide things in frames in the movies."

"Movies?"

Memory shook her head. "Oh sister dearest, I have *so* much to catch you up on."

Eloryn grinned and went over to the cluttered desk.

"What's this?" she said, lifting up a small box, wrapped like a present with a small envelope on top. She opened the note and read it.

More as requested. Use them well. I grow impatient.

Memory had come over to look over her shoulder. “See? You do have super detective powers.”

Eloryn rolled her eyes as she pried at the lid. The box opened with a snap and revealed a row of neatly laid out darts inside.

Eloryn reached to her neck. “Those are the same sort of darts the Wizard Hunters used to block the Spark of Connection.”

“That’s weird.” Memory pried one out and held it near her eye, examining it. “They look like iron. It makes no sense that iron would stop magic from working.”

As though to demonstrate the point, Memory pulled out her knife from a neat pocket in the waist band of her new outfit that looked made just for it. The way it was concealed there made Eloryn think it had been inspired by how Roen used to carry his fine electrum sword.

When she held the two pieces of metal together, the small dart wriggled from Memory’s fingers with a life of its own and flung itself at the nearby blade.

Eloryn gasped.

“Magnetized?” Memory said. “More sense being made now. Hey, can I try something?”

Memory got a wicked look in her eye, and before Eloryn could reply, Memory jabbed her in the shoulder with the dart. It pricked lightly through her skin and wooziness rushed through Eloryn as her Spark of Connection closed down.

“Mem!” Eloryn clutched her sister’s arm for support and Memory helped ease her down to sit on the bed. “Some warning would have been nice. And you better have a good excuse for doing that.”

“Warning takes away all the fun,” Memory said, her eyebrows wriggling cheekily. “We are pretty sure normal iron

draws magic into humans. And it looks like magnetized iron draws it out, like the change in polarity affects the way it funnels magic. It's just drawing magic out of you, right? So maybe the Spark of Connection is just a small bit of magic that's been put inside each human."

"It matches existing theory on the subject, yes. And it's a small bit of magic I would like back now please." Eloryn reached to collect the arrow-head she now carried in her purse, but Memory grabbed her hand.

"Wait, we haven't gotten to what I want to try yet. We already know that holding iron can re-start the spark. I want to try giving you some of the magic in me. I won't be casting anything, just sharing."

Eloryn frowned. "It sounds a little too close for comfort to me. You must be mindful of your oath."

"Oh shush. There's no behest for this, and it's behests I'm not allowed to do. It's just a little involuntary overflow."

Memory held her palms up in front of Eloryn's chest. "Okay. Now make me angry."

Eloryn laughed. "How shall I make you angry?"

"Tell me more about Hayes's scumbucketry, or Avall's women's rights issues, or the vampires stealing my friends, or talk about Mina, or…"

A glow flashed between them and Eloryn felt her spark re-open.

"It worked," she said, a little breathless.

Memory's face was closed for a moment as she breathed out an angry pant, then she shrugged and smiled. "And no fairy army banging down the door demanding my head. So we're all good."

"You really aren't fond of Mina, are you?" Eloryn asked.

A frown reappeared quickly on Memory. "She's only the most awful girlfriend ever, or whatever she is or was to Will."

Eloryn hesitated. She had grown increasingly worried about Will's situation with the fae the more she got to know him. For all she'd read about how the fae can claim human children or partners, Will seemed to fit that description. It was only the amount of freedom she'd seen him have that made her believe it wasn't true. Most humans claimed by the fae are taken to their world and kept there, or so the stories went. Like Lugh. Perhaps Will was simply friends with Mina and the sprites, and until Eloryn knew better, she decided it wasn't worth worrying Memory about.

"Still, we've not found any more clues regarding Providence. These darts are made to target human wizards, not the fae," Eloryn said. She held the dart up to the light of the nearby window to examine it. "Do you think magnetized iron would be safe for fae?"

"Clueless. Why?"

"Because these are also engraved with runes, the same old type of magic that Providence used on you and on Thayl's hand," Eloryn said, placing the dart back in the box and closing it up. "I'm guessing this little gift came from her, trying to hasten the death of the Wizards' Council so Thayl's debt would come due."

Memory rubbed her temples. "Makes sense. I just need to know what the hell Providence wanted."

Eloryn looked around the room again. Thayl hadn't been a well-organized man. Every surface and shelf was overcrowded and cluttered. *There must be more in here to help us, but where to start?*

"You told me once I needed to be more inventive with my magic. I need to start experimenting some more, correct?" Eloryn said.

"And I will live vicariously through you as you do," Memory agreed.

Eloryn nodded, and began speaking in the magic language. *"Reveal to me, anything of Providence. Anything of Thayl's relationship to Providence. Make yourself seen."*

The box of darts on the desk gave a small rattle and then glowed a rich golden light. Beside it, three books down in a stack, a thin ledger book shimmered briefly too.

Memory pulled the book from the stack, letting the rest of the tower collapse behind it. "I was wrong. Sherlock's got nothing on you."

Eloryn tsked and carefully picked the fallen books back up. She loved any books too dearly to see them dumped onto the floor.

Both girls stood shoulder to shoulder as Memory began flicking through the loosely bound documents. They appeared to be letters, from someone who signed only with a rough X, outlining expenses to be paid and the development of missions they were undergoing for Thayl.

"And this is?" Memory asked.

"Maybe my behest failed."

Memory stopped flicking, and started leafing back the pages. "No, I'd say you didn't fail at all." Memory pointed to a sketch of a long hooked tool.

"That's the same thingamabob Roen brought up from the iron stash."

"It's a leatherworker's awl," Eloryn said. She took the ledger

and began flicking ahead again. They soon found details of other iron items they'd seen in the depths of the castle. Eloryn skimmed the handwriting throughout, drawing in all the details she could.

"Thayl was hiring this person to collect iron for him. He even gave the hunter leads, told him to seek out wizards in hiding, or anyone seen as being powerful with magic. Thayl must have worked that part out when he first began hunting wizards. He also provided this hunter and his men with the spark-closing darts and... Oh."

Eloryn put the letters down on the desk and stared straight ahead, trying to calm the shudders that racked her frame.

"What is it?" Memory asked.

Eloryn took a deep breath. "It mentions the hunter's dragon. The last letter says the hunters were going to the mountains west of Maerranton following reports of a man seen there matching Alward's appearance. They were the ones who chased us. Led by the man with the lion's hair and scarred face. All this time I had believed I was the cause of our discovery, that it was my folly that brought the hunters to Alward and me." Eloryn shook her head.

Memory put an arm over Eloryn's shoulder and squeezed. "Why is it always the good people who blame themselves for what bad people do?"

Eloryn put an arm around her sister as well. After another deep breath, she felt lighter than she had for months. "So now we know they were hunting for iron as well as for wizards. And delivering it to Thayl, who hoarded the artifacts in the palace depths."

"Not all of the iron down there was from him, though,"

Memory said. "Will said the fae didn't go there even before Thayl. Hundreds of years at least. But there's the interesting thing. Even if Thayl didn't put all the iron down near the lake, we know for sure he added to what was there, and that he was actively seeking more iron. He might have done exactly what I did, find a place the fae didn't go in order to store more iron there. Even if he was using it to recharge his magic, he didn't need so much, and yet he kept seeking more and more." Like an unconscious action, Memory drew her own iron knife again. Her expression was chilling. "There's only one other value in hoarding iron that I can think of."

Eloryn looked at the knife in Memory's hand, remembering the searing effect it had on a banshee's skin. "Defense against the fae. But to want so much, it wouldn't have been just for himself. There's iron enough there to fight a battle."

Memory looked grimly at her sister. "What if Thayl knew what Providence was? What if he had some idea of what she was going to ask of him to repay his debt? What if the iron was to prepare for that?"

Eloryn's voice was quiet. "A war with the fae?"

Memory shrugged and pinched the bridge of her nose. "But if Providence is a fae, and presumably a dark fae, why would she want to make a human start a war? Why not just do it herself somehow?"

"You've said Hope was always trying to turn you against the unseelie fae."

Memory muttered an interruption. "Not that I need much turning."

Eloryn's head tilted. "There is some great animosity between the seelie and unseelie courts. Perhaps Providence was actually a seelie fae, planning to have humankind and unseelie set at war?"

"Maybe? I don't know. But why else? Unless for some reason Thayl thought he needed that much just to deal with Providence alone." Memory threw her hands up in the air. "Thanks for nothing, Thayl's room."

Eloryn collected up the ledger and box of darts. "We know more now than we did before. These were important clues. We will work it out."

Memory groaned. "Okay, okay. Trying to be optimistic. Will is still trying to get some more info about Providence from Mina and the sprites. He's got her interested in it now. Says she's keen to gossip about it, so we'll see what there is when he comes back."

"Roen and Peirs may find something also. I hope they will all be back soon."

Memory smiled in a way that did not disguise her worry. Eloryn knew that her own expression must be a mirror image.

CHAPTER SEVEN

The heavy rain from earlier in the day had ceased, but had left the ground thick with mud that clung greedily to each footstep. Clouds still covered the sky and the moon glowed through the mist like an ominous ghost of the sun.

Roen and Peirs stood together just outside of the pool of light cast by a streetlamp. They chatted quietly and casually, observing the people around them, before moving on to their next location. For three nights they had done the same thing, loitering outside of taverns and inns, wandering through the pebbled streets until the early hours of the morning. During the days they sought out Peirs's contacts and questioned people on the street for clues.

Peirs sighed and tilted his head, indicating to Roen it was time to move on. There were a few taverns around Caermaellan that the fae frequented, and they had been watching Myrddin's Cup that evening.

"We'll find something soon," Roen said.

Peirs snorted wryly. "We better."

They had the exact same exchange every time they moved on in their search. Roen could see the lines of stress etched around Peirs's eyes and tight lips, as though every day they didn't find the stolen children, Peirs felt another child die in his heart. Roen grabbed Peirs's arm and pulled him to a stop.

"We will find them," Roen said, putting every ounce of hope and sincerity into his words that he could.

Peirs shrugged, gazing up and down the street as though looking for answers. "Should we be doing this differently? Should I be sending guards to knock down every door in the city? I'm open to all suggestions."

"If I learned anything in my time as a…" Roen still hesitated to say it, but forced the word though. "…thief, it's that when seeking something precious, it's often best to do it quietly."

Peirs ran a hand through his hair. "I just can't think straight. Don't know if any decision I'm making is the right one." He closed his roaming eyes for a moment then looked at Roen. "You know, I was probably the age you are now when Thayl first took the throne as he did. I was no noble, didn't have much of a say in the whole affair, but it still made me angry. Angry enough to act. I never meant to be the leader of the resistance, but it sort of just happened." Peirs sighed and his breath formed a cloud, hanging in the icy air between them. "It's funny how we end up where we end up. Now a slip of a girl is our queen, and

made me captain of her guard. I know some don't believe in Memory, but I have from the start. I could see it right away, something special about her. By the fae, she's still a child, but she sure is an extraordinary one. I'm just some nobody desperately terrified of letting her down."

"I know you've made her proud so far. She thinks of you as family."

"As she does every one of the children we still need to find." Peirs hung his head, his face hidden in the shadow as he began walking again.

As Roen turned away to follow Peirs to their next tavern, he finally caught sight of their target. A pair of gaunts, tall and gangly, squelched through the mud toward the entrance of the inn. They walked boldly as though they had little care of being seen. The suits they wore were threadbare and grayed, the fabric of the pants shredded to the knees, but one had a new bright red handkerchief in its breast pocket that stood out like an open wound.

"There, see? What did I tell you?" Roen said, calling Peirs's attention back.

Peirs blinked as though not believing it. "Now I guess we wait and see if they try to take someone."

"Not at all." Roen grinned. "Now, we track them."

Roen quietly led Peirs across the street to where the gaunts had passed by, and pointed to their elongated footprints in the mud, each one a pool filled with murky water.

"We track them back to their origin from here," he said. "Much better than trying to follow the gaunts themselves and having them flee or fight us."

Peirs checked over his shoulder to where the gaunts had

disappeared into the tavern. "What if these gaunts aren't from the same group that's taking people, or if they've come from somewhere different to where they take their victims?"

Roen nodded. "All right then. One of us will follow the tracks, and one of us will follow the gaunts."

"I'm not as quiet as you for following after the unseelie beasts, but I probably have less chance of following their footprints well. That's our best shot, since we haven't tried it before. You track, I'll trail."

Peirs held out his hand and Roen shook it before they each headed their separate ways. Roen flicked up the hood of his long leather coat, and began tracking the creatures' steps.

His thoughts quickly turned to Eloryn and how she was able to follow a path by turning invisible footprints into pure light. He hadn't been back to the castle in days, but it felt like much longer since he'd seen her. He would have liked her to be by his side now, as he always would, but they needed to find a solution to stop Hayes. And he needed no magic to track the gaunts; it would be easy with the thick mud, as long as it didn't rain again.

Roen moved quickly, his eye on the creatures' marks, pausing only briefly when the path forked to spot the way to go. The gaunts had taken a circuitous route that led him under dank bridges and through empty parklands, until he reached the outskirts of the city where tight terraced housing made way for larger estates with mansions surrounded by vast walled in gardens.

The trail led to a building that sat on a small hill. It was hunched and crooked from disrepair. Weeping willows lined the property boundaries with draping leaves that whispered in the

wind.

No one seemed to be around, and Roen crept closer to the house, ducking between overgrown blackberry brambles and tumbled stone walls.

A dozen steps from the front door, the movement of figures in the dark made Roen duck for cover behind a cracked marble fountain. A gaunt had appeared from around the other side of the house, heading to the entrance, dragging a dazed girl.

This is it then, the place they are bringing the stolen people.

Roen froze, listening. *Did someone just call my name?*

The gaunt had disappeared into the house, taking the girl with him, and the door slammed closed.

"Roen!"

It was Peirs calling him. But Peirs was meant to be following the other two gaunts.

The other two gaunts…

Roen spun around in his crouched position. A bright flash of red moved in the dark in front of him- a bright handkerchief against tattered clothes. Two gaunts towered over him, the ones they had seen at the tavern. As he had tracked the gaunts, the gaunts had tracked him. One slashed its arm through the air, smacking Roen across the jaw and knocking him onto his back. Roen tasted blood on his tongue, salty and metallic.

Peirs ran up from behind them, still too far away. "Brand them! Brand them!"

I can't.

Roen grabbed for the iron dagger he carried. The gaunt in front of him stretched its black maw wide and loosed a wailing cry. The cry was matched by others, more and more howling at the intruders.

Hands grasped Memory's shoulders, shaking her roughly, waking her from sleep.

She struggled one eyelid open and saw Eloryn standing there. She looked so upset that Memory made an effort to shake herself awake. Will also waited next to Eloryn, looking equally concerned. Memory hadn't seen him for a while. He must have just gotten back.

"What's going on?" she asked, her voice croaky from sleep. She rubbed her eyes.

"It's Peirs, he's returned. But Roen hasn't," Eloryn said.

Memory was out of bed and getting dressed in a worried, half asleep blur. Clara rushed in soon after, in her bedclothes, and helped lace Memory into a thick leather corset, designed to provide light protection for fencing. Eloryn had dressed already, and Memory wondered how much magic was used to speed her into the practical dark colored riding outfit she wore.

When she'd done helping Memory dress, Clara brought Peirs in on Memory's request.

"You found it then?" Memory asked while pulling long leather boots on.

Peirs bowed. He looked ashen. "We did."

"What happened to Roen?"

"He was captured by the gaunts. They swarmed on him, too many for me to fight, so I fled, to bring help." Peirs took a knee. "Forgive me, Your Majesty."

"You did the right thing. If you'd both been taken you'd both be lost to us. At least we know where everyone is now." Memory helped Peirs stand again then said to Clara, "Get Erec, tell him what's going on."

Clara finished winding her wild mass of bed-tangled red hair into a knot at the back of her head, then nodded and left, her white night gown fluttering behind her.

Memory collected her iron knife from under her pillow and strapped it into a custom sheath on her new belt. She also pulled out the hooked awl and pushed it into Will's hands.

His hands didn't close around it. "I can't carry iron. The fae won't be happy."

"Things have changed. We know more about Providence. I want you carrying iron from now on. Please do that for me."

Will took the awl.

Memory looked from him to Eloryn, who stood like a deep breathing statue beside them, then to Peirs. "Peirs, what happened? Where are the gaunts hiding out?"

"They are in an old building, one the locals say is haunted, and is avoided by most. It's a human's property, but disused. That's why we hadn't been able to find them in any fae territory. It was surprisingly easy to track them there, almost as though they wanted to be found. Roen and I were separated and I was too far back to help when they took him."

Eloryn looked at Memory. "Could they be luring us in?"

"Does it even need to be said? But there's only one thing to do with a trap, and that's spring it. Besides, what else would we do? Leave Roen there? And all the other people they've taken? Shyeah right."

Clara returned, along with Erec. She cleared her throat as

way of announcement, then helped Memory slip on the leather jacket that matched her corset.

Erec gave his brother a look that seemed they were speaking silently together, then turned to address Memory. "You've found where the children have been taken?"

"We're going now," Memory said.

Erec cleared his throat. "If you intend to mount a rescue, Your Majesty, I have to advise against your personal involvement, or your sister's."

"You can advise my ass, Erec. I know it's important for the queen to stay alive, but this is more important. Not just for Roen, but to find out who is behind all these kidnappings, and maybe even more. Doesn't the king ride into battle alongside his army? Are you going to keep the two most powerful magical talents of Avall from assisting?"

Eloryn shot Memory a look.

I know, I know. No magic for me.

"I'm going," Memory said.

Erec looked to Eloryn as though for support.

She shook her head at him. "As I am also going."

"I'm afraid I'm with them, brother," said Peirs.

"I'm with Mem," said Will.

Clara stood beside Memory, her fingers on her lips. "I... I'm…"

Memory put a hand on her shoulder. "We need someone here to organize for incoming rescues, okay?"

Clara pouted her full lower lip. "I'm sorry that I'm not brave like you."

Memory laughed. "We're not brave. We're stupid. You're probably the smartest of us all."

Clara gave the smallest smile. "Just come back to me, and bring everyone home with you."

Erec said, "I suppose I'll have to go to keep you all safe then? I'll organize some of my men to join the party."

"And quick," Memory said. "It's time to get our raid on."

CHAPTER EIGHT

The carriage sped through the empty streets of Caermaellan. Over the clatter of the wheels and hooves on cobblestones, Memory heard a nearby clock tower ring for two in the morning. She could also hear the dozen or so guards on horseback escorting them. More empty coaches, larger and slower than the sleek model Memory rode in, were driven behind, in the hopes there would be survivors to bring home.

It had felt like a lifetime since Memory had driven these streets, distant days of going to school or visiting her homeless shelter, or her night with Dylan where he compared her to the moon. Memory wondered where he was now and wondered when her life would slow down enough to go back to school again, to continue her magic classes with Bedevere, to continue with her life.

When the lives of those I love are also safe. That's when.

"Everyone has iron?" Memory checked again.

Eloryn and Peirs across from her, and Will, beside her, all confirmed.

"Are we dumb to do this frontal assault style? Do we have any other more reasonable plan?" Memory asked everyone.

Eloryn looked out the window for a long moment. "The faster we're in, the better. If it's a trap, they are expecting us one way or another. But we've got iron, so we're at an advantage. The property they've been using doesn't belong to the fae, so it doesn't count as their territory. That means the second they try and attack us, we're in our rights to defend ourselves and Brand them. Whether the gaunts seduced their victims or not, they are in the wrong by law and it's our right under the Pact to stop them."

Memory glanced at Will then back to Eloryn and Peirs. "Well, you two can Brand. Will and I will stick to iron."

Peirs frowned, but said nothing.

A knock came from the window through to the driver's seat- Erec signaling they were about to arrive.

Memory looked to each of her friends in turn as she buttoned up her coat, the polished brass slippery under her fingers. "It's important to find evidence of who is running this place, to find out who Providence is or any clue about what's going on here, but remember, first and foremost this is a rescue mission. Roen, Maeve, the kids, we get them all out alive."

They shared silent nods, and the carriage came to an abrupt stop.

Eloryn took a breath so deep her whole chest rose and fell. "I will use my behests to help make all of us faster and stronger when I am able, but my main focus will be on finding Roen, finding the captives."

Erec opened the carriage door and Peirs stepped out first, followed by Memory, Eloryn, and Will. The team of guards dismounted around them, their horses nickering and restless from the fast ride.

As Erec gestured orders to his men, Peirs stepped up beside Memory. "I know you want to save the little ones as much as I do, but don't let that lead you to do anything foolish. Stay close by me. Be careful."

Memory bumped her shoulder into his and droned, "Yes, Dad."

The house stood silent and grim before them, a shambling mess of grey timber webbed with dead ivy that hung like tattered shrouds. No sound, no movement, no light showed from within.

Memory led the march up the steps to the front door, Will close beside her.

She found herself nose to nose with Mina.

"You? What are you doing here?" Memory said. *Providence couldn't be Mina, no way.*

Mina flicked her chin away from Memory, ignoring her. "Will, come with me."

Will's jaw twitched, but he spoke calmly. "I'm staying with Memory."

"No, you come with me, now," Mina shrieked, and her fiery hair whipped to life. "You are not going in that place!"

Memory stared Mina down. "He said he's coming with me. Just give him a break, would you?"

"You're not going in there. You're not, you're not," Mina said. She snatched Will by the wrists, shaking him. "Why are you being so awful? I don't want you to go in there. It's not safe. You can't."

Will pulled his hands free, stepping away from Mina and closer to Memory. "I'm going wherever she goes."

Mina's glow flared, anger shaking the fairy dust off her in tides as her breath caught in sobs. Memory had never seen her so flustered. There was something different, almost hectic about her. *Maybe she really does want to protect Will from something, something in that house. As much as I want to protect Will from her…*

Mina swiped her arm to grab Will again and Memory held her hands up to calm her. "Will, look, just go with her. It will be okay. I'll be okay."

Will looked hurt. "Mem?"

Memory leaned closer to him and whispered. "I don't want to see you hurt. It's okay, go. Go and find out what firefly has buzzed up this girl's butt. She clearly knows something we don't."

Will gave a single, slow nod, but his eyebrows were low and darkened his bright eyes.

Mina snatched his hand in hers, and the two of them vanished in a shower of fairy dust and swirl of Veil mist.

The confidence Memory had been feeling a moment before vanished with him.

More and more she wanted Will by her side. It felt right. It felt like home.

I'll just have to get through this so I can see him again soon.

Memory waved a signal to Erec, who took half of his men at a sprint ahead of her and barged through the splintered front door. Her heart started pounding as the door broke through.

No turning back now.

Memory, Eloryn, and Peirs went next, the rest of the guards taking position behind them.

A dull, earthy odor like old mushrooms hung in the air inside. The entrance hall was narrow, and doors to each side had been barricaded off, leaving only one direction to travel. All who could cast the light behest did, and the darkness gave way, showing wallpaper hanging from the walls like sloughing skin and a carpet littered in dead leaves and rodent carcasses. Portraits of the past human residents still hung on the walls, their faces slashed away by claw marks.

"Onwards," Eloryn ordered, and the group moved forward down the long tunnel. The ceiling above them had collapsed, leaving a gaping hole to the second floor.

Memory looked behind them and found the front door almost out of sight. The hall continued on much farther than she thought it would, leading them deep into the cavernous house.

"We're being forced along. Can we break through any of these doors? Search the rest of the house?" she asked the guards.

One of the guards lifted a small battering ram from his back, and held it between him and another man. The first strike at the door beside them seemed to shake the whole house.

"We've rang the doorbell now," Memory muttered.

Peirs grunted, "Where are the blasted creatures?"

The guards struck the side door again, and the frame began to split, a crack of space showing into the next room.

"Up front!" Erec called.

With disjointed movements, a mass of gaunts stepped up into the light. Memory counted at least six before shadows hid

any more that stood behind them. They hissed at Erec.

"And behind," a guard at the rear replied.

Whipping around, Memory saw her fears confirmed. More gaunts. They'd been blocked off on both sides in the narrow passageway.

Eloryn held her wisp light high and walked to the front to face the gaunts. "Back away. Let us through or be Branded."

A soft scraping sound echoed down the hall, like dry leaves blowing across dirt. As it built, Memory realized it was the gaunts, all of them, laughing at them.

The gaunt closest to Eloryn snatched for her. Erec pulled her back out of reach.

Eloryn gasped, and grabbed the iron arrow head she wore on a necklace. She tore the necklace free and held the iron out defensively.

Erec spoke in a tone cold and quiet. "Bronmarbh Aileadh."

The gaunt howled breathily as the mark appeared on its forehead. Its companions joined the cry and surged forward in attack. Long, wiry limbs flailed, swiping at any human within reach.

The guards at the back of the group rushed at the gaunts behind them, and those in front followed Eloryn forward, striking at the other assailants. The cries of dark fae and men, and the putrid smell of iron burning fae flesh filled the space. The guards used their daggers, unable to draw their swords in the small space, and the gaunts struck back with sharp talons. The unseelie fae from behind had broken through the guards at the back and fought with them up and down the corridor.

Memory tried to move forward, but was pinned between the backs of men, fighting gaunts on either side. Peirs kept shifting backwards, keeping her behind him and against a wall. She could hear him grunting as he clashed with the slashing gray arms of the creatures.

Eloryn and Erec were pushing forward with the main group, making headway with the iron they wielded and Eloryn's behests.

Memory saw a gap in the fighting, and ran to join them, but the body of a guard flew through the air straight at her.

Peirs stepped in front of her, taking the full force, but the momentum knocked him into Memory and they both hit the door beside them.

Already weakened by the attempts with the battering ram, it smashed inwards, and they fell into the side room and into darkness.

Memory fell hard on her back and her head cracked onto the ground. Her vision darkened and blurred and she widened her eyes and tensed, trying to fight off the black pull of unconsciousness.

The sounds from the corridor grew quieter as the fight sprawled further away into the house.

Memory strained to sit up, pushing away the sharp broken wood and crumbling wall that fell around her. She couldn't get her bearings in the dark room. She almost called a light behest before stopping herself.

"Peirs, can you cast some light?"

He coughed, and spluttered a raspy, "Àlaich las."

The wisp lightened the room, hovering beside Peirs's hand which was limply draped on the ground. They were alone, everyone else had spread out into the rest of the house. The room they were in had been cleared, all its furniture stacked

around the edges, blocking windows and other doors. On some walls, holes had been broken through, claw marks showing on the sides. Holes just large enough to squeeze a person, or fae, through.

Peirs groaned beside Memory, and the guard that hit them lay face down on her other side. She reached over to check on him, and felt no pulse at his neck. Memory took a deep breath to calm herself.

Peirs coughed again and Memory looked down at him where he still lay beside her.

His chest was bleeding and he held it clutched in one hand. He saw her looking. "How bad is it?" he asked.

"I could lie and say not bad at all. But you're a big boy and holy hamballs it looks bad. Super bad."

Memory scrambled across the floor, ducking out the door to see if anyone was still around. She needed Eloryn, needed anyone that could heal.

The hall was empty except for an equal mix of bodies of guards and gaunts, sprawled on the messy carpet. Too many bodies. Too many lost lives.

Back in the room, Memory tugged down the old lace curtain from the window and shook the dust from it.

She folded it into a wad and lifted Peirs's hands away from the wound. She could clearly see the spread of four claw marks torn through his clothes, slicing into his flesh.

Peirs smiled crookedly. "I Branded the bastard back at least."

Memory pressed the fabric against the wound and lifted his hands back over it.

"Hold onto this, press it on firmly to stop the bleeding. I'm going to get help."

His hands flopped down weakly, sliding away from the wound.

"Crap." Memory took his place, keeping her hands against the old curtain to slow the flow of blood. The cream cotton lace was already stained red through.

"I've heard Maellan excel at healing magic. I know you're busy, but I'm not wildly keen on pain, Your Majesty."

Memory winced. She hadn't been able to heal anyone other than her sister before. And even if she could, she'd made the oath to not use her magic. *Damn fairies and their damn oath!* "My sister, she's the one that's good at that stuff."

Peirs's eyes rolled back and Memory squeezed his shoulder. "Stay awake, you'll be all right. The bleeding is already stopping."

"Probably means I just ran out of blood."

"Don't sass me. You're going to be fine."

Peirs blinked and seemed to have trouble opening his eyes again. "You always did have too much faith in me."

"Maybe putting lots of faith in people is what helps them rise to great things."

He smiled, but his lips were stained with blood, burbling from his mouth.

That is a very bad thing. Memory gritted her teeth. She should try, she had to at least try and heal him. Maybe she would be able to do it now. Screw her deal with the fae.

"Peirs, I'm going to have a go at healing you, 'kay? I'm not great at it like Lory, so keep your fingers crossed."

Peirs just stared at her. He was too still.

"Peirs?"

Memory squeezed his shoulder but he didn't reply. She shook him and he did nothing.

Peirs's wisp behest began fading.

Memory clutched for Peirs's wrist and found it quiet, no pulse tapping away under the skin.

A single, rasping sob tore up through Memory's throat and she covered her face with her hands, sitting still and quiet.

Sorrow swelled inside Memory and settled, large and heavy in her chest. She gave it a home there, alongside the weight of everyone else she had lost. She would carry them always, every one of them, even if she had to grow stronger to bear that weight.

The light faded out entirely and she held Peirs's hand in the dark, a dead man on either side.

She heard the crunch of feet crushing dry leaves behind her. No light of a wisp behest came with it. It was not another human. Memory reached for the knife at her belt. Before her fingers closed around it, a heavy hand slammed into the back of her head and she collapsed.

CHAPTER NINE

Erec kept in front of Eloryn, so she could barely see past his torso. She spoke her behest to enchant the bodies of those around her to be faster and stronger, and with her iron as well they were making headway into the crowd of gaunts.

"Some are running for it," Erec yelled over the fighting. He looked at Eloryn, urgency in his features.

Eloryn shared his concern. If the gaunts' plan to corner and capture them failed, they might turn on the captives. They needed to chase down the runners and stop them from getting to their prisoners first.

"Quickly," Eloryn ordered, waving the guards around her forward. "*Quickly*," she said again in the magical language. They surged onwards, chasing the remaining gaunts through the dark house, sped faster by Eloryn's behest.

The floorboards strained and crackled under the charging footsteps. Eloryn pushed to the front of the group, leading the charge. *I have to get to Roen before the dark fae do. Please don't let it be too late.*

Eloryn took a face full of cobwebs and wiped it away. The corridor came to a dead end, blocked by half a dozen armoires piled atop each other in a splintered mess. A hole had been clawed in the walls on both sides and one above in the ceiling.

"They've made this house a maze. Which way?" Erec said.

Eloryn changed the meaning of the behests she spoke, and the creatures' path was revealed to her in shining footsteps. "Two went right, one went up."

Erec signaled his men, splitting them off to the right and boosting some up through the hole in the ceiling.

As the space cleared of guards, Eloryn gasped. "Where is Mem, and Peirs?"

"They were right behind us," Erec said, looking back down the empty corridor. "Your Highness, it's my fault. It's my responsibility to protect the queen."

Eloryn looked back the way they'd come, then forward through the holes the guards had gone. Memory was behind and in danger, Roen and others were forward, and in danger. Memory was still with Peirs and some of the other guards. Eloryn hoped that meant she was fine. "Go back and find her, I'll continue on for the abductees."

"Your Highness, you'll be alone, are you sure?" Erec asked.

Eloryn hesitated. *No. I want to find my sister. She's too vulnerable without her magic.*

In the silent moment, Eloryn heard a soft sound that made her heart race. "Go and help Memory," she ordered Erec.

Erec nodded and ran.

Eloryn stood still, alone in the quiet, straining to listen. She stepped toward the mass of furniture in the corridor.

"Eloryn?"

It was like Roen's voice, but weaker, rougher. It seemed to come from within the barricade.

"Roen, where are you?" she called out.

Eloryn climbed carefully up onto the first armoire. It lay on its back on the floor and the doors bent inwards, creaking when they took her weight. Some of the other furniture on top of it shifted.

The glint of eyes shone from a dark gap between the cupboards. A low growl hissed, "Eloryn…"

It wasn't Roen's voice at all.

The creature launched itself out from the jumble of wardrobes, claws first.

Eloryn inhaled sharply and stumbled away. She turned to dodge the sickle-like claws and they caught in her hair, pulling it loose from its pins. She cried out as tearing hair made her eyes water. The gaunt swiped at her again. It was smaller than all the others had been, small enough to conceal itself in that slim shadowed crack, preparing its ambush, but it was no less strong.

Its fingers tangled in her loose hair, grabbing on and tugging her head down so her face turned up toward the hole in the ceiling. The gaunt's other hand was above her, claws splayed and slashing down at her exposed neck.

She had to say the Brand, while she still had a throat to say it, but she knew there was no time left. "Bronma-"

The gaunt froze, eyes wide. It gurgled a harsh cry as its arms went limp, releasing Eloryn. Black smoke and slime spilled from its mouth and it fell to the floor, revealing Roen standing behind it.

Roen held his iron dagger, and it was slick with gray blood. Squinting at Eloryn and the bright light from her wisp around her, he said, "You look like an angel, my love." He grunted softly, winced, and wobbled on his feet.

Eloryn blinked, letting herself believe her eyes. Her heartbeat grew strong. "You've sustained a blow to your head," she said gently, wrapping her arm around Roen's waist to support him.

Roen nodded. One side of his face had a trail of blood running from his hair line to his jaw and he waved at it weakly. "I escaped the beasts, but this left me too weak to get out of the house. I've mostly been hiding and waiting for my princess to come save me."

Eloryn smiled and sighed at the same time. "I think we're one for one on that count. Thank you," she said, placing a hand to her still intact throat.

Roen smiled in return, but his eyes were vague, haunted.

Eloryn pulled a dressing from the collection she brought with her for treating wounds until she had time to perform proper healing behests. She pressed the wadded cloth to the gash on Roen's forehead. "How do you feel? I can heal you now but it could take some time and we've yet to reach the captives. We've also lost track of Memory and Peirs."

Roen just stared at her. "Come here."

He wrapped her in his arms, burying his head into her neck.

Eloryn felt tears aching for release in her eyes. "I worried I'd lost you. I shouldn't have let you go."

"Let's never lose each other, no matter what. Nothing will part us again."

Eloryn's tears burst free. "I promised I would solve Hayes's demands before I saw you again, and I haven't."

"Never mind. Let's just run off to sea together and be pirates."

A breathy, rich laugh of relief escaped from Eloryn. She squeezed Roen tightly, but could tell his grip was loose, looser than the strong embrace she knew him to have. "I can heal you now," she offered again.

Roen let her go and smiled. "I will keep. And I know where the gaunts are holding everyone. Let's go."

Roen led Eloryn through the hole in the wall the two gaunts had gone before.

They soon came across the guards who'd gone that way, who had managed to dispatch the last of the gaunts. Their gray bodies and black blood mixed into the gloom and grime on the floor.

"This way," Roen said, and the guards followed. They squeezed through a narrow gap between two walls and around into a large ruined sitting room.

"It's down under there." Roen pointed to the center of the room where a round carpet lay underneath broken armchairs and a tipped over piano.

The guards began to roll back the rug. Roen shook his head and pointed again. "There. The piano."

The guards seemed confused at first, but together put their shoulders against the piano and slid it out of the way. A hole dropped into black beneath it.

Roen looked grim. Eloryn's body refused to move, to go

and see what would be found in that dark pit. She forced it to, leaning over the edge and calling the names of children who'd gone missing, names Memory had told her.

The small, weak voice of a child made everyone move for the hole at once.

The guards dropped through first, helping to catch Eloryn as she followed. Eloryn strengthened her light behest to clear all shadows from the space.

The enormous basement had the tang of blood on the cool air. Clean cut stone walls had chains bolted into it at regular intervals, where the bodies of humans, pale and drained, hung like a butcher's shop window.

Many were adults, but some were children. Eloryn sharpened her senses, and could see the faintest rise and fall of breath on their chests.

"They live." *Some of them,* a mournful voice amended internally. "Help them down."

The guards acted quickly, breaking the shackles and cradling the prisoners as they dropped free.

Across the other side of the room, a ragged group of captives shied away from the light. Most had blank faces, compelled or dazed or too traumatized for thought. Eloryn approached them slowly. "Be still, we are here to help. You are safe now."

Hidden behind the front row, a huddle of dirty limbs and rags in the corner began to move. A pale face turned to blink at Eloryn.

"Mem?" The girl with the mountain of messy dark hair was familiar to Eloryn.

"No, Maeve, but she's nearby." *I hope.*

Maeve unwrapped herself from the clutch of other children

she was hiding beneath her skirts and small body. She moved stiffly, as though she'd been fixed in that protective posture for weeks.

Eloryn stared, dumbfounded with grief and fury at what she saw in that cold stone room. Then she shook some sense back into herself. These people needed her to act, they needed her help. She began speaking words of magic. She could not heal everyone at once, or rid them of the horrors they'd experienced, but she could give them enough strength to move, to escape this prison.

Eloryn put on a friendly smile and took Maeve's hand, helping her get the other children to their feet.

Maeve mumbled, "It's lucky Mem's not here. This would break her heart."

"Or very seriously enrage her," Eloryn added.

Maeve coughed out a sobbing laugh.

Roen called to them from the hole above. "I've found a ladder to help bring people out. And Erec has returned."

Eloryn called back, "And my sister?"

Roen grimaced. "Peirs is dead. And Memory is gone."

CHAPTER TEN

Light flickered through Memory's eyelids. Her head ached and she forced her eyes open. Two gaunts carried her slung between them, one holding her wrists and one holding her feet. They were going down stairs. Her vision faded again.

She wavered in and out of consciousness. She saw snatches of her surroundings — tunnels, darker tunnels, dirtier tunnels — but had completely lost her bearings. Each time her eyes twitched open it took moments to even remember where she was and what was happening. She'd been captured. She was being taken somewhere. She had to fight back. And then darkness would steal her away again.

A slamming jolt shook her whole body, waking her up.

She'd been dumped onto a stone alter on her back. Her body still quivered from the impact. She took quick stock of her surroundings, but all she could see were close, dark, stone walls, and cobwebs. She wished for light. The fae had much better night vision than her and moved without any. The only light was a glow coming from the opening to the room, the color of early sunrise, but dim and distant. Still, it gave Memory hope. Maybe there was a window somewhere nearby, a door, some exit she could escape to outside.

"It's awake," said one gaunt. A splash of black blood on its cheek shone wet in the dark.

"Keep it still," the other replied. Its voice was strangely high pitched and gurgling despite its masculine appearance. "Remember what the master told us to do."

The creatures held her pinned, one at her arms, and the other pushing her thighs down. She may as well have been bound by metal bars for all she could move. Their sharp claws dug cruelly into her. Panic burbled aggressively in her chest.

The panic had a voice in her head, screaming, *Let go of me, let go, don't touch me!* Memory squinted her eyes, about to loose her magic on them.

She clenched her jaw so hard it made her aching head throb. *I can't. Calm down. I still have my knife. There has to be another chance to escape.*

Across her temple and down to her ear was a sore area that felt wet and sticky. Consciousness was a wild bird, struggling to fly off and leave her at any moment.

The gaunt holding her arms leaned close to her and sniffed at her head. "Can you smell that?" it asked the other dark fae.

The gaunt holding Memory's legs down, the one with black

blood on its face, growled a warning. "Leave it. This one is the master's. All the blood is the master's."

"That blood is mine. Keep off me, monster," Memory said. Both creatures ignored her.

"So full of magic." The dark fae sniffing Memory leaned closer, dragging a long, raspy tongue across her forehead. It scratched on her skin like a cat's. Memory cringed in disgust.

"Full, full, full of magic." Excitement rose in the gaunt's voice as it licked her a second time, sharp teeth grazing her skin. Its clawed hands closed tight on her arms, tearing into her skin. Memory cried out and wrestled against it, trying to break free.

"Stop it!" Memory said. The gaunt kept licking, getting more and more excited, more ravenous each time. Memory yelled at the other one. "Stop him, he's going to get you both in trouble with your master!"

The gaunt holding Memory's legs down hissed in frustration. It hesitated, then let go, rushed forward and pushed the bloodthirsty gaunt away. In return it howled in the face of the other, a berserk fury in its cry.

Out of their grasp, Memory wasted no time to take her advantage. She whipped her knife from her belt and slipped off the side of the altar onto her feet.

Both gaunts heard her move and turned on her. One roared so loudly it made Memory's chest reverberate and hair fly around her face.

"Just stay back and let me go," Memory said, holding her knife up in front of her as a warning. Her vision still swam and she worried she'd simply drop like a stone into unconsciousness again at any moment. "Just let me go. I don't want to have to use this. I don't want to hurt you."

Both gaunts now had bloodied faces, the one with black dark fae blood, and the one with Memory's blood red around its mouth. The one with black blood grinned. "That's your mistake."

It grabbed the bloodthirsty fae beside it and pushed it toward Memory. The gaunt flew at her so fast it was impaled on Memory's knife to the hilt before she could pull back. Dark blood spattered, warm and sticky like molasses onto Memory's hand. She recoiled, yanking her knife out of the fae. The knife had already done its damage. The wound foamed and hissed, smelling like burning hair. Thick smoke that sparkled gold within as if sparks from a fire poured from the hole.

Memory stared horrified as the gaunt collapsed in on itself. She stared too long, and the remaining gaunt lunged at her, knocking the knife from her hands.

The gaunt grabbed for her, snatching her around the waist and throwing her over its shoulder. Memory kicked at it and scraped her fingernails on its back but it had no effect. The gaunt's musty jacket hung loose on its bony shoulders, and Memory reached down its back and grabbed the bottom hem. Curling her legs up, she wedged her feet against the gaunt's chest and pushed off as hard as she could. She launched herself backwards, off the gaunt's shoulder, and pulled its coat up and over its head as she went.

Memory landed against the wall with a crack and yelled in pain. The gaunt stumbled blindly, trying to free itself from the fabric covering its face.

Got to get up, get away. Memory's feet slipped as she tried to get them under her. Her body ached all over. A hand closed over her arm. Warm. Human.

She looked up.

Will.

He looked angrier than she'd ever seen him. He helped her to her feet then turned on the gaunt. "You hurt her."

The gaunt got its claws into the coat material and tore itself free.

Will held the iron hook, pointing it at eye level at the gaunt. Memory bent down with a groan and reclaimed her knife.

The gaunt stared at them both for a long moment. *Don't you dare kamikaze yourself at us you crazy creature,* Memory begged silently.

"Doesn't matter. My master will have you anyway, soon." The gaunt threw the remains of its coat on the floor and vanished away through the Veil.

"Holy crapoly," Memory said with a big sigh. "I do NOT like those guys."

"You're bleeding," Will said.

"And apparently it's tasty, tasty blood. Thanks for coming to the rescue. How did you get away from Mina so quick?"

Will didn't say anything, just held up the iron hook in his hands.

Memory raised an eyebrow. "You didn't hurt her, did you?" *Am I entirely sure if that would be a bad thing?*

"No. Just threatened. Made her send me back, once she told me why she didn't want me to go into the house. And who these creatures' master is."

Memory and Will found their way back out of the labyrinthine underground tunnel system and out into the cool morning wind through a wooden hatch around the back of the house.

Memory stood for a moment, breathing the freshness of that air. She felt exhausted, and not just emotionally. She was certain she was concussed. She just wanted to sleep and sleep, as soon as she knew everyone was safe. Everyone but Peirs and all the men who'd already died tonight. Memory started imagining how many families would wake up this morning without a father. She slumped, leaning into Will's chest in an effort to stay upright. Will took initiative from there, and in a smooth scoop she was up in his arms, carried there in a strong embrace. Memory let her eyes close for a short moment as she listened to his heartbeat and tried to forget everything else.

Reaching the front of the house, a guard who had just helped a young girl into one of the carriages saw Memory and Will, and raced back into the house. Soon Eloryn, Roen, and Erec came rushing back out.

Memory's chest warmed and tightened at the sight of them. "Roen, you're okay. You're alive."

Will placed Memory softly down on her feet. She managed a few wobbly steps to greet the others and Roen met her in a just as wobbly embrace.

Eloryn quickly joined them, holding her sister strongly. "Thank the fae, you're all right. We were just about to track where the creatures had taken you."

"You found the captives, you saved them. Is Maeve out? Edele?"

"Maeve is fine." Eloryn hesitated, and stepped back. "We're

still checking for everyone else."

Memory broke away as well. She turned to watch the first coach of captives rolling off toward the castle, and more people being directed by guards into another. Erec stood by the door, his face gray and eyes red.

"Erec. I'm so sorry about Peirs. He saved my life, and I… I couldn't save his."

Erec turned his head to Memory, and pulled himself into stance of attention. "I know if my brother had to give his life for anyone, he would have chosen you. He believes, believed greatly in you."

Memory just nodded, and watched as Erec returned to his duties.

Memory stared at the carriage in front of her, the smaller, faster one she'd arrived in and it felt suddenly so unfamiliar, as though it were years since they'd first arrived there that night, or that she expected to see a car there instead. She blinked, her eyes blurry.

"Let's go home," Eloryn said, putting an arm around Memory's waist and leading her forward. "There's lots of healing to be done, after tonight. But it is over now."

Tears flooded Memory's eyes and she blinked them away, refusing to let them fall. "No. It's only just beginning. This place, it was Finvarra's."

Eloryn stopped mid step. "How do you know?"

Will looked over his shoulder at the steps of the building. "Mina let it slip when she took me away. That's why she didn't want me to go in. Way too dangerous, out of bounds because it was the unseelie king's. She's been listening for gossip and that's what she heard."

Eloryn's eyes sought from side to side, the questions in her mind clear on her face. "Why? Some think him mad, but to do this? Why?"

Memory's voice was hard and low. "Mina heard that Finvarra believes drinking human blood will prolong his life."

Memory watched as guards brought out the last of the survivors. There weren't many. The driver climbed onto the carriage, ready to go. The few survivors Memory saw looked in pretty bad shape, mentally as much as physically. She wondered what horrors they'd endured, all just to keep one twisted old king alive. Memory kept hearing how the fae were dying, but this was absolutely not the right way to stay alive.

"Now we know it was Finvarra who was Providence, and Hope," Memory said. "And me and Thayl, we were just some other experiment of his, turning us into a battery to steal the magic from to charge himself up with new life."

Roen frowned. "You think that's what Providence would have asked of Thayl after his bargain was complete? To take all that power for himself?"

"Sure. Think about it. Finvarra couldn't go to the human world himself to gather up all that magic. He had to send a human to do it for him. And he found just the right sucker with Thayl."

Erec joined their group and notified them that the house had been cleared. Another troop of guards was on the way from the castle for a more thorough sweep, and to remove the dead for burial, but it was time for them to leave.

As they climbed up into their own carriage, Memory said, "The only thing I can't work out is why he wanted me to be queen. Why was that so important? It wouldn't have anything to

do with nabbing my magic to keep his ticker going."

Eloryn stepped into the carriage next, taking the seat beside her. "If anything, you being queen would make it harder for Finvarra to harvest the magic from you. Far more protections and politics in place. But that is our problem now as well. Finvarra is the king of the Unseelie Fae. There is not a move we can make against him for justice for this that wouldn't risk war, or risk the Pact itself."

CHAPTER ELEVEN

All living captives from Finvarra's blood lair were brought back to the palace for medical care. Both Eloryn and the wizards of the Council worked without sleep for two days to heal the survivors. Once well enough, they were also questioned on any further insight into what Finvarra had been doing. Most knew nothing, too dazed, compelled, or simply traumatized to remember anything other than an overwhelming sense of horror. Most remembered very little beyond being taken by a handsome man or woman who then turned out to be a gaunt. Those that remembered more never saw any fae except the gaunts, who would bleed the victims and take the blood away.

Memory had searched the survivors for one person in

particular; a little girl called Edele. She wasn't there. It had been so long since Edele had been taken that her fate was clear. Eloryn could see the ferocity of emotions that discovery caused within her sister. Eloryn was proud to see Memory keep her sadness and rage reined in, but even a couple of days later, the teapots and crockery on their morning tea setting rattled just by being within proximity to Memory.

Eloryn had arranged for them to have some time with just the two of them, while Roen and Will spent some time together as well, and the sisters sat at a neatly set up table on the emerald lawn of the palace's private gardens. Eloryn poured out some chamomile tea for her sister. "All of Finvarra's captives have made a full recovery, physically at least, and there have been no further reports of people going missing from Caermaellan since."

Memory rubbed her forehead with the palm of her hand. "But we still have to deal with him. Somehow. And Hayes, somehow. Your wedding is meant to be in just two days and all we have are somehows."

"We'll find something. We have to."

"You know what I want to do? I want to get both Finvarra and Hayes in front of me, then take a crap on my fist and punch them both in the mouth."

Eloryn coughed up her tea. "That was the singularly most graphic, disgusting and violent thing I've ever heard."

"You've led a very sheltered life."

"And yet I can't help agreeing with the sentiment." Eloryn sat back in her chair and looked up at the sky. The clouds hung so low and dark, barely any daylight shone through and the temperature was dropping tangibly. A hawk circled high above.

She wondered what she must look like in its eyes. What their problems would seem like to that animal, so wild and free. "I've almost finished rebuilding the Round Table. I wish all problems could be solved by fixing, rebuilding, or creating. Violence and conflict lead only to more of the same. If only there were some way I could heal Hayes's heart, to take away his greed or ambition or any grudges he holds against me for my actions."

Memory leaned forward. "Can you? You are so good with your magic, and you can heal bodies so well. What about minds?"

Eloryn paused. *Could I?* She wasn't sure at all if it was within her power, but she saw the possibility there, and the hope. "If I could, wouldn't it be wrong for me to change a person's thoughts and feelings without permission, for my own gain?"

"Pfft. Always having to bring logic and ethics into the argument. Okay, think of it this way- would it be wrong to cure someone of blindness without permission?" Memory's mouth twisted and she made a smacking sound with her tongue. "Without permission. Yuck. Yeah, those words just taste bad together. I guess even good things done without permission turn bad, don't they?"

Eloryn placed her teacup carefully back onto the saucer and regarded her sister for a moment. "You've suffered more hurt than many. Even with permission, is this something you would seek out? To have your hurts healed, taken away, or forgotten?"

Memory looked down, the tiniest smile on her mouth, so small it looked sad.

"A week or two ago I might have said yes. But no. I wouldn't. If it meant forgetting those I've lost, then no. I never want to lose them."

Eloryn bowed her head. A small service had been held for

Peirs just the day before. Memory wanted a grand event, to honor him, but Erec requested it be kept simple. Even still, the small graveyard overflowed with people coming to say goodbye. Erec was Peirs's only blood family, but there were the members of the resistance Peirs led, every guard from the castle, and every child from Memory and Maeve's orphanage mourning for him.

Afterwards, when everyone had gone and Memory thought she was alone, Eloryn saw her placing out a small marker in the graveyard for Edele as well.

As though sharing thoughts with her twin, Memory touched the corner of her eye to clear away a tear. "If it meant not being the person I am now, I would not. I'm the person I am now because of the hurt and the happiness I've lived through. I've lost parts of me before. I never want to lose anything again."

Eloryn's smile grew as her sister spoke, and grew so wide it almost forced tears from her eyes.

Memory kicked her under the table. "Quit it. You're making this all awkward now."

"I don't mind. You make me feel that somehow, everything will turn out fine."

Memory leaned to the side, looking past Eloryn. "This doesn't look very fine. Check it out. What's going on?"

Eloryn turned around to see Roen being escorted to them by Bedevere and a rank of guards. Will followed a small way behind.

She stood to greet them.

Bedevere looked deeply troubled, and Roen's expression matched.

Bedevere bowed to Memory and Eloryn in turn. "Your Majesty, Your Highness, I'm sorry to interrupt you but Hayes

has been found dead in his cell."

Memory got to her feet too as Will came to stand beside her. "No way. You mean, naturally? Or…"

Eloryn looked at the guards again, keeping close rank around Roen. "You can't believe Roen had something to do with this."

Bedevere bowed his head. "It seems as though Hayes was poisoned. There is a witness that has reported seeing Sir Roen near Hayes's cell. Or someone that looked like him," Bedevere amended. "Given that he also has motivation, he will be considered a suspect until the investigation is complete."

"How long will that take?" Memory asked.

"Not long. We will be utilizing all techniques available to the Council. There are no secrets to magic. I wish I could oversee the investigation myself, but I'm afraid I also am considered to have conflict of interest, if not motivation, myself."

Eloryn nodded. She still missed his brother, Waylan, as well. "Is there nothing further we can do other than wait?"

"I fear not," Bedevere said.

Roen tilted his head, seeming more embarrassed than anything. "They want to confine me to quarters for now. Apparently I'm considered of little risk of escape due to my lack of spark. I asked to be taken to you. If I must be confined to quarters, your quarters are much more accommodating than my own."

Eloryn's lips twitched into a small smile. She already knew it couldn't be him who murdered Hayes. She just had to trust the investigation would also prove his innocence. Taking him by the hand, she began leading the way back to her chambers. The guards parted, making way for them and Memory and Will following.

Bedevere stood back and watched them leave. "At least this has solved the dilemma of the marriage contract."

Eloryn turned back, answering over her shoulder. "We never wanted it solved this way."

Bedevere bowed low. "I know. For all Hayes did to my family as well, I am not happy to see him ended this way. There is no honor in this."

Memory pulled the thick, fur-lined cloak tight around her shoulders. Her teeth rattled as she puffed out a breath, watching it form mist on the air and mingling with the delicate snowflakes falling around her.

"Come back inside. You'll get cold," Will said from behind her.

"Like you can talk," Memory responded, shaking her head. Will still only wore a single layer of clothing, just one thin, button down shirt and pants. No shoes. She swore he didn't feel the cold at all. Snow fell all around them, soft and gentle, as they watched from Memory's balcony. Enough had fallen to start giving the trees and ground of the palace gardens a light blanket of white. "It's so beautiful. They say this is the first snow to fall in Avall since before the Pact."

"I've never seen it snow here before," Will agreed.

"The Pact and the fae in Avall changed its whole climate from a cold wasteland to temperate paradise. Clara says people are taking the snow as a bad omen, that too many fae are dying

or gone, and Avall is reverting to the harsh land it used to be." Memory paused to try and catch a snowflake on her tongue.

Will stared out into the hunting grounds where he used to spend more time. Memory wondered if he was thinking about Mina, or the other fae he knew. She wondered whether they were slowly dying as well.

"I think it's the iron," Will finally said.

Memory nodded slowly, frowning. "I've been thinking that too. The rest of the world is so rich with iron, and Avall has barely any now, not even raw iron ore. They had to get rid of iron for the fae, but they've screwed themselves over by doing it. It's like the rest of the world is one huge magnet and Avall is a tiny magnet and the huge magnet is sucking away and hogging all that hippy earth blood life force magic the fae live on. I've been hoping that I'm wrong, because what could we possibly do about it? We can't take on the whole rest of the world. 'Hey rest of the world, stop making steel and stealing our magic!' Can you see that working? Nope."

Will turned his back on the forest and looked at Memory. "Think about how fast industrialization is happening. It's going to get worse. Faster and faster."

"I've seen the flow of magic in the Veil. It's like a tide, flowing out of Avall." Memory stared at Will's eyes, icy blue and rimmed in dark lashes, they seemed to belong in this weather, like a black branch covered in snow. He reached out and brushed a thumb across her mouth.

Memory drew in a shaky breath.

"Your lips are turning blue," he said.

"I'm fine."

"You always say that."

"It's always true."

"Always?"

Did Will just step closer to me, or does he just suddenly feel a lot closer? Memory had to tilt her head up to look at him. A snowflake hung in his earth-brown hair right beside his cheek. His gaze on her was intense. "Are you really okay, after losing Peirs, after almost losing Maeve? After those gaunts caught you?"

Memory shivered, and not due to the cold. Will knew her too well. She'd been telling herself she was fine, but the whole event had left her shaken. To be held down against her will was nearly more than she could bear. It brought back too much pain.

She began shaking her head, ready to say the words again. *I'm fine.*

Will did step closer then and wrapped his arms around her shoulders, pulling her toward him. Memory gasped and hot tears flooded her eyes. They poured over her eyelids unchecked, darkening the thin fabric on Will's chest where she pressed her face.

"Damn it," Memory mumbled between sobs.

"I'm sorry I wasn't there. That I couldn't stop them touching you." Will's breath warmed through her hair as he spoke.

"I don't expect you to protect me all the time. I need to be able to look after myself."

"I know. But I want to protect you."

Memory clenched her fist around the cloth on Will's back.

He squeezed her tighter as well. "I want to be there for you when you need me most."

"You are," Memory said, sniffling away her sobs. "You're here with me now."

Will held her like that as the snow fell on them. After a few

moments, Memory stood back, wiped her nose and took a deep breath. "I need to fess a few things to Lory and Roen. Will you come with me? Moral support?"

Will simply nodded. Memory held out her hand to him and led him back inside to the joining door between the sisters' chambers. She paused there for a moment.

"What will I do if it was Roen who murdered Hayes?" she asked in a small voice.

"Do you think it was?"

"Most of me says no. No way. But part of me knows that we weren't finding any other way out of the marriage contract. Roen and Eloryn had to be getting desperate." Memory looked at the wall between her room and the corridor as though she could see straight through it. She knew if she could, she would see a troop of guards out there, keeping Roen confined in Eloryn's quarters until the investigation was complete.

"I'm Roen's friend. He's like a brother to me. But I'm also queen and I have to be fair and treat any crime as it should be. Ugh. If this isn't just the shittiest shit-tastic shit storm ever." Memory wiped her face again and puffed out a long breath. "Okay, let's do this."

Memory opened the adjoining door without knocking, and found Eloryn and Roen holding each other in the middle of the room.

"Aw, come on! I was hoping to catch you guys up to something much naughtier," Memory said, waggling her eyebrows at them.

Roen smirked. "What's happened? Have you heard anything about the investigation?"

"Not yet. I actually have something else I wanted to talk to you both about."

Memory panicked as everyone quieted to listen to her. She prolonged the task by getting everyone to sit down, and asking if anyone needed something to drink or eat, or more cushions, until Will gave her a stern look. Memory stopped fussing and stood still in front of her friends.

Then she told them everything about her past in the other world. Her time in the group home. The abuse she suffered there. She glossed over most of the details, until she got to the time right before she was brought back to Avall. The time she was beaten, and her magic killed the man who had been abusing her.

Memory shifted on her feet. They felt numb underneath her and she stared at them instead of looking at her friends. Anyway, I had to tell you. You might have already known, or guessed, but I had to say it out loud. I know it's the big cliché thing. Poor girl sexually abused in her past. But that's because it happens all the time. Happens too much. When it shouldn't happen at all. Never. Ever. *Ever.* And if I could do anything to stop it happening again, to anyone, I would. And now I'm a ruler maybe I can."

With a deep sigh, Memory dared to look her friends in the eyes again. "Now here I am, meant to be a ruler, someone who decides right and wrong, creates laws and defends justice. How can I do that when I'm a murderer?"

Eloryn had been sitting very quietly, staring at her hands in her lap. A long teardrop wound down one of her cheeks. She looked up at Memory with enormous sadness in her eyes. "I saw it happen. When I shared spirits with you, I saw flashes of your past. I didn't know for sure, then, because it was all so horrifying and confusing, but now you've explained the details it makes more sense. It wasn't murder, not hardly. It was self-preservation only. You did nothing wrong."

"I believe Eloryn. I saw how you looked when you first came to Avall. Beaten all over." Roen stood up and took her hands. "You've got an amazing heart, Memory. A quality many rulers overlook. I trust you to make just decisions."

A knock at the door startled all of them.

Memory answered quickly and found a page waiting there. He announced that the investigation had been completed, and they were all required in the Round Room immediately.

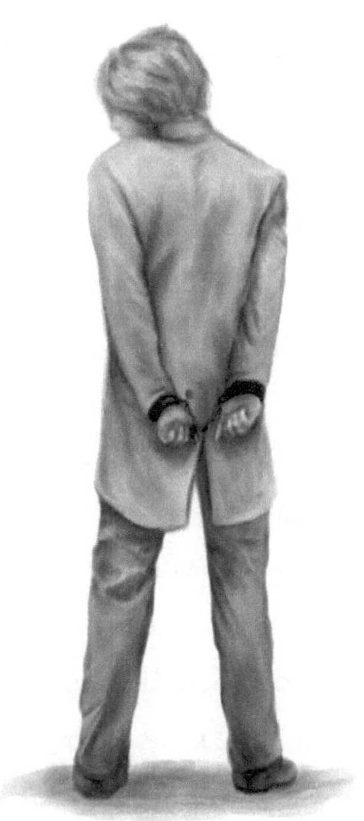

CHAPTER TWELVE

The troop of guards, including those escorting Roen and Memory's normal bodyguards, led them to the Round Room where Bedevere and a number of other wizards waited for them.

Memory saw another young man standing in the center of the room, bound in shackles. From a distance, the shade of his hair and angle of his jaw made him look just like Roen.

"Dylan?" she said.

He turned to look at her. His eyes were wide and eyebrows low, a combination of terrified and furious.

Bedevere gestured to an older wizard beside him "Madoc has completed the investigation and proof has been found of Sir Dylan Faerbaird's guilt in the matter of Hayes's murder. The fugitive was then captured whilst trying to steal from Hayes's chambers and flee."

Memory glanced at Roen beside her, worried about what reaction he'd have to seeing his brother like this. Roen seemed more confused than anything.

His voice was low and sharp when he asked, "Dylan, why have you done this? Are you trying to hurt our parents even more?"

Dylan's head bowed, but with a shake he lifted it again, staring furiously at Memory. "Hayes ruined my chances at having a comfortable life by his scheming to set me up with her. A life for which I'd already sacrificed a lot in order to keep." Dylan's glance flicked briefly to Roen before he turned on Memory again. "It was all Hayes's idea, he forced me into relations with you, Your Majesty. I was trying to get him to clear my name but he refused. He spoiled my future. He had to pay."

Memory gaped. "You killed him for revenge?" Her brain ached, trying and yet unable to comprehend. *Can any desire be so destructive as vengeance?*

"I don't care whose idea it was to pair the two of us up. But what you've done now, there's no coming back from that." Memory walked forward to stand in front of Dylan. "Even after what you did to me, I could have forgiven you. Truly. I'm really into forgiveness these days. You had a chance to reconcile with your family. *Your family*, Dylan. But now I must sentence you for this terrible crime."

Dylan rasped out a rough laugh, his eyes growing wider, wilder. "Why? I did you a favor! I know the old man was trying to marry the princess. I removed your problem. I was trying to help you."

Roen spoke from beside Memory. "You were only trying to help yourself. It's all you know how to do."

Memory turned to look at Roen and thought about how he would have to deliver this news to his parents and her heart broke for him. Five of his brothers had been lost in battles, and Dylan had left them by choice, wanting riches and comfort over a life in hiding with his family. And now he was more of a criminal than Roen ever had been. She wished she could simply remove all the anger and greed from within Dylan, and return him to his parents as a beloved son, and no one would have to suffer. But she knew in her heart no magic could do that. But maybe time could.

She sighed. "Would I be right in assuming the standard punishment for murder in Avall is some sort of execution?"

Bedevere nodded solemnly.

"Not any more. Dylan, your crime is one of the worst, but you will learn nothing from dying and teach nothing to others. And I couldn't live with myself if I took another of Isabeth and Brannon's sons away from them. You will be imprisoned, and you will work to help make Avall a better place. We're going to introduce Avall to some things called community service and rehabilitation."

Memory called the guards to take Dylan away. He craned his neck as he was taken, watching Memory. The look on his face was confused, possibly even relieved. She hoped he would take her mercy and use it well.

Roen put a hand on her shoulder. "Thank you. For all that he is, he is still my brother."

Memory still watched the empty doorway. "I know. But I didn't save him for that reason. I believe people deserve a chance to right their wrongs."

"I hope he lives up to your expectations. Even as a child, he was always selfish, deceitful, and even cruel. What if some people are born that way and can never change?"

"I have to hope that they aren't. To bring myself away from the darkness inside me, the darkness that almost killed me, I have to try and always see the best in people. Maybe if I can see it, I can reflect it back for them, to let them see what they could be. Maybe that is all they need to change."

Roen squeezed Memory's shoulder and then strode across the room into Eloryn's waiting arms. He lifted her off her feet and she giggled in utter joy and relief.

"Are you sure this is a good idea?" Clara asked.

Memory shifted the skirts she'd gathered into her hands to get a better grip on them and clear them away from her legs. She picked up her pace, her friends following along. They were already more than fashionably late. "Good idea? No. It's more the kind of idea that would make a bad idea feel good about itself."

"It is a good idea," Will said. "Just be careful."

"It would be better if I weren't running late," Memory said. Roen had been giving her sword fighting classes, and the two of them got too caught up in training, forgetting the time. Changing from the fencing uniform into a formal gown wasn't a short procedure either. Clara was still adding accessories and finishing Memory's look as she chased her along the corridor.

Memory stopped outside of the Round Room and wriggled her gown back into place. Eloryn helped brush some crumbs off her shoulder from the last minute snack Memory had scoffed down on the way.

Memory peeked around through the entrance and saw the King of the Unseelie Fae, the Queen of the Seelie Fae, and the room full of their followers, seated inside. The circular table, which Eloryn had finally completed repairing, was laid out in a range of the castle's finest delicacies, fruits, candies, and treats that both human and fae could eat, interspersed with tall, happy floral arrangements overflowing with multicolored roses from the palace gardens. Memory could already hear the larger party started downstairs in the grand ballroom, and wondered how it looked at that moment, filled with humans and fae mingling under shining chandeliers.

She sighed. "There are these movies back in our world with this super-secret agent who always meets his nemesis face to face and sizes him up at some big fancy do. I figure holding a big mixer like this, having a bit of a formal meet and greet with the fairy nobility in a friendly and diplomatic environment is a good way to get our eyes on Finvarra and maybe even get some info out of him."

"Do these meetings normally work well for this, *super-secret agent*?" Eloryn asked, her head tilted in a curious, if long-suffering, expression.

Memory cleared her throat. "Yeah. Uh. All the time."

Will frowned at her. "I'll be right here if you need me."

Memory felt the urge to throw her arms around him, to kiss him or do something that showed him how grateful she

was of his presence, both there now and in her life as a whole. She swallowed hard and thanked him awkwardly before turning away and entering the Round Room.

Aine and her companion Lugh both stood as Memory and Eloryn strode into the room. Nyneve matched them on their feet, but it took a few longer moments for Finvarra to get off his chair, groaning and struggling at the effort to stand for the entrance of the human ruler.

"Thank you all for coming," Memory said, trying to sound confident and warm. "It's my intention to build better relationships between our races, and have asked Your Majesties here tonight to help me in that cause."

Memory took her seat around the table from the fae rulers so she could face them both. Aine smiled graciously as she took her seat.

Finvarra grumbled as he returned to his. "Words. Just words. Heard them all before from your predecessors. What are you going to do that's different? You've already got unseelie blood all over your hands."

Memory bristled and clenched her jaw to keep her mouth shut.

"Father, please," Nyneve gripped his wrist and he grumbled more beneath his breath, but soon quieted.

Aine folded her elongated golden fingers on the table in front of her and looked across at Finvarra. "It is true, that more fae blood has been spilled recently than for a long time before. But the fault is not human alone, that is obvious."

Memory paused for a long moment, letting the fae watch her and wait. "The Pact is being violated more and more often. I've seen fae who don't give a damn about it or whether they

are Branded. Humans are defending themselves more violently because they are seeing the fae becoming more threatening. If we're going to fix this, I need to understand why. Why are so many fae now willing to break Avall's laws?"

Finvarra and Aine both stared, mouths closed into thin lines.

"Because we are dying," Nyneve said. Her voice was deep and hard edged with pain.

Memory bowed her head to her. "I've heard the rumors, and seen evidence. It's all the iron, isn't it? Out in the rest of the world, drawing all the magic away from Avall."

Nyneve's eyes narrowed slightly and she nodded. "Avall is meant to be our sanctuary. Our own world, the lands of Tearnan Ogh, are a timeless place. Eternal, but lifeless, it has long ago lost the natural magics of life needed to sustain us. That's why the fae needed Avall and why we formed the Pact. But as this land too is sapped of all its life force, we will surely die."

Aine waved her hand dismissively. "Great human civilizations have come and gone before. The expansion and progress of the other human lands that is causing this imbalance may end at any time now, burnt out in war or plague or any other form of human weakness. This will not be the end of the fae, despite what those who are behaving rashly believe."

"We'd cling on a lot longer if the humans of Avall weren't using up what little magic is left," Finvarra said, spattering out the words.

"What do you mean?" Memory asked.

He eyed her up and down, distaste curling his lips. "Humans and their magic, their *behests*, using up what we need to stay alive on their frivolities. And you, the worst of them, all that magic stored within you. It's an atrocity."

Like you can talk. You made me this way. Memory glared back at him until Eloryn cleared her throat and Memory tried to form a more diplomatic expression.

Eloryn said, "Have the fae truly known all along that the rest of the world did not become a hell?"

"It did become a hell," Finvarra replied with a fierce wave of his clawed hand.

"Maybe to the fae, but not to humans." Eloryn shook her head. "You openly misled the people of Avall all along."

Aine shrugged her delicate shoulders in a graceful roll. "Have the people of Avall suffered in some way? I am sure Avall is much better off now than it would have been without the Pact. You've lost nothing from being disconnected from the iron hell."

Memory watched wisp light fall onto the glittering cheekbones of the fairy queen and wondered how something so beautiful could be so empty of heart and reason.

"That shouldn't have been your decision to make," Memory said. She felt like banging her head on the table in front of her. Any chance of uniting the races had been lost the minute they started talking, and she'd learned little other than just how selfish and oblivious the fae could be. "If you'd told humans earlier, let them know all along what was happening, we could have worked with you in finding some sort of solution."

Memory stood up and ducked a very small curtsey. "I think that's about enough for this meeting. I still wish to help if I can, but assistance only comes with honesty. We can't hope to help each other out with lies and secrets still hanging between us."

She directed her words straight at Finvarra, but received

only a vague grumble in return.

Memory waited at the door as the fae left the room, heading downstairs to the larger party. As Nyneve walked past at the end of the line, she touched Memory's hand softly. Memory looked up and was struck by the deep black of her eyes, lined in bright silver eyelashes. The serpentine scales on her silver flesh seemed to form swirling patterns down her cheeks and neck.

Nyneve leaned close and whispered, "I still have hope the humans will be able to help the fae, too."

She smiled a small, soft smile at Memory before following her father.

CHAPTER THIRTEEN

Will leaned on the wall, waiting for Memory to finish in her meeting. He felt far too visible standing in the open, well lit corridor like this. After so long in the woods, adjusting to life indoors again with other people was taking longer than he liked. Even being in a room just with Memory's new friends all at once felt crowded and uncomfortable.

He could hear someone walking up behind him. The man's scent, like soap and the spiciness of cloves, and soft fall of his feet, told Will instantly it was Roen.

"Are they done yet?"

Will listened, and heard Memory stand up and end the meeting. "Almost."

Roen glanced sidelong at Will as they waited, his hands plunged deep into his pockets and shoulders pulled in. Eloryn had left Will and Roen together for a while once, but they hadn't really talked. Will wondered just what Memory's new friends thought of him. He knew he was different now, that his life with the fae had made him different, much like Aine's consort, the human man Lugh, had been made different.

But he knew he had to make an effort to fit into this new life, for Memory. And he wanted to for himself as well. Deep inside, he knew it wasn't long ago he'd all but given up on his own life. He was Mina's and lost all hope that the girl he waited for would ever come back to him. But now she had, now Memory was in his life again, he wanted to take his life back, to make his own decisions again and see where that life could take him.

And while ever he still carried iron, Mina wouldn't be able to do anything about it.

Memory walked out of the Round Room then and smiled at him, and his heart's rhythm sped. Her rich purple hair was so at odds with the misty green formal gown she wore, but she looked so confident that it worked for her. In the past, her hair color and piercings always seemed to be a mask to hide behind. Now, she owned them. She was herself, and also someone new, someone better.

Memory bumped her shoulder against his as he stepped into place beside her and they continued with Eloryn and Roen down to the ball downstairs.

"How did it go?" Will asked.

"We all made it out of the room alive, so I'd call it a success," Memory said.

A herald announced the entrance of the queen, princess,

and their partners as they reached the grand ballroom, and Will tensed as the crowd paused to stare at them and applaud. Clara had helped him dress as formally as any of the other human men out in the room, but it didn't help. If anything, the layers of shirt, overcoat, jacket and silky scarf left him feeling breathless, strangled.

Memory glanced at him. With a clearly fake yawn, she gestured to some seating in the corner, partially obscured by a draping curtain. "Want to sit down with me for a while? I'm exhausted from the fury hamster in my chest."

Will crooked an eyebrow.

Memory gestured to her chest, her hand going round and round. "Like my insides are an insane angry rodent, running like crazy on its wheel of fury all day. So let's grab a seat."

Will glanced out at the crowd again, then nodded, his mouth gone dry. *So much for taking my life back. A room full of people and I feel like running away.* He followed Memory around the edges of the busy room, and noticed she kept looking back at him, checking he was okay. By the time they sat down he was smiling again.

Memory kicked her crystal encrusted slippers off and put her feet up on a chair. She wriggled toes covered in sheer lace stocking and slouched against the backrest.

Eloryn and Roen had gone together straight out onto the dance floor and were already spinning joyfully between the other dancers. Wide hooped skirts gusted and twirled to the rhythm of the chamber orchestra. In between the humans in their suits and silk gowns, sprites and other fae creatures did their own, less structured dances. Most were seelie fae. While the unseelie had been openly invited, few seemed to accept the invitation, although Memory did identify one banshee in the mix. Tiny pixies flittered above the crowd, creating streaks of light and glitter in their path. A group of sprites at human size danced together in a ring in the center of the room, shimmering like fireworks.

Memory watched Eloryn and Roen dancing with a deep, wistful expression. Will almost asked her if she'd like to dance, but panic rose in him again, followed by a deep self-loathing that he was too scared to be the fun and sociable partner Memory deserved.

The fae royalty had already arrived and been announced into the gathering, and Will watched as they took their seats on a raised side section, reserved for royalty, above the general crowd.

The party-goers who were not dancing were cooing and fawning over the children serving food at the event. Memory and Clara had arranged for Maeve and the orphans to learn how to waiter the event, as another chance to build some bridge between the nobles and the poor of Avall. Mostly the party guests just seemed to think the little outfits the children wore were cute.

"Look at him," Memory said in a whisper just loud enough for Will to hear over the noise of the ball. She flicked her chin across the room at Finvarra, currently being served by the two redheaded orphan girls, Isa and her sister. "He's looking at them like they are the food."

While watching, someone else caught Will's eye. He frowned. Mina stood across the way, just standing, glaring, and fuming at him.

He felt for the small iron tool he carried in his coat's breast

pocket, reassuring himself it was still there. Regardless, he doubted Mina would act out in a setting like this. The very fact she couldn't seemed to be making her even angrier.

When Memory leaned across from her chair and put a hand on Will's knee, laughing at a young man trying to hit on Clara, Mina stomped a foot and took a few steps toward him.

The midnight haired daughter of the unseelie king, Nyneve, interrupted Mina's path. They seemed to exchange a few words, and with one last look at Will, Mina followed Nyneve away.

Memory was giving two thumbs up and a lewd grin to Clara across the room. She turned back to Will, gasping with laughter.

"Hey, do you want to…" Memory paused, a slight frown over her smile. She glanced at the dance floor, then again at Will. "You want to get out of here?"

Will bowed his head. "Yeah."

Will and Memory talked long into the night, reminiscing and laughing at how strange it was that Memory now recalled their past more clearly than Will did. They dragged cushions and blankets out onto Memory's balcony and sat there together, wrapped up in a huddle, watching the stars and a new, light fall of snow, until they fell asleep in each other's arms.

Memory woke up in her bed the next morning. Inside her chest the fire of the stored magic still burned as usual, and a warm happiness sat beside it.

Looking around, she wondered where Will had gone. Since

raiding Finvarra's lair, Will had been nearly constantly by her side. It felt like that was how it should be, and even though she couldn't see him now, Memory was confident that Will would be close by.

Smiling, Memory climbed out of bed, greeting Clara who had come to help her prepare for the day. She was meant to be meeting Eloryn, Roen, Maeve, and a handful of other people their age who stayed at the palace, for a brunch in the palace gardens. It had been Eloryn's idea, in order to make some new friendships, to normalize their lives a little. Memory had invited Will, but he seemed reluctant. It was clear he still had trouble being in crowded situations, which made Memory sad for him, but she knew he would need time to adjust to the changes in his life. She was happy to give him as much time as he needed. He had waited so long for her, after all.

Memory dressed in one of her new outfits, which were much faster to get on without help than the gowns in her wardrobe. The tailor had managed to create a new pair of jeans for her, although the denim wasn't really denim, but rather a soft canvas dyed gray-blue. She pulled them on. Over a collared cream shirt, she clipped a royal purple and cream striped corset closed then sat down to put on a little make up.

"Have you seen Will this morning?" Memory asked Clara.

Clara worked on brushing Memory's hair and pinning it into a braided up do. She had bobby pins between her teeth as she said, "He's already out in the grounds with the others."

Memory jerked her head in surprise and Clara scolded her, taking out a few pins and redoing the section again.

"Will? My Will?" Memory asked.

"Yes, *your* Will." Looking above her head in the dressing

table mirror, Memory could see Clara smirking.

Memory tried to stand up, and Clara pushed her back onto the seat.

"Is my hair done?" Memory asked.

"Almost. What's the hurry? You're the one who slept in. Overcome with a sudden jealousy that *your* Will might be interacting with other people?" Clara was downright grinning now.

"No, just…" *Just what? Worried? Proud? Or Jealous?* Memory wasn't sure. She just knew she wanted to be there with Will. "Can I go?"

Memory stood up as Clara tried to hold her head still to slide in one last pin. "All done."

"Ouch," Memory grunted, then placed a quick kiss on Clara's cheek. "Thanks, Clara."

Memory was already dashing out of the room as Clara giggled. "You're welcome."

Pulse tapping in her throat, Memory ran all the way through the palace. Breathless, she dashed out into the private grounds at the back of the castle, near the hedge maze. The air was chilled and dry and made her throat ache. The sky was clear blue, and a light fall of snow remained from the night before, making topiary hedges and shrubs look like cakes dusted in icing.

On the large area of mosaic pebble paving, a long table had been brought out and spread with tiered food stands. A dozen people sat around it, including Eloryn. Maeve was standing aside with Erec who seemed to be on guard duty, but paying more attention to her. Memory also recognized Laudine and another girl from the finishing school.

They all watched a fast, dangerous looking swordfight taking

place between Roen and Will. Everyone smiled and clapped when one of the two fighters made an impressive move.

Boys, Memory thought.

Will hadn't noticed her yet, and she watched quietly from the side of the yard.

A small hollowness of jealousy opened in Memory. She didn't want or expect it, but seeing Will interacting with other people so openly brought it anyway. He had been something that was hers, just hers, and that was changing. Only a moment after, happiness filled that space, flowing into her like taking a deep breath. It rushed inside her with the realization that Will had stopped being *hers*, and started being *his*. Seeing him adjusting to his new life, embracing his new life, made Memory swallow back a happy sob.

Will had Roen on his toes. They each had a fencing sword, and Will mimicked the formal style Roen used, but his height and reach had him at an advantage. One or two times Roen made a show of shaking out his sword hand after a particularly strong blow from Will clattered their blades.

Then with a wicked grin, Roen stepped up his performance. He smiled like he'd been so clever to trick Will into thinking he had an easy win, until Will flicked out his other hand and the small hooked tool he held in it, and with one twist, disarmed Roen and left him knocked flat on his back in a flurry of snow.

Memory was running again. She ran so she didn't have time to hold herself back.

Will saw her coming only a second before she jumped up into his arms. She pressed her lips against his, her hands threading their way into the wild hair she loved so much.

Memory heard the dull thunk-thunk of Will's two weapons

fall on the ground behind them as Will brought his arms up around her and pulled her close to him. A low growl came from the back of his throat and he kissed her back, lips pressing hard on hers.

A round of polite applause from the bystanders brought Memory back to reality. She dropped down with a bashful smile and rose-flushed cheeks.

Memory giggled at their audience, then smiled up at Will.

He still had his eyes closed, smiling and panting deep breaths.

When he opened his eyes and looked at her, again it was as if they were the only people there. His lips shivered a little as he said, "I wanted to dance with you at the ball. I should have but I was scared. I don't want to be scared anymore. For you, and for me, I don't want to be scared to live my life. And I want to live my life with you. Whatever the rules, whatever might happen, I don't ever want to be apart from you again."

"Worlds couldn't keep us apart," Memory replied. "Tried and failed already."

Will laughed.

Memory turned and noticed the sword and Will's iron hook lying on the pavement a few paces behind them. She moved back to pick them up for him.

Only one step away, a rush of air filled the space between Memory and Will. In a burst of whipping winds and the ember filled gray smoke of the Veil, Mina appeared.

Her eyes were wide and gleaming as they looked down at Memory, frozen in shock there where she bent to pick up the weapons.

Will has no iron on him. Memory's heart pounded. *He has no*

protection.

Mina's hair whipped around her as though she were caught in gale force winds. "No! You cannot have him. He is mine. He ate food from my hands. I saved him and his life is the debt he owes to me. I own him and will keep him far from you forever!"

Memory grabbed up the iron hook near her fingertips and swung it back at Mina.

But she was already gone.

And so was Will.

CHAPTER FOURTEEN

Memory's knees hit the ground.

Eloryn, Roen, Maeve, and Erec were all standing around her. She wasn't sure when they had come over. Had they tried to stop Mina too? They were all too slow.

Will is gone.

Everyone was talking but Memory couldn't hear. A dense humming filled her head and her magic boiled, ready to explode. Eloryn put an arm around her shoulder.

Memory realized she was holding her breath and gasped air in. It struck like a knife in her chest and she bit back a cry. The world came back into focus.

Her voice came out as a harsh whisper. "I was wrong

before."

Will.

Her hands formed fists, pressed against the crushed grass. "This is what having your soul broken feels like."

"Oh, Mem," Eloryn said.

Clenching her teeth, Memory took a deep breath and stood up. "I'm going to get him back."

Erec watched her for a moment, then hurried away. The other guests at their brunch were standing back, faces white and fearful. The iron awl hook that had been Will's protection was still held in Memory's hand, her fingers rigid around it.

"She must have been watching, waiting for a chance to get to him," Memory said. "The minute he didn't have iron on him... How could she even do that? It can't be allowed. She said she owned him. She doesn't own him. No one *owns* him."

"I'm so sorry," Eloryn said. "But she could own him. Under fae law, if she saved his life, if he ate fairy food, she could own him. Everyone in Avall knows to be careful not to lose themselves to the fae like that, but coming from your world, he would have been easy for Mina to claim."

"You're telling me this now?" Memory grunted.

Eloryn looked at the ground. "I didn't know. All I know are fairytales of humans being claimed, stories parents tell at night to stop children going near the fae. Or stories of those who go willingly, like Lugh. Will seemed to have so much freedom, living in the forests in Avall. In the fairytales, the fae always steal the child away to Tearnan Ogh, the fairy realm."

Memory's face ached with unspent tears, tears she refused to shed until Will was back by her side again. She looked up at her sister. "No. That's not it. You didn't doubt what was happening, you just didn't think I could cope with knowing."

"I..." Eloryn stuttered then looked at her feet. "I'm sorry."

Memory couldn't blame her. She wished her friends, her family, would trust her more. She felt she'd showed them time and again that she could be strong. But she'd also shown them how very weak she could be. They'd seen her at her darkest and she knew it would take a long time to gain their confidence again.

I will show them how strong I can be.

After a deep breath, Memory said, "Tearnan Ogh... Is that where Mina has taken Will now?"

"That would be my guess," Eloryn said.

Memory saw Erec return. He'd brought Bedevere back with him.

Memory eyed them. "You're worried I'm going to run off and do something cuckoo banana pants, aren't you?"

"Well, I wouldn't necessarily use the term cuckoo banana pants..." Bedevere said in his dry voice.

Memory forced another deep breath into her tight chest that seemed to have forgotten how to breathe on its own. "Don't worry. I'm not going to be *that girl.* I'm not going to dump everything else in the world for one person, for a boy, for... love."

Bedevere just bowed his head, waiting.

"What do we need to do, to make sure everything is in order here in Avall? I can't leave Avall in chaos again, so that's our first job, to do everything we must to make sure it won't be. I want things stable here in case I'm gone for a while."

"Your Majesty, if you travel to Tearnan Ogh to recover Sir Will, you may not come back at all," Bedevere said.

Memory held up a hand. "I'm getting Will, and we're coming back. That's happening. I need you to help me make sure everything is set right here before I go. Can you do that for me?"

Bedevere simply nodded.

"Then let's get started." Memory marched back toward the castle, and everyone fell in line behind her.

"Mem, stop and think about what you're saying," Eloryn protested. "I know you want Will back, we all do, but going into the fae lands is beyond dangerous, it's…"

"Stupid?" Memory asked.

"Suicidal," Eloryn finished, her tone cold.

"We've dealt with nasty fae tactics before."

Eloryn's chin tensed and she grabbed Memory by the arm. "Travelling into the fae realm is entirely different to dealing with the fae within Avall. It is one hundred percent their territory. One false move and a human can be Branded, but has no power to Brand in return. You would be vulnerable to their every whim and trick. Humans simply do not travel into the fae realm unless they are taken by the fae. Even royalty and dignitaries are not safe. That's why all official meetings between our races are held here in Avall."

Memory pulled her arm free and continued up the stairs into the palace. "I'm not leaving Will as a prisoner to that crazy sprite."

"Then we will go with you."

Memory stopped her march. "You just told me it was suicidal. Why the hell would I let you come with me?"

Eloryn stopped too, eye to eye with her sister. "Because if you don't I won't tell you how to get into Tearnan Ogh."

Memory matched her sister's look. "Bedevere will tell me."

Eloryn held a hand up to the wizard but held her sister's gaze. "Don't you even dare."

Bedevere made no sound or move.

Memory huffed. "Then I'll work it out on my own."

"And how much longer will that take?"

Every second Will was gone scratched a sharp tally mark on Memory's heart. Would Mina punish Will for choosing Memory over her? What would she force upon him or make him do? The thought of Will as a slave to that sprite twisted Memory's guts.

Memory was torn; she didn't want to put her friends in danger but she knew she would need help.

Roen spoke from behind Memory, breaking the staring battle between the twins. "You may find this hard to imagine, but I think we've all become fond of the fellow. Will's our friend too. We all want to do what we can to bring him home."

Memory whimpered a little then steadied herself. "We're all going then. And we'll keep each other alive, just like we've always done."

Erec cleared his throat, breaking the intense look the three friends were sharing. "Your Majesty, you say you're going, so you are, and I'll spare my objections. But you must also spare your objections to my coming with you. I failed to protect you in the gaunts' lair, and I plan not to fail again."

Memory shook her head. "If you come with us, you could die, and I can't have your death on my hands. Not after Peirs."

Erec, who had been standing at attention, relaxed his posture. The move somehow seemed to give him more authority. "Travelling into Tearnan Ogh, you could all die. I will go and I will do everything I can to keep us all alive. That is my decision, and should I die it would not be at your doing."

Memory smiled and gave him a small nod. "Anybody else? Anybody?" She looked around with a wide grin, caught Bedevere's gaze and pointed him down. "No. Not you. I need someone to keep the rest of the wizards under control."

Bedevere bowed. "The realm of the fae is not the one I wish to explore, so I am happy to stay, if saddened to see you leave. You are our queen. We would send a legion of men with you if you wished it. But I know you do not."

"Then you know me well. Saving Roen, Maeve and the others, that was different. We had to stop the kidnappings, find out who was behind them. This is personal. So we settle what needs to be settled here in Avall, we work out a plan, then we go and get Will." Memory started forward again, climbing the steps into the palace two at a time. "We've got a lot to get done, so let's get it done. I don't even know how we get to fairyland yet. Do we eat magic cake till we're shrunk all itty bitty and wash ourselves down a drain with our own tears or what?"

Reaching the halls of the palace, both Bedevere and Erec called staff over to them, sending messages off in different directions before taking their leave and heading another way themselves. Roen and Eloryn continued beside Memory.

"You have some strange ideas of magic," Eloryn said. Her slippers made hushed sounds pressing into the long carpet runners that had been brought out to cover the cold marble floors when the snowy weather hit Avall. "The fae have doorways similar to Veil doors, spotted throughout Avall wherever they hold territory, such as within fairy rings. They use these doorways to travel between Avall and Tearnan Ogh. Fae can generally traverse through the Veil as they wish within Avall,

much as you could, but to travel between worlds they use the established doorways. Mina would not have taken Will directly to Tearnan Ogh when she vanished with him, but to a doorway first and then through that."

Memory thought back to her trouble with trying to force a doorway through to the rest of the human world, how much harder it was to break through than skimming within the Veil in Avall. "These doorways, do they stay in the same place?" she asked.

"Not exactly, but close. They shift very slightly, as though there is an ebb and flow displacing the join between the worlds."

Memory took a deep breath and her pace grew more confident, faster. As much as she declared unwaveringly that she would bring Will back, she was terrified she couldn't, that she had no idea where to start. Not anymore. "I know where to start looking."

CHAPTER FIFTEEN

The woods were cut through with the horizontal orange beams of the setting sun. The light cast long shadows and created sharp contrast against a black and white ground of sludgy leaves and spots of melting snow. The cold air was scented with woodsmoke, and the trees above Memory and her friends leafless, showing the darkening sky above.

Eloryn, Roen, Erec, and Clara trailed after Memory silently as she led them on through the forest. They were all dressed and prepared for a long journey. Even Eloryn had chosen pants, and brought the satchel that had once belonged to Alward, which curiously seemed to fit more food and supplies than expected. Memory refused even the suggestion of a skirt, and instead wore tough leather riding pants and knee-high boots that buckled tight three times up the sides. The deep purple coat she wore matched her pinned-back hair, and had its own mini-skirt length bustle at the back and double breasted buttons of brass.

She had left off the corset, breathing would be fairly important today after all, and had been hard enough to do since Will had been stolen away. Six days it had taken to wrap up her affairs as queen so Avall could continue on while she was gone, or if she never came back. Six breathless days.

The new government Memory had been working toward was already close to complete. Between them, and Lanval, who she'd left as her replacement, if she never came back, she felt confident Avall was in good hands. Honestly, she was more confident in the adults she'd put in charge than she was in herself as a ruler anyway. She felt good that the people of Avall had someone as their leader other than a seventeen year old girl with possible mental health issues. She had found a desire in herself to lead, and a desire to lead changes and progress in Avall, but knew she wasn't ready. She was little more than the Maellan-blooded figurehead and knew it, but those desires had become one more reason she wanted to live- to grow old and wise enough to rule well, one day.

And she wanted to grow old and wise with Will by her side. *Worlds couldn't keep us apart.* She would get him back. And then she could breathe again.

That morning, Memory had said her goodbyes to Maeve and the children. Maeve had wanted to come with Memory, to help however she could, but Memory needed her to stay and look after the other kids. She couldn't bear for something to happen to them again.

Saying goodbye was hard, especially when Isa clung to Memory's leg and had to be pried off, crying and screaming, by Maeve.

Clara, on the other hand, had flatly refused to say goodbye. "I'll say goodbye when it's time to say goodbye, and then I will say see you soon."

"It might be a long way out into the woods," Memory objected weakly. She didn't want to say goodbye either, but knew a foray into the fairy realm was no place for Clara.

"I'm perfectly capable of walking. It's just the hunting grounds anyway."

Memory watched her now, tripping over more sticks than she managed successfully to step over. Erec kept close beside her to keep her upright, a gentle smile on his face when he caught her arm each time. Memory started to wonder if the damsel in distress act was for his benefit. It worried Memory to be leaving Clara out here alone after saying goodbye, she would have arranged an escort to take her home again if she'd had more notice, but she felt better knowing she had a way to call home and check on her.

That had been the last thing Memory did before leaving. On their way out of the palace, Memory took her friends to the chamber that kept the Speaking Mirror.

The piece of magic mirror in Caermaellan castle was a long, thin sliver, shaped almost like a scimitar and about that size. Memory reached up and reverentially placed her hands on either side of the frame that held it, and lifted it from the wall.

She could see Eloryn's eyes pop wide as she brought the frame over her head then threw it on the floor.

The frame broke apart and the Speaking Mirror shattered

into pieces.

Eloryn cried, "Are you insane? That is priceless! Irreplaceable!"

"So are you." Memory crouched down in front of the wreckage, and collected out the five largest pieces. One for her, and one for Eloryn, Roen, Erec, and Clara. That left a few small pieces for those remaining in the palace as well. She stood back up and passed them around to her friends, careful to not let the razor edges slice their hands.

"When magically connected, each part of this mirror can see and hear the other parts, right? I didn't break the magic, I just made more pieces. One each, so we won't be out of contact."

Eloryn stared at the triangular shard in her hand. The mirror glinted and sent sparks dancing up onto her cheekbones. She choked on words that she couldn't quite get out. "But… it's…"

Memory shrugged. "If you guys had mobile phones or walkie-talkies I would have used them instead, but we use what we've got."

"Only Erec, Clara, and I can use them anyway," Eloryn said. "You know you and Roen can't without someone to make the magical connection."

Memory nodded slow and deadpan. "I did realize that. I figure it's still worth it for you guys and was hoping you could set it up now and keep the line open. Connect yours to Roen's, and mine back here to Clara and the Palace. That way we're always connected to someone if we are separated, and if we're together then all is good anyway."

Eloryn hesitated, still pouty at the destruction of a precious magical artefact. Then she sighed and spoke her behest words to connect the mirror pieces. Memory held hers up, and could

see part of Clara's red hair in the icicle shaped mirror. There was barely enough mirror to see a complete eye when Clara also held hers close to her face, but when she spoke into the mirror, her voice came through clear and loud to Memory's piece.

Roen and Eloryn tested theirs as well, and Erec flipped his around in his hands. "I sure feel left out," he said.

"You can connect yours to anyone whenever you want," Memory said.

He grinned and tucked it away in a pocket on his vest. "Details."

Memory put hers away as well in a pouch on her belt. "We all have iron. We all have a speaking mirror. We have a plan. I think we're ready."

In the hunting grounds, Memory stared at the small ring of red and white spotted toadstools in front of her. It sat within lush green, needle-thin winter grass and a spray of white wildflowers.

They were ready, they had a plan, but the next step, literally, was a scary one.

Eloryn stared as well. "Do you think this will really work?"

Memory shrugged. "Only one way to find out."

"Why must you be so flippant? If this doesn't work, you will be lost."

Erec, Roen, and Clara stood across the ring from them, and all looked up at Memory for her reply. She didn't want to lose herself, or lose them. But she'd already lost someone and that had to be fixed.

"It works, or it doesn't. I'm doing it anyway, so why ask?"

Eloryn turned from the fairy ring to stare at Memory, her green eyes squinting, assessing her. "I just want to know if you are doing this because you truly care for Will or just because your pride is hurt."

Memory felt the verbal slap in those words. She took a deep breath to let the stinging fade. There was no question anymore what the truth was. "I care for him," she said. "As deeply as you care for Roen. Don't ever question that again, Lory."

Eloryn grinned a little slyly. "I was just waiting for you to finally admit it."

"You little trickster!" Memory shoved her sister's shoulders with both hands, laughter in her words. Pointing at the other three who were all grinning as well she said, "Go on, get. Time for you lot to hide."

Roen and Erec patted Memory on the shoulder as they walked past, and Clara kissed her on the cheek. Eloryn just nodded to her, her expression serious again. Memory returned the nod and tried to wear a hopeful smile. She watched them disappear behind thick tree trunks, the echo of Eloryn's behest words settling in the cool air as her magic concealed them further.

Letting out one long, deep breath, Memory clenched her jaw. *Life as a flower couldn't be too terrible, could it?*

She stepped forward and instantly she felt the tug and pull of the fae magic there, enclosing her within the small ringed space. Reaching out her hands, she ran them around the edges of her confines, feeling the firmness of the air there. Memory leaned her whole body into it, pushing as though to escape. She wondered if this was how being in a padded room might feel.

After ten minutes of pushing and prodding and waiting, Memory started to get anxious.

Clearing her throat, she called as loudly as she could, "Oh bother, I seem to be trapped."

The sun had fallen low, and shone directly into Memory's eyes. A rustle of leaves had Memory squinting into the light and a silhouetted shape crept toward her, haloed by the golden glow of the sunset behind.

"Hello human." A soft whinny shook the words as the fae creature spoke. The faun stepped close to the fairy ring, the white fur around her cloven hooves muddy and spotted with wet leaves.

"Hello… furry thing."

The faun regarded Memory with all black eyes, spiked with silvery lashes. "Stumbled in again, did you? This time, you are mine for reals. Isn't that how you said it? For reals? You belong to me now." Lips covered in a soft white down pulled up into a satisfied smile.

"Oh no, oh dear, alas, you've got me now," Memory said, the back of her hand against her forehead.

"You are mocking me?" The faun shifted, her legs coming up and her hooves pawing at the ground. Silvery dust fell from her eyelashes as she snorted. "I think I will turn you into a flower this time. Let the bees have you."

Memory barked a laugh. "You're such a bluffer! You got me with your lies last time, but I know what fairies can and can't do now. Got myself an education."

The faun gazed at her, body rigid with what looked like anger, or confusion. "You know nothing."

Memory began ticking off items on her fingers. "I know you guys are all strong and nearly immortal, can glamour appearances, and travel through the Veil, but unless you learn human magic there is very little else you can actually do."

The faun showed its teeth in a truly cheeky grin. "Maybe I

hoped I could just glamour you to look like a flower, and you'd be so shocked you'd fall down dead from fright."

Memory raised an eyebrow at the faun's honesty.

The faun's grin widened. "Flower or not, I still own you now."

"So are you going to keep me as your pet, or what? Take me back to Tearnan Ogh? Can you even do that with your puny fairy magic?" Memory folded her arms, unimpressed.

"Of course I can! Don't know if I will though." Her long nose wrinkled and trembled as she sniffed the air. "You still stink of iron."

Memory nodded out into the trees. "Actually, this time it's not me."

As if sensing what was about to happen, the faun jumped and turned to run but was too slow.

Memory could hear Eloryn's behest words as she sprang the trap. A thin, web-like iron cage encircled the faun, trapping her within its toxic framework. Every piece of iron they carried had been given to Eloryn, and she used her magic to stretch and spread the mass of them large enough to hold the creature.

Erec, Clara, Roen, and Eloryn stepped out from hiding and into a circle around the cage.

The faun shrieked and her body started to swirl with Veil mist, trying to escape through the Veil. But it was obvious she had no strength surrounded by iron, and the wispy smoke evaporated uselessly. In panic she lashed out, kicking at the cage and her hoof sizzled at contact.

Clara gasped and turned away. Memory's stomach clenched violently, watching the little thing buck and shudder. "Just stay off the bars, calm down!"

The faun's eyes widened to completely round black orbs and her goat-like ears hung down. She shrank herself small, desperately trying to keep clear of the iron web. "Let me out!"

Memory made calming gestures with her hands. "Make a deal with me and I will. You will take me and my friends into Tearnan Ogh. You will be our guide there, will not harm us or knowingly lead us to harm, and you will return us to Avall. And then you will be free again."

"Free?" The faun sagged against the ground, her body shuddering and heaving with sobs. Perspiration foamed and curdled on her snowy coat. "Taking you there, it will be death for me. The members of the court will kill me for taking you to our lands."

Memory stepped back, knocked by the words. Would her quest mean death for this creature no matter what? Was that a price she was ready to pay? She stared at the creature's black eyes, unseelie eyes, trying to feel only hatred for it. She couldn't. "I will make sure you are safe."

The faun huffed. "That is a pretty lie."

Erec stared down spitefully at the creature. It was clearly easier for him to hate the white beast. "My queen does not lie. Make the deal, beast."

"I don't want to die!" the faun cried, scaring a flock of black birds from the branches above. They fled into the darkening mauve sky.

Memory had worried that the faun, after being trapped, would simply welcome death as the gaunt she'd once faced did. But her behavior seemed like that of a child. A small terrified child. It looked young, but that was no indicator for an immortal creature like the fae. Still, Memory wondered if maybe it wasn't as old as other fae she'd known. It trembled as Memory moved closed to the cage. The faun really was afraid of death, and Memory knew it. She wished she did not know it, because it gave her the leverage she wished she didn't have to use.

She tried to speak kindly. "Agree to the deal, and maybe you will die, later, at some time. Or maybe you won't. Maybe you will live. But if you do not agree to our deal you will die now."

"I will Brand you." The faun's voice was a desperate whisper.

Eloryn frowned, clearly troubled by everything. "You can't. We have not touched you and not attacked you. We're offering to free you, not hurt you."

Erec sniffed and lifted his chin. "Say the words if you must."

The faun gasped, and stuttered, its eyelids screwed shut. "Bronmarbh Aileadh."

Memory tensed, scared that maybe it would work, that they hadn't followed the law thoroughly, that their loophole wouldn't protect them. But it did. Not one of them was marked with the Brand.

"Monsters. You are monsters," the faun whimpered.

Looking down at the huddle of white fur, shivering on the muddy ground, the faun seemed so small and childlike that Memory did feel like a monster then. But she knew the fae were tricksters and would change how they looked for their own benefit. She remembered the banshee who looked like a child before it transformed and attacked. She remembered Hope, looking the mirror image of herself before she brought the tower down around her and her friends. Her lips grew tight. *Monsters? The unseelie fae are the monsters.*

Memory's voice turned cold. "Do we have a deal?"

The faun gathered herself up onto her knees. "So be it. I

agree to your bargain. May it be everything you desire. This is our binding deal."

"Our deal is binding," Memory finished, sealing their agreement under fairy law.

Memory signaled Eloryn who spoke her behest words. The behest was long, and Memory knew it was a complicated one, that even Eloryn, who normally could create new behests on the fly, had to plan and run past Bedevere for confirmation. The iron webbing retracted, forming back into molten lumps, and then finally into their original forms. Memory's knife, Eloryn's arrowhead, Clara's button, Roen's dagger, and a spearhead for Erec. They collected their pieces off the ground.

The faun staggered to her feet, her eyes still wide with pain and body coated with sweat and a smell that reminded Memory of nickels rubbed together in a hot palm.

Memory worried the faun would flee, vanish into the Veil, and everything would have been for nothing, but the creature remained. Sullen, she stared at them with frightened eyes, standing back a few feet and wrinkling her nose as they put their iron away.

"This is goodbye then," Memory said, looking at Clara.

Clara fidgeted with her fingers, her face pale already from watching the caged faun. "I could… I could come with you."

Memory dropped her head and raised her eyebrow in an 'oh really?' expression.

Clara smiled a small, embarrassed smile. "To be honest, I'm not sure right now if I'm more scared to go with you or stay behind without you. Oh I wish you didn't have to go. I cannot stand to see you all walk away knowing you may not come back. You are heroes, every one of you, and I'm just…"

Clara blinked back the tears that stood in her eyes but one fell anyway, leaving a long gleaming trail down her cheek, highlighting her freckles.

Memory blinked back tears of her own. Clara was like the mom Memory never had. A young mom who did outrageous things with her daughter, but a mom nonetheless. Would she ever see Clara again? Would any of them?

Yes, she told herself. *We will all return, safe and sound and with Will.*

Memory gave Clara a quick hug. "Go back to the palace and make me some of those delicious pastries with the custard and hot caramel inside. We'll be back before they get cold."

The faun snorted, her velvety nose pointed into the air. "If you are ready to go we need to go now." *Before I lose my nerve and break a binding oath,* went unsaid but Memory heard those words anyway. Maybe they were the faun's, or maybe her own.

None of them spoke for a long moment, inhospitable glares passing between the humans and the faun.

Eloryn moved to stand beside the white fae, slowly, as though approaching a feral cat. "What's your name?"

"Shonae," the fae replied, huffing and backing a step away. "What does it matter to you?"

"I'm Eloryn, that's Roen and Erec and Clara. Memory you already know."

"I wish I did not."

Memory felt her top lip twitch into a sneer. "We all wish a lot of things." Eloryn gave her a look but Memory ignored it. Will was more and more lost with each passing second and she had no time to make their guide feel better.

"We are ready to go," she said.

"To our deaths, then," Shonae said and turned around. Her white tail flicked up as she waved a swirling Veil door into existence in the middle of the fairy ring and trotted through.

Erec took the lead, one hand on the spearhead sheathed in his belt. Eloryn looked at Memory and then Roen. Roen stepped forward and Memory felt a twinge of envy at the protective arm he put around Eloryn's waist. It was overcome by worry though, worry she really was taking them all to their deaths. Her friends she loved the most, who had just claimed the love between them, who were so happy together, about to start a life together.

They stepped through the Veil door one at a time. Memory went last, waving to Clara as she left the human world.

CHAPTER SIXTEEN

Small strands of loose purple hair tickled Memory's cheeks and lips, brought to life by the wild winds within the Veil. Pressure built and popped in her ears and she stepped clear, out into the land of the fae.

She took a deep breath to clear her lungs of the tightness of Veil travel and the air tasted rancid and dry on her tongue, like mud and burned sugar. Her stomach curdled. Blinking, Memory shivered at what lay before her.

The world of the fae. Tearnan Ogh.

In her mind she'd imagined rainbows and sparkling streams where unicorns frolicked around pots of gold, or some other fairytale images. But the world she saw was bleak and lifeless. A shadowed husk of a world.

She'd heard the fae speak of how their world held none of the natural life force that the human world did, the life force they needed to survive, but to see it in reality shook Memory. It disturbed something deep within her and scared her in a primal way. What could have caused their world to become like this? Did the fae pay for their immortality with the death of their world, or did they kill it carelessly the same way humans seemed to be doing with their own?

Murky ink-black puddles and pools made a patchwork pattern across dead, cracked ground. The water rippled occasionally as some loathsome creature turned below the black surface. Angular, broken trees with immense, hollowed trunks, turned gray with petrification, crowded around them. Their buttressed roots forked out into the water in woven cages. Memory touched the nearest tree to her and it was cold like stone.

No one in her group moved, frozen, as they stared at the world before them.

Shonae watched them in return, the corner of her furred lips turned up in a small smirk. "The wilds of the Unseelie Court. My… home." The smirk faded.

Memory frowned. *This wasn't the deal, not where we needed to go.*

But Eloryn nodded slowly. "Your home. We would have needed a seelie fae to be able to take us directly to the realm of the Seelie Court."

"Then how to we get from here to the Seelie Court? How long will it take?" Memory asked.

"Don't fret human, I want to be free of you as fast as possible. We will travel the briar path. It won't take long." Shonae

sniffed the air and tucked her shoulders up close to her neck. "This way. Keep quiet."

Shonae broke away from them, leading off across the rough ground. Her hooves beat swiftly along the dirt and the group of humans had to walk fast to keep up with her but she always kept well ahead, just within sight. Memory knew Shonae did not want to be too near them because of the iron they were carrying. It would sap her strength, which was the last thing either of them wanted. Memory needed Shonae up and moving. She needed to get to Will. Yesterday.

Under Memory's feet, the path sparkled lightly, as though the dirt was made of crushed glass. The hazy mist filled the air and pooled on the ground in thicker swirls.

Memory felt a strange surge of relief as she passed by a small tuft of flowers, growing in an odd arrangement along the top of a fallen log. Maybe there was some life left in the world. The flowers were star-shaped translucent bells, hanging from long stems, and tinkled sweetly in the light breeze. Memory reached to touch one. It slid gracefully over her fingertip so smoothly that it took a few seconds for the pain to register. Memory cried out and clutched her finger, staring in shock at the thin razor cut the flower had sliced there.

From the front of the group, Memory heard Shonae chuckle.

Eloryn dashed over beside Memory and clutched her hand as well, working swiftly to wrap the finger in a bandage. "Don't let your blood drop on them. And don't touch anything else."

Memory just nodded, staring at the plants. She could see now that they weren't real flowers at all, but finely spun glass and fairy gold, made sharp as a knife. Raising her head, she looked

out behind the log and saw a wide field of the faux-flowers, spreading out into the stone forest. "This place officially receives my stamp of creepability. I don't even want to know what would happen if my blood dropped."

"At least we don't seem to be headed that way," Roen said over Eloryn's shoulder.

"No, instead we get to travel through the hopscotch of deadly black swamps," Erec said cheerfully from behind him.

"Fantastic," Memory said, and they all moved along after Shonae again.

The farther they walked, the closer the dark waters seemed to close in around them, until soon they walked along a thin pathway between the growing swamp.

Along the curved roots of one massive tree, white shapes fluttered like butterflies, then blew away. Just ash on the wind.

From the tops of the poisoned pools rose a dense mist that coalesced into shapes as they passed them. Faces leered at them, and voices rang out from visages whose mouths vanished long before the wails that came from them did.

There was something so terrible and sad about the sounds that Memory wanted to stop walking, lie down and weep tears into the lifeless ground. She could feel her pace slowing, her breath catching.

This is just fairy tricks, horrible monster tricks. Her resolve hardened and she ignored the mist, staring ahead at Shonae only, keeping her eyes on her guide.

In front of her, Eloryn gasped. "Alward."

Memory had never known Alward alive, only seen his dead body briefly, but she still recognized him there in the swamp. Grayed blonde hair tied back in a ponytail and round glasses

balanced on his nose, he seemed real, solid, as he struggled against a sea of ghostly faces surrounding him.

"Ellie!" he cried.

"Steady," Roen murmured.

Eloryn winced and looked away. "I know. It's not real. It's an obvious trick." She spat her accusation out at the world around them. "As if we'd fall for something so simple."

Memory nodded, proud at Eloryn's strength. But still she could see her sister's mouth move, as though saying silent spells to keep herself strong.

"It wasn't him," Memory said in a low voice.

"I know that, Mem."

"It still hurt though."

Eloryn's eyes closed for a short moment. "Terribly."

"I'm sorry."

Eloryn gave her sister a small smile. "They won't take us so easily."

There was an echo of evil laughter and a plump raven with a white streak from beak to tail soared overhead. It landed, tangling its wings in a skeletal tree branch before uttering hoarse caws at them.

"Ellie!" the raven cried, its voice a mix between bird and human. "Ellie!" The caws came faster, harsher, sounding like the laughter.

Eloryn's face drew still. "Come on, we're moving too slow. We stick together with all our iron and they can't touch us."

Memory knew she was right but she also knew that the fae were hardly finished. They would throw whatever they could at them in the attempt to get them to split up. The iron had unsettled them. They were desperate to divide the iron's strength, and the group's as well.

Patches of grass along the path rustled as they walked along. Shonae seemed to avoid it, bounding and hopping around it as she led. Memory tried to do the same, but missed a step, and the black grass she placed her foot down on shattered and crumbled, as though it had been burnt to a crisp so fast it had kept its shape perfectly until touched.

Ahead across the black swamp and through the trees, a huge patch of vines reared up in a wide screen that curled around on itself in a way that made Memory's stomach do the same.

Shonae stopped, sniffing the air, her wide nose twitching.

"Is that the briar pathway?" Eloryn asked.

"No. Beyond there."

Shonae craned her neck, looking off to either side. The vines seemed to spread as far as they could see in each direction.

"Let's just go through then," Erec said, drawing his iron spearhead into one hand, and larger bronze sword into his other.

"Wait!" A voice rang out from behind them.

"Clara?" Memory squinted, and saw a figure running up the path behind them, a shadow within the mists.

"Could she have followed us here?" Roen asked warily.

"It's probably not her. It's probably another trap," Eloryn said.

A small shriek reached them and the figure stopped moving.

"What if it's not?" Erec growled. He took a few steps toward Clara. "We shouldn't have left her behind. She's come after us."

"Erec!" Clara cried out. "Help me, I'm stuck. Something… something is holding me." Her voice was broken with sobs.

"It's probably not her," Eloryn said again, but she didn't sound sure anymore.

Erec seemed sure, and began running.

Roen's arms shot out, gripping Erec around his waist. He wrenched side to side, trying to break free.

Memory's heart jumped into overdrive and she began fumbling for her pocket.

"Please! It's hurting me!" Clara's cries ripped through the air and the shadowed shape down the pathway writhed and crumpled.

Eloryn came and stood in front of Erec, still bound in Roen's arms, staring him down, trying to talk him down. He began to still.

"It is not her," Roen whispered.

Down the pathway, the mist thinned, clearing a view straight to the person there.

"It is her!" Erec roared, ripping at Roen's hold again.

It did seem to be her. Clara, just as they'd last seen her. Her feet had sunk into a boggy spot and a heavy figure made of fog and black water shot up from below her. Dark tentacles wrapped her body and grabbed her by the throat, squeezing so hard that her friends could see her flesh pinching closed.

"Clara," Memory called out. "CLARA!"

The small piece of mirror in her hands flashed and the image shifted. It spoke back to her.

Erec's arm flailed out and cracked against Roen's face. Blood trickled from a split in Roen's lip. Erec broke free, stumbling down the path to Clara.

Memory ran in front of him, holding the speaking mirror up in front of his face. "It's not her. Clara is safe, back in Avall. Look. LOOK."

Erec stopped in place, panting heavily.

Clara's voice came through clear from the broken glass. "Mem? I'm so sorry, it took me a moment to realize why my pocket was yelling at me. Is something wrong?"

Erec met Mem's eyes. He looked away again, down to the ground. "I'm sorry. I'm sorry, I was foolish."

"It's okay," Memory said to him. Then to the glass she said. "We're all okay."

"Well, don't scare me like that then!" Clara scolded.

Down the pathway, the imposter Clara giggled in a sharp, high pitch. She merged with the larger monster behind her, coalescing into a single immense scaly form that slunk away back into the dark waters. The disturbing giggle continued to echo around them.

"Sounds like you're having a wonderful time," Clara said, the edges of her freckled nose filling the small mirror.

Erec had walked back and muttered a few manly mumbles to Roen and they shook hands. Both of them were covered with sweat and the blood coming from Roen's lip had already begun to dry. "Let's keep together," Roen said. "The fae are not going to stop trying to trap us until we are out of here so let's get out of here."

"Agreed," Memory said.

Eloryn already had her eye on the next hurdle, the thick tangle of vines ahead. She'd approached them, and started speaking her words of behest.

Shonae eyed them all carefully.

Memory took a deep breath. They were all still together, so far.

"Hello! Hello? Are you still there? Is this thing broken? Oh, of course it is broken…"

Memory grinned. "Sorry Clara, just wanted to check you got back to the palace okay."

"I'm just sitting on my bottom while you're all off in Tearnan Ogh, and you call back to see if I'm fine? Other than being worried to death about you all, everything is just splendid."

Memory laughed at Clara's tone. "We're doing great. Fairy tricks at nil points. See you again soon. More than just your nose that is."

The mirror filled with Clara's poking out tongue, and Memory chuckled as she put it back in her pocket.

CHAPTER SEVENTEEN

Roen rubbed his jaw, where Erec had landed his elbow a moment ago. His mouth still tasted of blood, but he couldn't be angry at Erec. He'd almost run to help Clara too. If it had been Eloryn instead, he knew he'd have gone.

He clapped his hand onto Erec's shoulder. "We're not doing too badly."

Roen wasn't sure he believed it. They'd barely made any progress, and had only just survived the fae lures so far. They had to do better than this or none of them would get home, just as his parents feared. When he'd explained to them where they were going and why, they'd asked him not to go, ordered him, begged him. He was their last son, and he knew they thought him travelling into the land of the fae meant he was lost to them forever as well. But he had to do it. For Memory. He owed her so much already, and deep down, he really believed Memory would get them all home safe again, somehow.

The mist had closed in on them again, as though taunting them, and Roen suppressed a shiver.

Eloryn stood in front of the wall of vines, and when Roen went to join her, he felt another tremor in his belly. The dense undergrowth seemed to be alive; it quivered and vibrated as Eloryn studied it.

"These vines do not look normal," Roen said.

Eloryn looked back at him, her forehead creased into her cute frown of concentration. "I'm certain they are an enchantment. They are not a living plant, but some kind of fae magic. I might be able to clear them away though."

She began casting, the air around the vines turned slightly blue, icy crystals forming like a spray of lichen across the twirling tendrils. The vines crumbled and turned to dust, and then they regrew as fast as they had died. Eloryn paused and shook her head. "Something else then," she said and tried a different spell.

"Aren't you going to help us get through here?" Roen asked Shonae.

"No," she replied, watching Eloryn intently.

The battle between Eloryn and the vines went on for long minutes. The vines would wither only to spring back to life. They made a groaning cry with every death and shrill scream with every rebirth. The air stank of fetid sap and dead leaves. The ground gave off a boiling black oil every time the vines landed on it, dead and tangled.

Memory clapped her hands to her ears. She spat her words

at Shonae. "You're supposed to be our guide to get us to the Unseelie Court. Can't you help us through this?"

Shonae just raised an eyebrow and brushed her wooly hair from her cheek. "I know what I'm meant to be doing."

"I got it, I think!" Eloryn was panting but she was also smiling. There in front of her was a cleared section, a long tunnel leading into the vines. She headed for it. "I am going through."

Roen's breath caught.

I know what I'm meant to be doing.

His heart pounded so hard he felt his ribs could crack.

You will be our guide there, will not harm us or knowingly lead us to harm.

"El, no! Stop!" Roen yelled.

Vines that had appeared dead and fallen near her feet sprang to life, snatching Eloryn up into them. She turned, trying to escape and Roen saw her face, just long enough to see her eyes bulging in fear and her arms pinned helplessly to her side. Her face had gone a dusky red color, all breath squeezed from her body. She was pulled to the ground and dragged off into vines which closed up tightly around her.

Memory screamed.

Roen found his iron dagger in his hand, and hacked blindly at the vines. His hair whipped around his face as he screamed. Erec was there beside him, slashing with his sword, alternating with the iron spearhead.

Roen felt the ground tremble beneath him.

A wild fury filled Memory's face and her breathing came in harsh snorts.

"Mem, calm yourself. The iron is working. El is smart. She has iron too. She'll look after herself till we get her back." He made his words sound strong, despite the part of himself that hoped Memory would explode, scorching this land till nothing remained, to punish it for taking Eloryn.

Hold on, El.

Memory screamed again, a rough, frustrated scream, and launched herself at the vines as well, slicing with her iron blade.

At each touch of iron, the vines burned and shriveled and stayed that way.

The vines dropped away and Roen pushed through. On through the thick wall of vines they all crashed, tripping where the creeping tendrils lashed around their ankles. One thick vine caught Memory around the waist, slithering and tightening its grip like a serpent. Smaller ones came to join it, twirling like whips. Erec cut her free just as they began hoisting her up into the vines overhead.

They broke through the final tangled screen and tumbled out the other side.

Eloryn was there, wide eyed and panting. In her hand she held her arrowhead, still pointed defensively at the vines, her arm coated in ash and black slime up to the elbow. Her coat had been lost and her ivory shirt was now gray and blood-stained, ripped apart off one shoulder. Long blonde hair had come loose of its ties and fell in tangles.

Roen fell to his knees beside her, scooping her up into his lap and burying his face into her neck. She clung back fiercely.

"Tell me you are safe, that I've not lost you and gone mad with grief," he whispered.

"I'm here," she whispered back. "But we are not safe."

Roen realized then that they weren't alone. The glassy clinking of metal and shifting of heavy feet in the crackling, dead grass told him all he needed to know before he looked up.

They were surrounded.

Memory stood protectively between where Roen held Eloryn on the ground, and the ring of huge creatures on horseback staring down at them. *No, those really aren't horses.* Certainly not like any horse Memory could recall having seen before. They were tall and shaggy, shaped like black lions with clawed paws and whip-like tails, and heads like a horse but covered in hard, shiny scales and sharp beaks. It was hard to tell because they were folded away behind the riders' legs, but Memory thought they might even have wings.

The knights themselves were all in heavy armor of black lacquered leather which gleamed and sparked in the dimness, covering whatever their true form was beneath.

Some carried spears and others had bows, arrows nocked, all tipped with the translucent yellow of fairy gold. All aimed their weapons at the humans.

Shonae crept forward out of the vines, keeping her distance from the humans and their iron. She bowed deeply, groveling to the ground in front of the mounted fae men.

Her head turned to the side and she hissed across at Memory, "Bow, fools. These are King Finvarra's soldiers. Bow and at least your death may be quick."

Memory shook her head. She would not bow and have her life taken. "Let us pass. We are just travelers. Our business is

with the Seelie Fae, not with you or your master."

Not yet, anyway, Memory amended internally.

"We know who you are," one of the knights said. Its voice was deep, gravelly, and monotonous, like someone fighting throat cancer.

"Then you know attacking the queen of the humans of Avall is probably a big deal and shouldn't be done."

"Do you think we would be here without orders? You are nothing here." The knight who spoke drew closer, leading his steed up in front of Memory. Foam spilled around the creature's lips, and it snorted hot breath and spittle across Memory's cheeks. She turned her face to the side but held her ground.

Roen got to his feet as well, helping Eloryn up beside him. They stood defiantly beside Memory, with Erec on her other side.

Memory wanted to whisper to Eloryn. She needed advice, she needed some brilliant magic plan to get through this, but the knight stood too close to them, staring down. She was sure he was smirking at them beneath his helmet. The knights weren't making a move yet, as though they were waiting for something, but there was a fight coming, Memory was certain of it.

Memory might have softened a little, but the girl she used to be never shied away from a fight. She lifted her iron knife, holding it against the thigh of the dark fae knight right in front of her.

Led by her action, each of her friends held out their iron as well.

"Let us pass and no one has to die," Memory said. *Wow, I even managed to sound like I'm not about to pee my pants.*

The white streaked raven from the swamp flew overhead,

cawing in long taunting notes.

The knight in front of Memory lifted the visor of his helmet and glared at her. His eyes, fully black, were set in ghostly white wrinkled skin that seemed to drip like old wax across his face, revealing long, yellowed teeth in a protruding jaw. "Humans, walking in our territory, in the Unseelie Court, bearing iron against us. Well…"

The fae knight's all black eyes shifted. Without pupils it was hard to tell where he was looking, until he reached out a gauntleted finger and pointed crookedly at Roen. His lips curled into a vicious grin and he said, "Bronmarbh Aileadh."

Memory's heart stopped. Her chest tightened until her breaths came in tiny, short gasps as she waited, hoping, wishing it wouldn't work. Then she heard Roen howl in agony.

"Roen, no, no!" Eloryn was screaming as loud as him.

He had crumpled to the ground clutching at his forehead, his shoulders shaking violently.

When he turned his face up and screamed into the sky, Memory could see the rune-like mark of the Brand there, burnt into his skin.

Memory's eyes were wild, searching for answers, screaming for Eloryn. Her sister must be able to fix this, there had to be a way to fix this.

The knight in front of her was swaying his finger between the rest of them as though playing a cruel game of eeny-meeny-miny-mo.

Eloryn was lost in her own grief. She stood beside Roen, his hand gripped in hers, and began turning her magic against the fae before them. There were no plants, no animals, no life force of magic left in the world to help her. But she did have her iron arrowhead.

"Mem," Roen croaked from beside her. "Just take El away. Get her to safety. Please."

Memory nodded, all the while knowing that Eloryn would go nowhere without Roen.

It only took a moment, and two more words, for it to be too late anyway.

The knight's finger came to rest pointing at Eloryn, and he spoke the words of Branding again.

"Bronmarbh Aileadh," he crackled.

Eloryn cried out, and kept speaking the words of her behest through gritted teeth as the Brand burned itself onto her forehead.

The arrowhead in her hand began to melt, spreading and spinning and stretching into a long filament. As she fell onto one knee, Eloryn flicked her arm, sending the thin iron wire whipping out at the knights in front of her. It lashed across three of them, skimming uselessly over their armor. Their steeds weren't as lucky, and toppled so fast Memory was sure she was hallucinating.

A roar went up from all the knights and their beasts.

Memory knew there was nothing left to do. It was time to fight.

Lory. Roen. Memory's chest flamed and she roared at the useless magic inside her, magic that couldn't free her friends from their Brands.

She ran forward, plunging her iron knife into the gap between the knee guard and thigh armor on a knight in front of her. Sizzling smoke and gray ooze spilled around her blade as she pulled it back, whirling to find her next target.

Memory tried to make sense of the erupting chaos of death and battle around her. Did they have a chance to run? Was there a leader she could take down?

Erec had downed another lion-horse and its knight fell below the beast, his armor stained with dark thick blood.

Memory could see Shonae, scrambling away across the ground, the ashy dirt staining her pure white fur.

Roen and Eloryn were fighting back to back. Some of the knights had dismounted, beating them with the blunt ends of spears, knocking them to the ground.

Memory saw then that the fae men carried ropes, black and slick like the vines they'd just passed through.

Eloryn struck out again with her thin whip of iron, and screamed more words of behest as she did so. The iron danced and twitched in the air, striking into the vulnerable joints between the knight's armor. Some fell, but more came. More and more. Too many.

The knights had not been there to kill them; if they had been they would have been dead already. They were so outnumbered, despite how many fell to the iron the humans wielded. The knights were there to capture them, no matter what the cost, but that revelation didn't help Memory.

The words of Branding were croaked out again, barely audible over the screams of battle.

Erec. Memory felt her eyes burn with tears.

One of the steeds bucked in panic through the fray, knocking Memory away from her friends. She tried to push back, fight her way back to Roen, Eloryn and Erec, but arrows rained down. One pricked her upper shoulder and blood bloomed quickly, dripping down her sleeve. Her left arm drooped, pain making it useless to her. Another barrage came from the air and Memory ducked and rolled away, taking cover behind one of the fallen animals.

Roen and Eloryn were screaming, lashed with rope and being dragged away from each other.

"Mem!" Eloryn's cry shattered through the air. She struggled against the knight holding her. His hands were like claws and they yanked her up onto his steed which twirled, paws digging into the dry earth.

Memory could see Erec, fighting still within a crowd of unseelie fae, drawing all their attention as he refused to fall.

Memory stood from behind her cover, ready to run and help him, or Roen, or Eloryn. One of them, somehow. She wasn't sure where she was going, only that her mind burned to *help them. Save them. Fight.*

A strong hand wrapped around her arm, cold fingers digging in firmly.

Memory tried to yank free, and turned to see a cloaked figure.

"You can't save them now. Run, fight later," silver lips said, shimmering under the shadow of the hood.

Nyneve? Memory stared into the black cowl, wanting to argue, but she was given little choice. Nyneve ran, dragging Memory behind her with unbreakable strength. She ran straight for the dark vines. They shrank away from them, clearing the way as Memory remembered the trees cleared their way from Eloryn the first time they met.

Shonae appeared, running frantically beside them, arms hugged around her chest and eyes wide. The vines gave off a low-pitched moaning, the sound hungry children made at the sight of food, and Memory had to hold her breath to keep from throwing up.

The three ran along the length of the wall of vines until Memory was out of breath, and when her legs failed her, Nyneve let go of her arm and Memory fell with a crack onto her knees, gulping air.

The moment she was able to stand, Memory turned back the way they had come, but hands wrapped around her wrists and held her tight.

Memory screamed and fought the cloaked figure, determined to go back and save her friends.

"Quiet, before you get us all killed."

Nyneve loosened her hold, and Memory pushed free, looking up at the unseelie princess. Her hood had fallen back while holding Memory still, and her midnight hair tumbled around her silver snake-skin face like inky shadows.

Her black eyes swept the area around them, silver eyelashes shining in the thin rays of light coming from the western edge of the sky.

"What are you doing here?" Memory coughed out.

"Trying to save your life." Nyneve placed the cowl back over her face. "I have little time, I cannot be seen with you and it cannot come to light that I helped you. If we are caught there will be no hope for your friends."

Did that mean there was some hope? Memory blinked back tears. "I'm covered in the blood of creatures I killed and just lost the people I love the most in the world so maybe you should talk real plain. How, how can we save my friends?"

Nyneve looked down her straight nose at Memory. Her face held little expression, like a fine silver statue. "Finvarra has captured your friends to get to you. He will keep them alive until he does."

That's why the fae Branded them first. Hatred made Memory's insides flame.

Nyneve's face softened then, and eyelids fluttered down slowly. "I want to help you. Branding is a horrible death. An unfair thing. I saw it happen to someone I loved, once, long ago." Her twig-like fingers rested on her heart. "I know what has been done to you by my father. Finvarra is… evil. He's grown old and twisted and I fear for his mind. I want to help you and your friends, but he is still my father, and still my ruler."

"I'm sorry you had to watch someone you loved die from Branding." Memory was, and what was more she was pretty sure she was about to understand that particular pain very well soon.

"Let's not let it happen again." Nyneve turned to the side, away from Memory. With her face obscured by the cowl Memory couldn't see her expression, but she sounded choked, as if she was crying, or maybe laughing. It was funny how alike the two could sound.

"Only the monarch of the offended race can lift a Brand once made. You can challenge Finvarra for the lives of your friends. You have one turn of the sun and moon to get to the Unseelie Court and fight for them before the Brand takes its toll. I will help you as much as I can when you get to the court but I have to go now." Nyneve looked over at Shonae, and Shonae shivered visibly under her gaze, making her body small as though to hide in plain sight. Pointing behind the small faun, Nyneve showed Memory a tunnel of twisted sticks and dry brambles, woven into neat and intricate patterns and filled with a golden glow. "There is the briar path. You must take it. Listen to me, and listen well- do not tarry. Finvarra wants you, but he is unpredictable in his insanity. He could kill your friends at any time. That's why I have to go back now. I will try to keep them safe from him, but I cannot keep them safe from the Brand. Twenty-four human hours and it will kill them."

"Twenty-four hours," Memory repeated. The words tasted like blood in her mouth.

Nyneve nodded. Just like that she was gone, only a faint ripple of air left where she had been standing.

Memory stared around her, unable to think or even want to.

All she wanted was to crumple, to let the weight that had

built inside her finally break her down and let her become nothing, to become more dirt and ash on the ground. To become something that didn't feel pain.

She felt utterly alone.

A soft scratching on the ground beside her reminded her she wasn't.

"Will we keep going?" Shonae's voice was a soft whinny. She had shuffled over close to Memory, but leaned back as though she could be struck at any moment.

"You're still here?" Memory mumbled. "What happened? Did you forget which direction you were running in?"

"We made a binding oath."

Stupid oaths, Memory cursed. She'd held back her magic, not knowing how to use it, not wanting to break her oath to the fae. Maybe with it, she could have taken the upper hand in the fight, but not before Roen was Branded, or Eloryn. She might have saved them from being captured, but they'd still be Branded, and Memory would too be Branded, hunted, or killed by the seelie fae for breaking her oath.

"Stupid snot-licking, hatred-vomiting, kitten-killing, ass on backwards OATHS!" Memory roared, cursing the sky and kicking at the dirt.

Tears blurred her vision and that time she could not stop them from falling. Warm wetness spilled down her cheeks, ran across the bridge of her nose, down her neck.

Shonae's voice was soft. "Keeping our oaths is what keeps the peace."

"Do you think this is peace?" Memory bellowed. "Everyone is fighting! People are dying, fae are dying! Finvarra is a raging lunatic and I saw my friends get Branded and dragged away!"

She turned on the faun, bearing down on her as the fae backed skittishly away. "And you, you KNEW about the vines, didn't you? I trusted you!"

The faun squealed. "I am not allowed to tell humans of such things. It is forbidden. I tried to keep my part of the oath. I did not lead you into the vines, into the danger. I am here because I am still trying…"

"They were BRANDED!" Memory screamed. "Do you know what that means?"

Shonae's dark eyes flared with warning and her floppy goat ears stood straight up. "Yes, I do. Do you?"

"Yes!"

"Then why do you just stand there screaming?"

Memory's jaw dropped. "Because I… am venting and… totally freaking out… Because this is all my fault." She took a step back from the cowering white faun. "And I don't know if I can fix it."

Shonae said nothing. From the distance came the sickly rustling and whimpers of the vines, as though they were still trying to reach them. Memory wiped her eyes and took a long breath. Her whole body ached and her spirit was crushed, but not gone.

I'm going to save them all.

She dried her eyes on her sleeve. "Let's go, the clock is ticking."

Still holding her shoulders up defensively around her neck, Shonae asked softly, "Where would you have me take you first?"

It was a hard decision. Who did she love more? Was that the question? Would answering cost any of them their lives?

They were at the briar pathway. Beyond it would be the

Seelie Court.

Will was there. Memory could get him back first, and then together they would be able to save Eloryn, Roen and Erec.

"Same as before. To get Will from the Seelie Court. I will need his help to save the others, and… and I need him." Tears pricked her eyes again and she swiped them away with the back of her hand, angry at her inability to control her emotions.

She turned her sodden eyes to the path before her. The briar path. Having just battled through the disgusting tangle of black whipping vines, travelling into another pathway of sticks and thorns seemed greatly unappealing. But at least the briar path was actually shaped like a path. Thick trunk-like vines that looked eons old, dry and lifeless, wrapped in spirals, forming a tunnel just wide enough for two to walk side by side. Dry silver sticks were layered and woven, twirling like fractals into a misty infinity. A smooth sandy floor shimmered like diamonds in the low light.

With a small nod from Shonae, Memory followed the faun into the briars.

CHAPTER EIGHTEEN

How long have I been here?

Will shook his head, trying to clear his eyes and thoughts. Both were blurry, drunk with the bitter-sweet passion of fairy foods. In his years knowing Mina, she mostly left him in the forests of Avall, the neglected pet she came to toy with on a whim, but she had brought him to Tearnan Ogh on occasions, mostly to show off her human to the other fae. He was a status symbol to her. Few fae had their own humans anymore. He was Mina's, Lugh was Aine's, and he knew of only one other. Mina would bring Will here, flaunt him around the Seelie Court, and then banish him back to solitude in Avall when he seemed too needy. It wasn't his fault humans needed to eat regularly.

In all that time, he never worked out where fairy food came from. He never saw anything growing in the fae world, no real trees to grow those incredible fruits. The fae themselves didn't really eat, or if they did it was purely for pleasure, not for sustenance. He suspected the food Mina used to lure him as a boy, the food she now kept him drunk on, was created from pure magic. Maybe created from a fae's life force itself. Maybe that was why if you ate it you became bonded to them.

He didn't really care. He just wanted the strength to fight it.

He barely had the strength to sit up. He lay on his back in the softest of downs. Something white and so fluffy it was barely there under his fingers, cushioned around him like a cloud. Overhead was a ceiling of branches with silver and gold leaves woven into seven-pointed star shapes. Colors shifted and flashed, reflecting off the metallic screen like living rainbows. He couldn't see anything else. His eyelids fluttered, falling closed.

He tried to gather his thoughts one at a time, lining them up, creating a wall of lucidity to protect himself.

I am Will.

I will find Memory again.

Worlds can't keep us apart.

Something tickled his lips.

"My sweet pet. You seem hungry."

Will could feel Mina snuggle in beside him. He growled, trying to push her away.

"Aw," Mina simpered, her voice sickly sweet. "Don't be like that."

Will forced his eyes open. Mina's face was right beside his, her amber eyes flickering with sparks of gold, lighting them from within as she smiled.

"Let me go back. Send me back to Avall," he said, as it felt he had done a hundred times.

"No," she said simply. "I don't think we'll ever go back there again."

Mina ran a fingertip around Will's lips. He lifted a leaden arm and brushed her away.

Mina pounced, landing across Will's chest. He could feel the skin of her thighs pressing into his bare stomach, and she dangled a blue cherry-like fruit over his mouth.

He tried to turn his face away, but she turned it back.

Mina hissed. "Behave, boy! Or I will cage you!"

As weak as he felt now, Mina was easily stronger. Her fingernails dug into his cheeks as she clawed at his jaw, pulling his mouth open, and the fruit dropped in.

Will roared, summoning every scrap of resistance he had. The fruit already melted into his mouth like chocolate in the sun. He wrenched himself up, throwing Mina off him.

She shrieked, cursing him.

He tried to find a way out, but his vision grew milky, fading.

He landed on the floor, and everything he knew fell away.

The tears helped Memory keep going. Some of her anger and fear ran out of her along with the salty wetness, splashing on the powdery path. All the emotions she had not dealt with came to the surface and she let them run.

Inside the briar pathway, the darkness was lit by giant webs

strung across the floors and walls, shining gold with their own luminescence.

Shonae reached out with her downy fingers, and tugged at one long thread. It twanged softly as it pulled free of the rest and she began winding it around her narrow waist.

Memory watched, curiosity overriding her sadness. "What are you doing?"

"The web of Rump of Steel-skin spiders is valuable. I can trade this well, if I live through my obligation to you." Shonae flicked a look at Memory and flicked her tail at the same time.

"Rump of Steel-" *Rumpelstiltskin, spinning hay into gold… Everything is so connected.* Memory examined the webbing, spotted like glowing nightlights through the gloomy tunnel. "Is it actually real gold?"

Shonae snorted. "Not human gold. This is what fairy gold is made from."

Shonae tugged the webbing again, and a spider the size of Memory's face fell free of the tangled twigs, slipping down the thread into Shonae's hands. Memory gasped, but Shonae just gently brushed the iridescent gold arachnid away. It fell on its back onto the sandy ground, spindly legs twitching, until it righted itself and disappeared again into the briars.

Memory watched the thorny walls around her with a new level of paranoia.

Overhead, the branches looked dangerous and thick with thorns, safely just out of reach. Shonae warned Memory that would not always be the case. Neutral territory or not, the pathway demanded its price from those who travelled it.

"Everything has a price," Memory said. She'd learned that long ago, a world away. There, the prices were different and the

rules were too but everything cost something.

Shonae eyed her for a moment. "I have an obligation to you and I will fulfill it. You want to save your friends? Yes? Then let go of all that anger and that greed because that will be what gets them killed, and me too."

"Greed? I don't want anything for myself!"

Shonae huffed. "Then why are you here?"

The question was a good one. It cut to the very heart of Memory's anger. They were there because she had wanted Will back by her side and her friends were all suffering because of her actions, because of her greedy determination to have what was hers.

But was Will hers? She loved him. She knew it deep down in the bottom of her soul. But Will, he belonged to no one. He was a human being, not an object.

From that moment on, I was yours.

She knew that Will had given himself to her, as the greatest gift she could ever desire, but a gift she could not keep. She may have come here for the wrong reasons, but she would make them right. "I'm here to free my friend, not to take him for myself. Any claim I have to Will when I take on firefly-face Mina, I will give up to give him his freedom."

And when he is truly free, would Will still choose me?

"Hmm." Shonae snuffled, still winding thin strands of web, creating a neat spool like a belt around her middle. "I've only known humans to be greedy."

Memory barked a sharp laugh. Talking with Shonae, as odd as it was, had improved her mood. She wondered why the creature was giving her breath to the conversation. She was under no obligation to talk to Memory. That was not part of their deal. Although the faun had been challenging with her words, they were never spoken unkindly.

"And I've only known unseelie fae to be evil monsters," Memory shot back.

Shonae tilted her head. "Would you call a snake or spider evil? They are creatures of nature, same as the unseelie, same as all fae, same as humans. We are as we are and all have our place in the balance."

Memory eyed the skittering shapes of elongated legs creeping above her through the briars. "Snakes and spiders generally only bite when threatened, and only some of them are outright aggressive. Most of the time they are more scared of us than we are of them."

Shonae tilted her head back the other way.

Oh… Memory frowned.

Shonae's furred lips seemed to have the smallest of smiles on them.

Memory knew that she was right on some levels. She thought she hated all the unseelie fae, but what did she really know about them? She hated them based on her own limited experience, but were her reasons all personal and did they have any truth to them? And what about her experiences with the seelie fae? With Mina, or Aine?

A Rump of Steel-skin spider skittered across the ground beneath Memory's feet and with a clenched jaw she made an effort not to stamp down and squish it. It seemed to hesitate, angling its many eyes toward her, before rushing off again.

Memory watched Shonae walk in front of her for a while, the slight sparkle to her wild mane of wooly white hair, the long, black claws protruding from her furry paws. "What is the

difference? Between seelie and unseelie fae, I mean. Both courts have all different kinds, and as far as I've seen you're all just as tricksy as each other."

Shonae lifted one shoulder. "Unseelie fae, we were born of the night, which gives us the shadows in our eyes. Seelie were born of day."

"So you don't get to choose?"

"Choose what?"

"Whether you are seelie or unseelie."

"No."

"So you are born good or evil and you get no say in the matter?"

Shonae's lips split, showing her teeth as she nickered loudly. "Would being born on one day or the other force a man to behave a certain way? Humans are just as capable of dark and light, of choosing their own way. We are not as different as you would like to think. The night gave me black eyes. That is all."

That is all. The cold nausea of confusion and uncertainty had started to spread in Memory's stomach. It was so much easier to hate the unseelie fae, to hate all of them, to think of them as monsters. But she'd hate even more to do so and be wrong. "That is really the only difference between seelie and unseelie fae? Your eye color?"

Shonae's grin vanished. The web she'd been winding came to an end, and she snapped it from where it was anchored to the curling tunnel. "I know your kind find the seelie fae more fitting to your ideas of beauty."

Memory paused. Was it really that simple? Did humans make the unseelie into monsters with just their thoughts and imagination, a prejudice that made the unseelie fight back and become the monsters they were perceived to be? Could it be as simple as visual bias?

Memory hopped forward a few steps so she was within Shonae's field of vision. "What do I look like to you?"

"Like a human."

"Do we all look different?"

Shonae wrinkled her nose as she often did when Memory came close. "Of course, but none of you is very pretty."

"Thanks a lot." Memory chuckled. "You look like a white deer-girl to me. Not as scary as some other unseelie I've seen."

"I am still young."

"Yikes." Memory's first reaction was to imagine the hideous transformations this deer-girl's body could take as she aged. But she had to stop and think- even if Shonae changed, if she looked like a troll or a banshee or some other monstrous fae she'd seen before, inside, wouldn't she still be the same being who spoke with her so thoughtfully now? It was only appearance. That was all.

"I'm sorry," Memory said. "For trapping you like we did. I realized then that you were young. You were just as scared to die as I am."

Shonae's black eyes opened wide. "I did not know you were afraid to die."

"Of course I am. Most people are. I think it's why we're so stupid all the time."

"I never knew humans feared death. You always seem to court it."

"Court it?"

Shonae rolled her hands in the air, as though that would help her explanation. "You always do things to put yourselves

near death. Things that make no sense. Like jumping off the castle walls with just the gust of your skirts to protect you from a fall to the earth."

"You… saw that?" Mem said. The recollection of the deep sadness she'd felt in that moment, when she was ready to give everything up, filled her eyes with tears again. "That was… that was something else. I get what you mean though. In the other world people jump out of airplanes—big flying machines that go across the sky."

"That is a myth."

Memory wanted to laugh but she could see by Shonae's face that she believed that something like an airplane was simply a myth. "In that world fairies and magic are myths."

"We will be a myth in this world too, soon enough."

Just that morning, Memory might have said good riddance. She wasn't so sure now.

A loop of thin, dry wood hung low, spotted with thorns. Engaged in the conversation with Shonae, Memory ducked away too slow and a small sting flared on Memory's cheek. She covered the cut with her palm. The tunnel walls felt closer than they did before, and again she had to dodge away from a branch extending close to her face.

"The path is getting smaller," she said.

"And it will get smaller again," Shonae nodded.

"And, why?"

"To start a journey is always easier than to finish one."

Memory shot a glare at Shonae. When did fairy riddles start making so much sense?

"Frotz," Memory swore as a thorny stick caught on her sleeve, pricking through to her skin beneath. "Is all the plant-life in Tearnan Ogh this bloodthirsty?"

"There is no plant-life in Tearnan Ogh. It is enchanted to move like it still lives, but it is all dead. The briar pathway is but a ghost. A ghost who takes payment in life to sustain itself." Shonae folded her hands across her waist, protecting her Rump of Steel-skin web, but made no other attempt to protect herself from the thorns closing in on them. "It will take what it demands. Don't fight it, and don't use your iron to cut through. This is the price we pay."

"No wonder this highway is so bare," Memory grumbled.

"It once was full of life. Fae would travel the briar pathway all across our world and others. Now those who are left remain in Avall and their own courts only. All others have turned to dust." Shonae kicked at the diamond sand on which they walked.

Memory's stomach turned. *Please be speaking metaphorically, pretty please.*

The tunnel had closed in until Memory and Shonae had to walk in single file. With every step, hooked thorns caught in Memory's hair and clothes, ripping thin razor cuts where it met flesh.

Memory stopped trying to avoid them. There was no way to. This was the price she would pay.

The briars rustled, a mix of dry wood crackling and a low slurping, licking sound that Memory was sure was going to drive her crazy.

The briars dipped lower, closing in completely. Shonae pushed through, grabbing onto Memory's wrist and dragging her behind. Scratches covered Memory's face and hands, her red blood dripping into the ground. She thought she heard a contented sigh coming from the briars.

With a final push, Shonae and Memory broke through the thicket. Memory turned back to see the mess they had just fought through and saw instead a wide tunnel, looking just like the open mouth of the briar pathway they had entered on the other side.

"Typical," she muttered. "Still, we made it."

They had arrived at the court of the seelie fae.

CHAPTER NINETEEN

Memory picked a thorn from the back of her hand as she took in the landscape before her.

Neatly shaped trees of silver and gold were spotted in careful arrangements across a smooth, level ground, entirely paved in polished gold-streaked marble as far as Memory could see. The trees held no leaves, only blossoms studded along the bare branches. The flowers ranged from lilies to roses, all crystalline and glittering. Everything was too vivid, and the scent drifting down from the blossoms too strong, unnatural. A sprite zoomed through some of the branches, which tinkled and sang in its wake as it vanished again.

Up ahead, a palace loomed. A confection of milky quartz

and twisting silver created a series of pointed dome shapes and towers which combined into a massive structure, reaching higher into the sky than Memory could see.

Although she couldn't see a sun in the mauve tinted sky, everything shone brightly, casting flares of light off every surface. Memory shaded her eyes with a hand. "I guess there's a reason they call this the Summer Court."

Shonae was squinting, her eyes barely open. She hunched, cowering away from the light. "I will wait for you here," she said. "I cannot go any further."

Memory could see the fear held in her black eyes and hear it in the break of her voice. Even if Shonae had been allowed into the seelie court, she was terrified, and with good reason. Shonae had brought an interloper smelling of iron into her opposing realm.

"Stay safe. I'll be back soon," Memory promised, and began her march to the palace.

The paved ground felt slick under Memory's boots, and the warmth of light around her dried the cuts on her skin, making them pucker and sting.

She kept a close eye on her surroundings, worried a troop of seelie soldiers would rush out and capture her. The trees she walked by really did seem not just silver and gold colored, but actually made of silver and gold. Just one branch would have been enough to retire on in the other world. But she knew enough now to know not to touch them. More than anything, the precious trees made her sad. There was nothing real here, nothing alive. No wonder the fae were so keen to trick the humans of Avall into sharing their land.

Memory reached the wavy glass walls of the palace and

found the gate, formed from what looked like a single slice of a massive geode. It was open and she walked through into the grounds and there she started to see some life.

A range of seelie fae spotted the bright courtyard. Sprites, dryads, a couple of gnomes- Memory was starting to know the different types by name. She thought she even spotted what looked like a small horse shaped creature with a long curved horn on its forehead.

UNICORN! Memory gave herself a mental high five.

All the creatures kept their distance, watching her warily. Some even turned to flee, shocked by her presence. Memory watched them warily in return. They were all beautiful in her eyes, but she couldn't help wondering now what they really meant.

The courtyard itself was also beautiful, filled with a forest of columns that opened at their tops into more artificial trees. The sweet sound of running water and birdsong filled the space, and Memory saw the pristine fountains and caged earth birds those sounds came from. Small staircases and raised pathways disappeared in all directions around the courtyard, leading up and down and off into tunnels filled with light.

Memory kept on, straight up the largest, main path into the palace. She knew where she had to go, she had to find Aine.

Eloryn had explained that was the way to get Will back. Through the seelie queen, Memory could challenge Mina for ownership of Will.

Memory was glad of that. The palace was huge, and Will might not even be in it. He could be anywhere, but a queen should be in a fairly obvious place.

Memory climbed the steps and headed into the walls of

the castle. Crystals in the shape of flowers were set within the ceiling, lit from within and showering down fine sparkles of fairy dust. Silver, gold, and emerald streaks ran in rich veins down the stone walls. The light glittered and danced off those precious trails, and bounced back into her eyes, blinding her slightly.

"Where's a pair of sunnies when you need them?" Her voice echoed back to her and she shivered. The bravado was lost in the echo and her voice sounded as frightened as she felt.

It struck her that she missed having Shonae at her side. No matter what the faun was, she was company. Now, Memory was truly alone.

Not for long.

Memory's feet twitched, impatient, the countdown to her friends' deaths filling them with panic. Walking was too hard. She broke into a jog.

Chambers flashed by, some filled with fae, some empty. Will was nowhere to be seen.

Huge double doors ahead of her were carved in swirling patterns, pulsing with magic that made Memory dizzy. They opened as she approached.

Memory skidded to a stop along the silky floor.

The room she'd reached put any of the ballrooms at Caermaellan to shame. The chamber's ceiling was so high Memory couldn't see it, or maybe it had no ceiling, opening up to the bare lilac sky above. But there must have been something there, because chandeliers of diamond dewdrops hung down from impossibly long golden threads. The room spun with pearly colors and iridescent metallic glows, caused by the swirl and dance of the fairy-kind who filled the space. Though no music played, they moved together like an ocean, a surging tide

of giggling, glittering bodies.

Memory faced the members of the Seelie Court. They peered back at her and whispers broke out around the room and the waving motion stopped.

Moving slowly, Memory walked in, and the fae separated around her as though she were a ship breaking through sparkling ice.

In the center of the room, on a throne atop a high pillar, sat Aine.

Memory's pulse thundered and her breathing was too fast. She took a long slow breath and held it, willing herself to be calm, and then approached.

Although Aine's face was turned to the side, Memory could see the seelie queen's eyes tracking her as she crossed the floor to stand below the throne. The fairy's long hair tumbled like living bronze down from her high perch, all the way to the floor, and swished when she shifted position to address Memory. Her gown seemed to be made of the same type of cobwebs Shonae had been collecting, woven into a tight fitting, barely-there slip that dangled around her, the tattered tips ringing with small bells. She was impossibly beautiful.

Memory knew her own hair had been torn loose from its ties and fell in ragged, tangled clumps, and that her coat and plain pants were stained with bloods, unseelie black and human red, and the soot, slime and dirt of her journey.

She steadied her stance and raised her chin to meet the seelie queen's gaze.

"The human..." Aine let her eyes roam up and down Memory's appearance, "*queen* has come into my realm? What an honor this is. What, no gifts for your host?"

"I am sorry for coming unannounced, and the gift I will give you is my quick departure, after I have what I came for."

The fae around the room gathered closer, all eager to watch how their monarch dealt with the strange new human queen.

Aine's eyelids drifted closed and opened slowly as though bored. "And tell me, Your Majesty, what have you come for?"

"A fairy from your court has stolen what doesn't belong to her, and I've come to claim him back."

Aine settled into her throne, arching her back like a cat waking from a long nap. "I know the boy you mean. You speak nonsense. The human has long belonged to Mina. I saw her bring him here myself, long before you walked this world."

"But I have owned him since before he came to this world." The words tasted wrong on Memory's mouth. But she had to say it. The only way to free Will was to claim ownership of him.

A buzz of gossip spread through the assembly of fae.

Aine straightened up into a formal position. "A challenge it is then. Mina? Would you bring your pet here?" Aine called sweetly, the grin on her face dripping with venom.

Memory straightened to attention as well. Will was already here, and Mina too, in this room? Her eyes darted through the crowd, trying to spot him. Some movement to her right caught her attention, and the other fae parted to allow Mina to come forward, Will at her side.

Memory bit her tongue to keep her expression neutral and hold back her gasp. Will wore barely any clothing, his skin covered with rich gold paint, smeared in finger-painted patterns across his chest and shoulders. His eyelids were low, hooded, and looked only at Mina with a warmth that made Memory shiver.

Mina flared when she saw Memory, lips curling cruelly.

"Why is *she* here?" Mina asked. Her wings jittered, sending rainbow colored splashes across the faces of the onlookers.

Memory stared at Will, daring him to look up at her, to see her and remember her. To remember himself. His face was slack and his eyes held no emotion. His mouth hung open slightly, lips glossy and an aching color of red like they had been kissed hard and long.

Memory turned her attention to Mina. "I have come for my possession."

"Yours?" Mina's eyebrow raised high. She ran a fingertip up Will's thigh, smearing the gold paint there. Will's shoulders rolled with pleasure. "Will is mine. He ate food from my hands and is pledged to me forever."

"Too bad. He was mine before that, so any claim you have to him doesn't count." Seeing Will like this, so vacantly lustful, threw Memory. Her voice trembled and she realized she was close to tears.

Lock it down, girl.

Aine sounded greatly amused when she said, "If he is yours, it will be proved."

"I have proof." Memory began to speak, telling the court of the time that she and Will had shared in the other world, how she had saved his life and the promise he had made to her that day.

"Will owes me a life-debt, he is mine until I release him. I have proof Will promised to be mine—forever."

Memory walked close to Will and lifted his arm. It was heavy and warm and he barely reacted to her touch. Memory held his arm high, to show his wrist and the tattoo that was on it to the crowd around them, putting her wrist and matching tattoo beside it.

The gossip and murmuring in the crowd quietened.

"A story and a marking. That means nothing," Mina scoffed. She wiped her finger across Will's lips, the paint she'd smeared off his thigh leaving them tinted gold. Then she swiped cross-hatched scratches along Will's chest. "I have marked the boy too."

Mina turned, her eyes daring Memory to respond. Memory almost responded with her fist.

Mina leaned back, purring softly as she nuzzled into Will's chest. He brought his arms up around her, spreading his palms on her belly and dipping his face to her neck. "I think everyone here can see that this boy is mine."

He. Is. Not. Yours! Memory screamed inside herself, but she knew she had run out of ideas.

"Will? Will, look at me. Please just look at me!" Memory yelled, starting to panic.

He lifted his eyes lazily, barely passing them over her before burying his head back into Mina's fiery hair. Those eyes were cobalt blue, deep and rich and dark.

Memory blinked. Her lips curled. "You think you own him? You don't even know what color his eyes are. Will's eyes flash bright, like lightning in a snow storm." Memory backed away from the man. "I don't know who this is, but it isn't *my Will.*"

Mina reared back, fairy dust shooting like sparks from her skin.

The fairy queen clapped slowly. "How entertaining! Seems you do own the boy, human queen."

The glamour dropped like a curtain. Will, the imposter Will, vanished.

Memory looked around desperately. "It was a test? Where is he? Where is Will?"

Aine flicked a limp wrist toward the nearby wall, and there, Memory saw a cage that wasn't there before. Or more like a box, with thick silver walls checkered with small clover-shaped holes. Those walls clattered and shook as though something struck them.

"Will?" Memory tried to push through but Mina blocked her way.

"Don't even," Memory spat. In a swift movement, Memory clutched a fistful of the sprite's hair in one hand, yanking her down as she kicked out her feet from under her.

The seelie queen shrieked with laughter, clapping her hands faster.

Mina crumpled, her wings flashing and fluttering as she hit the floor and stayed there. When she looked up her face was devoid of expression but there was still rage in her voice. "You take him from me and you will pay!"

"Mina! Your ploy didn't work. You've lost your pet. Let them free," Aine said sharply. "We honor our laws, here."

Mina argued back, but Memory wasn't listening anymore. She ran to the cage as it thudded again from inside.

"Open it!" Memory screamed.

No longer amused by the proceedings, Aine's voice was hard and deep, barely human. "Take him and go."

The cage opened, and Will was there, his bloodied fists still pressed against the wall.

Memory reached in for him, and he growled at her touch. His shirt was shredded down the front, hanging in strips off his arms and shoulders. His eyes, the brilliant blue she knew so well, flickered and roamed, not settling on her.

"It's me, Will. It's Mem. Can't you see me?"

He winced, shaking his head, gaze still not focused. "Mem?"

"Come on. You're free." Memory reached again for his hand, and took it in hers. His hand shook as she helped him up and out of the tight, dark space, and then tightened around hers.

"What have you done to him?" Memory yelled at Mina, who skulked below Aine's throne.

Mina hissed, and with a flick of her chin, vanished away.

Memory turned to Aine for answers.

The look on the seelie queen's face said she would get none. "I said take him and GO!"

The roar was so loud the floor shook beneath Memory.

Memory squeezed Will's hand and he followed her blindly as she led him through the silent crowd of fae around them.

No matter what, I have him again. Memory's heartbeat accelerated in relief but she dared not show it, or allow the smile that was tugging at her mouth to crease her face. She was seriously outnumbered and things could change at the queen's whim.

Just as Memory and Will reached the doorway, a deep voice spoke softly. "Water from the well down the stairs in the courtyard will clear his eyes."

Memory looked and saw Lugh standing before her; Aine's human consort, said to have been with her for decades, maybe centuries. He was like a golden god of a man, strong, tall, with shimmering silver-blonde hair. His expression seemed almost bored, but his eyes glittered with sadness.

Memory stopped and looked up at him, her heart swallowing itself. "What about... what about you? Is there anything I can

do?"

Lugh looked as though he could laugh, but his smile quickly became small and sad. "Child, strange as it may seem, I am here of my own choice. But thank you, and good luck."

"Thank you," Will said.

Out through the doors, Memory wanted to run. It was only Will's blindness that kept her pace slow and steady down the long glimmering corridor and out into the courtyard.

Across to her side, Memory could see a wide section of steps leading down into the earth in a V-shape, starting wide and becoming narrower as they descended.

"This better not be like the briar path again," she grumbled, and supported Will as she took him carefully a step at a time.

He said nothing, just let her guide him. The warmth of his chest leaning on Memory made her feel safe and sad at the same time.

Memory recognized the pants he wore as the same he had on when Mina stole him, but they were tattered and torn, worse than her own clothes. In a fit of self-consciousness, she suddenly remembered what she looked like, and what Will would see when his eyes worked again.

He won't care if I'm a mess. It's one of the reasons I love him.

The steps were level and smooth, as were the walls beside them. Fist-sized gems of brilliant aqua, set into the walls, cast a fresh light into the stairwell as they reached a depth the brightness of the world above didn't touch. There was no roof, just a cut in the earth that seemed to go forever, deeper and deeper into the earth.

Just when the sky above was nothing more than a thin ribbon, they finally reached the bottom. A small pool opened up before them, glowing with the same aqua light as the gemstones. Memory dipped her hands in to scoop up some water, and the scratches on her fingers washed away as though they were nothing but splashes of paint. She was desperate to wash her face in the magical pool, but reached her hands up to Will first.

"Tip your face back," Memory said softly. "And maybe duck down a bit. You're a freaking giant you know."

Will did as instructed, kneeling down and turning his face up to the sky, and Memory dripped the water into his eyes.

He blinked three times fast, then one slow, then looked straight up into Memory's eyes.

"You're okay?" Memory's voice was barely a breath.

"You saved me." He looked at her with wonder. "I owe you all over again."

Will got to his feet and reached for her.

Memory frowned, stepping away. There wasn't much space, and her back hit the wall.

"You owe me nothing. Will, you are free, of Mina, and of me. I release you of any ownership or any debt. You don't belong to me, or anyone, not ever again."

The wavering light from the water lit aqua lines across Will's face as his expression changed through shock, relief, confusion, and sadness.

He looked down at his bare feet. "Don't you want… can I still be by your side?"

Memory drew a trembling breath. She felt all of her seventeen years old, staring up at the most beautiful boy in the world. "I do. I mean, if it's what you want. Not for anything you feel you owe me. Only if you want to. Only if you want… me."

Will's gaze stole straight into her soul as he bent his face to

hers. "I want you."

The kiss Will placed on Memory's lips then was one that burned with the truth of what he just said. And as her lips parted to meet his again, they burned with love in return.

"I love you," Will gasped between kisses. "I have loved you so long. Since the day you saved me until this day. I've fallen in love with you over and over. I loved who you were. I loved who I remembered you were. Then I loved who you became."

"I love you too," Memory whispered, tangling her fingers into the dark twists of Will's hair. Will clutched at Memory, pulling her tight against his body.

Tears came to Memory and she let them run, tasting the salt of them between her mouth and Will's.

Gently, he let her go. "What's wrong?"

Memory brushed her hand down Will's cheek, wiping away a tear there. *Mine or his?* "You're free. That's the good news."

"I'm free," Will murmured, smile wide on his face and eyes closed. He opened them again and looked around and up the stairwell behind them.

His dark brows dropped low. "Where are your friends? Did you come alone?"

Memory sighed. "That's the bad news…"

CHAPTER TWENTY

As Memory explained to Will her journey through the fairy realm so far, and what had happened to the others, she pulled Will's iron awl from a loop in her belt and handed it over to him. His hand wrapped around hers as he took it, and he lingered there, feeling the fragile coolness of Memory's slim fingers in his. There was also a tremble there that made Will want to pull Memory into his arms and hold her again.

Memory had lost her friends because of him. She'd risked everything to save him, they all had. And he couldn't be upset because he knew he would have done the same if the situation was reversed. And he knew that together they would risk everything again to save Eloryn, Roen, and Erec.

Will dabbed the healing well water across Memory's face and his jaw grew tight. He knew Memory planned to save her friends at the Unseelie Court. And he knew he would go with her, anywhere. But he still wished that they could simply go home, be safe, where nothing more could hurt the girl he loved. He wished it with every aching nerve in his body.

But he knew a quiet, safe life was never the destiny of this girl. Maybe he'd always known it. She always had the fire of a hero burning within her. He could see her great and terrible fate on her as clearly as the scratches that marred her skin. He couldn't stop whatever was to come, but he would do everything in his power to protect the body and the heart of the young woman before him.

Will bent to collect some more well water and Memory held him back.

"That's enough," she said. "As nice as it feels right now, we're only going to get scratched up again. Plus we're on the clock."

Will nodded, and they strode up the deep stairwell and out of the Seelie Court.

A light breeze seemed to chase them from the court, out through the tinkling metal trees and over the tiled ground, so polished it reflected like a mirror. They found the briar pathway quickly, and a petite white creature emerged shyly from where she had been crouched in the shadows.

"Got him back, then?" she bleated, one long ear twitching.

Memory nodded. "Will, this is our guide, Shonae. She's… well… She's been helpful."

Shonae grunted, spat, and turned her back, taking the lead into the briar tunnel.

"Mostly," Memory muttered.

A giant spider skittered past along the twigs overhead, its shadow sending chills down Will's spine. Although he knew of the spiders and the briar path, this was all new to him. He'd never been through here before, because he'd never travelled outside of the Seelie Court. He'd never been free.

The concept still staggered him. For sixteen years he had been a pet to Mina. Neglected, toyed with, put on display, or put in a cage. He'd felt free, at times, when Mina had left him alone in Avall's forests for long stretches, but the choke of an invisible collar had always remained.

The girl he loved had freed him, and if he didn't think he could love her any more, maybe he could, for that.

They continued down the twisting briar tunnel until the entrance disappeared behind them. Just as Will took a deep, free, breath of relief, a familiar twinkle caught his eye.

"Stop!"

In a sparking explosion of fairy dust, Mina appeared before them, blocking their way down the narrow path. Fury lit her eyes like a fire within.

"I won't. I won't let you go." Mina stomped a foot on the ground. Her wings sent sparkling drops of red light into the air and Will had to squint to protect his eyes from the brightness.

"Mina, let us pass." Will's voice was firm and strong. "Go home. Don't make this difficult."

Mina came towards them.

Will saw Memory's fingers tightening on the handle of her blade. "You don't own him anymore, Mina. No one does."

Will put a hand on her slim shoulder, wanting her to back off—to let him handle this. She seemed to receive the silent

message and stilled.

Mina flew right in front of Will, clutching at the tattered remains of his shirt with both hands. There was desperation in her eyes as they stared deep into his. "You love me. I know you do. Say it and stay with me. Stay here. Be mine."

Will kept his gaze steady, locking eyes with Mina. "You saved my life. I will always thank you for that. But I am free now. I choose to leave."

Her eyes filled with tears. The glitter falling from her wings turned to dust, black and heavy. "Are you really leaving me? I love you, I need you. Please don't go."

"Mina, you don't love me. You don't know what that even means. You just know you want me, you want your pet. Love is not the same thing as thinking you should have what you want just because you want it. It's not keeping someone with you when they want to go. It's not spells or tricks or keeping someone in a cage. That is not love, Mina, and until you know that you are never going to know love in return."

"You don't know how I feel!" Mina's face twisted, anger tightening her lips until they spread, baring thin teeth. "I will not let you just walk away from me. You're mine!"

"He was released by your queen," Shonae said. She shook her head at the sprite, a small warning, fae to fae.

Memory had a look on her face Will did not like. She was testing the edge of the blade with one finger and eyeballing Mina as though she was trying to get a bead on where to stick that sharp weapon. "Stop being the bad ex and just go home."

The light in the tunnel grew as Mina hissed, her firelight glow raging under her skin. "You. Everything was fine before you stumbled out of the Veil. Stealing my boy." Mina's snarl

became a wicked grin. "Well, you have won Will, but you lost all your other friends to the Unseelie Court, haven't you? They won't be so easy to get back."

Memory said nothing. Her shoulders were rigid and her mouth pressed down into a thin line that told Will exactly how afraid she was that what Mina had just said was true. Will pushed Mina's hands off his shirt and walked back to stand beside Memory, his love for her like a magnet, drawing him in. "It's going to be okay. We'll get everyone home safe. Come on, let's go."

Will brushed the back of one finger lightly across Memory's cheek.

"No! You can't choose her over me," Mina shrieked. "I don't care what the queen said. You might be free, but that doesn't mean you're protected. If I can't have you, no one can."

Mina ran at him, screaming. A bright gold light flashed in her hand, her inner light reflecting off the wide fairy gold dagger she held there. It took a moment for Will to believe it was real, that Mina would really try to kill him. She was many things, but he didn't believe her truly capable of such violence. That moment of confusion brought the dagger to his chest, the razor edge of it cutting through the remains of his once fine shirt. Distantly he heard Memory cry out as though far away, despite being right beside him.

Will sidestepped, sliding with the thrust of the weapon, rolling away from it before it broke his skin. Will grabbed Mina as she passed him, his fingers slipping over her arm and her hair smacking him in the face as they spun together.

He grabbed her small wrist, applying pressure. The fae were strong but brittle, much like their gold.

Mina screamed again. "You are hurting me!"

"I'll break you if you don't drop the blade."

The dagger clattered to the ground.

Will let go of Mina and picked it up, holding it defensively against her.

Mina backed away, her face glowing with rage.

"Do you honestly think you are going to get away from here without a fight? I have more friends here than you do!"

A hum built in the air, and the light brightened until the glare made Will wince. Memory raised her arm to shade her eyes. "What's happening?"

Shonae nickered a gasping high pitched sound. "We're for it now."

Will's breath caught in his throat. "We have to run."

Sprites flew up the tunnel behind them, like swarms of fireflies. In their smaller form, they seemed no more threatening than a tangle of Christmas lights, but Will knew better.

He grabbed Memory's hand and dragged her along the briar path. Shonae ran beside them squealing as the flying creatures harried and tormented her.

Sharp stabs of pain marked Will's arms, his neck, and cheeks. The sprites buzzed about him, their tiny faces puckered with unholy mischief, their hands holding needle-like blades that sliced like paper cuts.

Laughter rang out from every corner. The buzzing of wings beat all the way inside his head. Memory fell, pulled to her feet by a mass of the tiny beasts in her hair. She shrieked in anger and pain.

Will hauled her to her feet, swatting at the fairies with his iron hook that Memory had returned to him. He kept a tight

grip of her hand.

They ran, beating their way blindly through the cloud of sprites. The sting of the fae's attacks blended with the scratching of stick and thorn as they crashed against the walls of the briar path.

"Don't stray," Shonae cried out. "Don't stray!"

Her warning came too late. In a burst of dry and broken twigs, Memory and Will stumbled out and clear of the briar pathway, with Shonae falling behind them.

Will blinked in the sudden darkness, trying to adjust. The sprites were gone, the attack was over. He closed his eyes to fight away the trails of light burned into his retinas. Opening them again he saw black trees hanging over their heads and dead grass below his feet. Behind them there was no sight of the briar pathway, no entrance, no thorny walls, nothing. "Where are we?"

"Lost." Shonae grunted. Her shoulders were hunched and she licked at a bleeding cut on her forearm. "We strayed from the path, and now we're lost far from where we should be and I'll never be rid of you."

Memory sat on the ground, catching her breath. "Mina and her buzz-buddies are gone at least. They forced us out here but didn't follow us. This looks like the unseelie lands. Is that why they didn't keep chasing us? How far could we be from the court?"

Shonae huffed. "How far could it be from one side of your world to the other?"

Memory scrambled to her feet. "No, don't be with your riddles now. Are you saying we're not going to make it in time?"

"We got shoved out of the briars mid pathway. We could

have come out anywhere." Shonae slouched and turned away.

Memory looked to Will with crushing fear in her eyes.

Will moved to stand in front of Shonae. "Please, can you try and tell where we are? Is there anything you can see?"

Shonae sighed, and turned her face up to the empty gray sky. She tilted her head side to side, her goat-like ears angling around independently.

"There's nothing up there. What do you see?" Memory asked, looking at the sky herself.

"Our sun is dim, nearly dead, but she is there."

Memory turned back to Will. "We're not going to make it in time."

Will didn't answer. He just wrapped his arms around Memory and drew her close.

She murmured into his chest, "I don't know how long I've been here, how long since Eloryn, Roen, and Erec were Branded. I have no clock to know when their Brands will kill them. Nyneve said a turn of the sun and the moon but I can't even see them in this awful world!"

Shonae sniffed, then leaped up onto an outcrop of rocks that formed a small peak, hopping up them like a mountain goat.

When she reached the top, she looked all the way around, and then extended one arm. "That's the way we need to go." She pointed with her long white finger. "But it will take at least three days to walk there without the briar path."

"Three days." Memory's voice was a harsh breath.

"Let's go then," Will said. He knew it was hopeless, but what else could they do?

"We could Veil door there. Maybe. I don't know if I can do it in Tearnan Ogh or where we are going but I can try." Memory

was babbling. Her face was pale and tired, and Will wondered how long it had been since she'd eaten or slept.

"You made an unbreakable oath not to use your magic. We only just escaped the Seelie Court. Let's not provoke them again." Will tried to smile, to win a smile from Memory, but it was a lost attempt.

"I have to do something."

"You will. I don't know how, but you will save them. You'll save everyone. You've always been my hero, and heroes always win."

He was rewarded with a small smile then. "We must have at least twelve hours left, right? So let's walk. We can walk for eleven hours, and then you can try your magic."

Memory nodded, and her whole body swayed. If it had been anyone else, Will wouldn't believe she'd last that long. But he knew Memory could.

"Deal," she said. "No backsies."

With a deadly serious shared look, they both spat in their hands and shook on it. And then they started walking.

Every step on the crackling, dead ground counted like a second ticking on a clock in Memory's mind. When they started out she'd tried to count in her head, count the seconds, minutes, to get some idea of how long they had walked, of how much time they had left. But there were too many seconds, and minutes, and her thoughts were too addled with panic and exhaustion.

We'll make it there in time, somehow. That became the new mantra Memory repeated over and over instead of counting as the three of them walked in silence. Maybe Nyneve could do something for her, extend the deadline. Something. Memory kept hope alive within the burning magic in her chest. The walking was easy enough, great flat plains of hard-packed, shimmering dirt with just a few twisted trees reaching high into the air like giant beanstalks. Memory cast concerned glances at Will as they went, seeking support. The determination and courage on his face when he looked back at her hurt almost as much as it helped.

Shonae told Memory to relax. This was daytime apparently, and there would be a night. They had at least until then.

Memory stared skeptically at the dull gray sky and wondered how they would tell the difference. She couldn't see the sun Shonae spoke of at all, only a slowly churning mass of monochrome clouds. There wasn't even enough light to cast shadows, but Memory supposed it could get darker. *Things can always get worse*, she reminded herself.

Something in the sky moved on the horizon, and Memory swallowed hard. *Say the famous last words? Of course I did.*

The wind picked up and there was a low whomping sound, ominous and drawing nearer. They all looked up, the small shreds of hope that had begun to settle on them shattering like thin ice on a lake.

There it was. The dragon.

CHAPTER TWENTY-ONE

"Just what we need," Memory sighed, reaching for her knife.

In the dim light his black scales had no shine, making the dragon look like a shadow or silhouette in the sky rather than a real creature. He was flying low, a loping, tumbling flight that lacked the grace Memory had once seen him possess.

Even still, he flew fast and would reach them in seconds. Memory's stomach clenched with fear at the thought of being bitten in half by those huge teeth, or set on fire by dragon breath. How badly would that hurt?

Memory knew they could not run or hide. She doubted they could fight. All they could do was wait. Will put his shoulder beside hers and they watched the dragon come to them. Shonae crumbled to the ground, her face down in the dirt in a deep kneeling bow.

The dragon landed in front of them. His feet hit the earth hard and skidded, sending puffs of dust flying up into their faces. Memory covered her eyes with her sleeve and Will coughed.

The dragon came to a stop lying on his side. Memory could see his wings were tattered. When the creature raised his head to look at the small group, it seemed to be with great effort.

Without moving his tooth-filled mouth, the dragon's words rattled into Memory's mind. "Hello human."

The massive serpentine beast made no threatening move or sign that it would hurt them. He just waited.

"Hello dragon," Memory replied, eyeing him with a confused frown. "Been a while."

The dragon blinked huge verdant eyes. "I have been watching you since you came to our realm."

Memory winced, both for the power of the dragon's voice in her head, and for her failures the dragon must have observed.

Will spoke, obviously hearing everything Memory heard. "Why? What do you want?"

"I am trying to decide what it is you are doing. If you mean to harm or help the fae as we draw to our end."

"I'm just here to save my friends. Standard search and rescue then we're going home. I wasn't even thinking about…" *I wasn't even thinking about anyone else.* Memory let out a breath like she'd taken a baseball bat to the chest. *My friends are in trouble, and I wasn't even thinking about anyone else.*

Memory took a step closer to the dragon. His scales were patchy, missing in places, moldering. "Dragon, are you dying?"

"We are all dying. You already know that." The words held

no bitterness. He extended a claw so carefully toward Shonae, scooping her arms onto it and raising her back to her feet.

Shonae shivered slightly, staring with round black eyes at the dragon, but she kept her fingers wrapped around his claw as though holding hands. Shonae looked so healthy, so alive, that it was hard to understand for Memory that she could be dying. Much like most of the fae. But seeing the dragon like this made the truth suddenly sink in.

The dragon tilted his head and Memory wondered how many of her thoughts he had access to. "My time is less due to my size. I need more magic to sustain me than the little ones. But eventually all of this will end."

"I've been so selfish." Memory shook her head, staring at her feet. "I am doing everything I can to save my friends but there are so many who need help. I should be doing more."

The dragon shifted, making a soft hushing sound in the shifting, glittered sand. "What does the fate of the fae matter to you? If you wish you can take your friends and go to the other lands. You can live there with the rest of the humans and never worry for the fate of Tearnan Ogh or Avall."

For a brief moment, Memory tried to imagine Eloryn and Roen adjusting to life in the modern world. Eloryn would probably love the internet. Could they live there happily? What about Erec, or Clara? Then there were Roen's parents and Lanval. Maeve, and the orphans. Bedevere and the Wizards' Council. The rest of the castle guards and staff. Memory's thoughts spiraled out, larger and larger, reaching farther. The teachers and students at the university and finishing school. The people she saw on the streets of Caermaellan, Maerranton markets or Elder's Bridge Inn. All the humans of Avall. Shonae… Aine,

Nyneve, Lugh. All the shimmering sprites of the Seelie Court. The banshees and trolls and gaunts of the Unseelie Court. The dragon. Every creature in Avall and Tearnan Ogh. How could she abandon any of them? How could she pick and choose who would live?

This entire world of the fae was passing into the shadows, and would take Avall with it. Avall had been created as a haven, but the constant drain of magic away to the rest of the world had wrought devastation on the fae, and it was only the fae that kept Avall habitable for the humans.

"What can I do?" Memory's words were a mere whisper.

"I think you already know."

Magic. Life. Like a bonfire, burning me away from the inside.

Memory nodded. Everywhere things and people were dying from a lack of magic. Could she give them hers? She took a deep breath, and reached to place a hand on the dragon's cheek.

"Dragon, would you let me gift you with some of my magic? I have more than I can ever use and it could save you."

His lips split, showing rows of razor tipped teeth, and a harsh gust of hot air rushed out along with a rumbling chuckle. "Oh you little human. No. I would not take your magic. It is too compressed into you, tangled up inside. Who knows what other *human* things I might get along with it?"

The dragon leaned slightly into Memory's touch, and Memory could feel the slow pulse of his life beneath his scales.

"Besides, I am old. Older than you can imagine, human, and I am the last of my kind. Life is just a series of lonely days and nights. There is no joy in it, no thrill. My mate is now dead and without her there is no love, no way to ease the stifling boredom that is centuries piling on top of one another. I am better off

dying, then I could fly free again with my mate and the others of my kind who have gone before me."

Having grown up believing dragons only to be a myth, the idea that Memory would discover they were real only to lose them again seemed too much to bear. It hurt to speak but she did. "Dragon, our worlds will not be the same without you."

"I agree." The sly humor in the dragon's voice was clear as it reverberated in Memory's head. She smiled at the dragon as tears streamed down her cheeks. Will took and squeezed her hand and put his other on the dragon's neck.

"Be strong, small ones. The worlds need you. And you need help now, so let me help you. I will fly you to the Unseelie Court."

"You are not a beast of burden," Memory said, reminding him of what he had once told her when she had a boon to request of him.

"No, but the time for old rules has past. The good fight for themselves and their friends. The great fight for everyone."

Memory bowed her head.

"I think you are worthy of a ride, or at least, one day, you will be," the dragon quipped. His words were light, but Memory thought she saw something on his wizened face, some emotion so close to human sorrow that it cut her to the very core.

Memory did not even bother to wipe away the tears that rolled down her cheeks. "I cannot thank you enough, Dragon."

The dragon laid himself low and Will helped boost Memory and Shonae up, then climbed up behind them. The dragon's back was smooth despite the scales and scars. Shonae took the webbing she had collected from the spiders and wrapped it carefully around the three of them and then around the dragon's

neck. They sat in a row with Memory up front, Will behind her and Shonae clinging tightly at the rear.

"For all the risk and danger you put me through on your journey," Shonae snuffled, "perhaps it is worth it all, to fly on the back of a dragon."

Memory brushed her hands across the metallic black scales she sat on. *Perhaps it is worth it all.*

The dragon shifted under her, and as he raised himself up Memory gasped at how high she was, there on his back. The tattered wings spread, lifted, and pushed downwards, creating mini-tornadoes of sparkling dust as they lifted off the ground. Memory had to close her eyes when they took off and her fear mounted as they soared over treetops and higher, until the ground had vanished below the clouds they rode through.

Memory wasn't sure the dragon would even have enough life left in him to get them safely to the Unseelie Court, but if he trusted her enough to let her ride, then she trusted him enough to try. Each dip and glide of the dragon's wings sent her stomach swirling, and she had to crouch low against the scaly back to shelter from the rushing winds. The Rump of Steel-skin web that she clung to felt too silky and delicate to be her tether on this creature so far above the world. She knew too well what it felt like to fall.

The warmth of Will's body behind her was reassuring, and after a while her thoughts took her mind away from her fear of falling off the dragon's back. Tearnan Ogh was dying, the creatures and people within it were dying, and there seemed to be no way to stop all of it. She could go back to the rest of the world if need be, and take her friends with her but what about all the other humans of Avall?

How would any of the citizens of Avall survive in a world they had so long been separated from? Time had passed, and the old ways that stayed with Avall long gone. Cars and nuclear weapons had replaced swords and horses; people ate food from paper wrappers and flew in steel tubes across the sky. Would the people of Avall be able to withstand those changes without going mad?

Maybe I should have helped educate people on the modern world, she thought tiredly. *I should have done… anything. I should have… Crudmonkeys! What is the use in thinking of what I should have done when it is obvious I need to do something right now?*

But what?

Memory knew even if she could take every human from Avall into the modern world, she couldn't take any of the fae. They couldn't stand the abundance of iron and steel there. *What can I do to save this land and the fae and the dragon? How could one person save an entire world?*

She wanted to save it. As strange and weird and terrifying as Tearnan Ogh was, it hurt her to think of it disappearing forever.

Memory wiped a tear away on her shoulder so it wouldn't fly back and splash on Will or Shonae behind her, alerting them to her uncontrollable emotions.

Will seemed to understand anyway. "Stop worrying. Just rest. You need it." His breath tickled her ear and his hand stroked her back.

He was right. She was beyond exhausted. They all were. Even the dragon swooped lower, floating on the updrafts and saving his waning energy.

Memory's head sagged to one side and her body relaxing into Will's. His heart beat below his skin and she felt it echoing

into hers as she fell asleep.

"We are here," Shonae said and Memory wished she did not hear the terror in her voice, wished she didn't hear her at all, that she could have slept one hundred years and given up all her worries and responsibilities.

But she knew no one else could do what needed to be done. And she was starting to understand what that was.

Since Memory had slept, the world had grown darker, black like the mottled scales of the dragon they rode.

The Unseelie Court came into view, a beacon of red fire light reflecting off dark crystal under the ebony dome of the sky.

Please. Memory said a silent prayer to anything that would listen. *Please just let my friends still be alive.*

CHAPTER TWENTY-TWO

The dragon dipped suddenly and Memory felt her stomach float up into her throat.

"How are you holding up?" she asked the dragon, hoping her voice, or at least thoughts, carried over the rushing winds for him to hear. "Are we okay for a landing?"

"Tired." The single word reply held a depth of emotion, the weariness of centuries.

Memory placed her hand on the dragon's neck, wishing she could do more for him. They soared toward the ground, lurching roughly through the air, and Memory tightened her thighs to steady herself.

The dragon skimmed over a vast boundary wall, a

shimmering fence of glistening black crystal woven like tangled tree roots. It seemed to sing as the air from their flight trailed through it. Reaching the inner courtyard of the castle, the dragon spiraled, slowing his descent as the unseelie fae in the area dashed for cover.

They landed hard but stable. As the disturbed dust cleared, all around them Memory could see black-eyed faces peering up in awe.

"You've made a big entrance, that's for sure," Will whispered into Memory's ear.

"Nice way to make an impression," Memory agreed. "I only wish we had some kind of plan from this point on. I'm basically walking right into a trap. As usual."

"Just be yourself. Save your friends. It will work out."

Memory grunted an unsure agreement then threw her leg over the side and slid down off the dragon in what she thought was a remarkable display of not falling on her face.

The dragon's head was close by her as she turned back to see Will and Shonae follow her off its back. She smiled softly to the huge beast. "Thank you."

The dragon's head dipped ever so slightly, and he poised to take flight again.

His wings were even more tattered than before. They were riddled with tears and holes, his scales were dulled and flaking and she knew he had cost himself much of his life by flying them through the night the way he had. Sorrow filled her, but before she could say anything else the dragon pushed down his wings and lifted into the sky.

Whispers blended with the sound of the dragon's flight. Hushed words buzzed around Memory and her friends as they

stood in the middle of the grand courtyard, right on the steps of the Unseelie Court's castle, surrounded by curious onlookers. Two humans had come to the court on the back of a dragon, accompanied by a young unseelie fae. Strange things were afoot and everyone wanted to know what they meant.

Memory looked up at the castle and tried to draw on her well of courage and found it almost dry, already consumed from constant use. *Shouldn't it get easier, being brave? Why do I always have to dig deeper?*

The castle itself was similar to the Seelie Court, if anything more organic and flowing in its lines and design. Darker colors were used, but they made a rich, warm impression rather than the haunted house of terror Memory had been expecting. But she knew that the terror lay inside.

She forced her feet to move, and to the main entrance they went.

Guards met them. The tallest of them stood in their path, a fairy gold spear held firmly in his hand. He, and the dozen guards behind, all wore the same high gloss black armor as the soldiers who had stolen her friends away, but this lot wore no helmets. The leader's long white hair fell to his waist, and his skin was gray as ash.

The knight narrowed his eyes, his silver tipped lashes veiling the pools of black below his eyelids. "We've been expecting you."

"Then where is the red carpet?" Memory said.

The smugness dropped from the knight's face as he tried to interpret her reaction and phrasing.

Memory squared up her fingers to frame the dark fae's face and squinted through at him. "And that look on your face is exactly why I love saying stuff like that. So, are you going to let us in?"

The knight hesitated. Not in a way that seemed confused, but a way that seemed torn, and troubled, and made Memory's stomach bubble. "Human queen," he said in a hushed voice. "You should return home."

"Let them pass!" The deep, regal voice called from behind the crowd of guards.

Nyneve appeared, and the men parted to make way for her. She strode through them, wearing a dress encrusted with thousands of diamonds, as though she were glistening sea-foam on top of deep black water. The shimmer of her dress and the shimmer of her lightly scaled, silver skin blended perfectly so it was hard to tell where the close fitted bodice ended and her flesh began. The skirts, though, billowed around her strong frame and trailed in a long train behind her. With her hair like nighttime flowing all round, she seemed to be the very embodiment of the starry sky.

"Your Highness," the men muttered in rough unison, all taking a knee.

Nyneve looked darkly at the head guard who had showed hesitation at allowing Memory and her friends to enter the court.

"They are here by invitation of one of our own, or so it would appear." Nyneve's eyes raked over Shonae, who trembled and tried to press herself into a corner. "They are to be allowed entry."

"They tricked me into compliance. They carried iron," Shonae stuttered.

"Iron," a knight said, disgust written on his face.

Nyneve raised her chin slightly. "Yes. The iron. You cannot

be allowed to bear it into the court, you must understand."

Memory reached instinctively for her knife in her belt. Without iron, they would have no protection at all, but what good was it to her now, truly? She could not fight her way with iron through every dark fae in the land to save her friends. It didn't protect them the first time.

Memory gave a single nod.

Nyneve waved for them to follow, and they walked into the long entry hall and to a small room to the side. "Leave your iron here. You can rest your thoughts, knowing no fae will be able to touch it, move or steal it, lest they be burned."

Memory and Will placed their iron artefacts onto the table. They met gazes, shared a worried look, and turned away.

"Hurry now," Nyneve said softly. "Your friends live, but they suffer. You must act quickly. You have the right to declare or accept a challenge from the monarch, to prove the innocence of your friends and remove their Brand." She waved them back out of the room, then followed, gown flaring around her.

Out in the long arched hall, Nyneve took the lead again. The walls were like dark mirrors, reflecting her, Memory, Will and Shonae as they sped along the corridor.

"A challenge? What kind of challenge?" Memory half jogged to keep up with the long stride of the Amazonian unseelie princess.

Nyneve slowed as they reached a wider section of hallway which met a huge door, or more like gate, made of woven silver vines and elegant heart-shaped leaves. She touched it softly and it began swinging open. "Trial by combat," she said.

Memory's heart lurched into her throat. The gate opened into a gargantuan domed room, filled with monsters of every form and shape. It felt as though someone had opened up a compendium of fairytale monsters and let the beasts spill from the pages into real life. Minotaurs and trolls, gaunts and green skinned crones, banshees and crooked, twisted, dark winged harpies. Memory tried to see them with fresh eyes, tried to see beyond their physical appearance and judge them without bias, but all she could see was monsters. Monsters, every one of them. Because they were here in Finvarra's court.

The chamber was formed of the same mirrored dark crystals as the rest of the castle, but within them sparkling shapes and clouds of color moved, like nebulae in space, adding color and light to the darkness. In the center of everything was a raised dais where grand seats were formed from crystalline tree roots that met in a thick, twisted trunk that held the largest throne of all—Finvarra's. He sat there, within the hollow of the sparkling tree whose branches spread up, up, twirling into the high ceiling as though it was what held aloft the very roof.

The creatures in the room squabbled and gossiped, argued and drank. The race of news was already spreading through the room and Memory heard whispers of her name, and "dragon" in the chatter.

As the gates swung into their fully open position they clanged against the wall, and then all eyes in the room were upon Memory.

Finvarra sat in his throne like a tumble of fallen branches, his body a mess of wiry limbs, sharp angles, and rough, ancient skin. He looked down at Memory and extended his arm, curling a sharp clawed finger at her to beckon her to him.

Shonae tugged at Memory's sleeve, cowering by her side. "As Finvarra has grown more cruel and twisted, so has he attracted

the worst of the fae into his court. I fear we will not walk free from here again."

Memory walked in anyway. The dark fae moved apart, creating a path for her. She could see something in their all black eyes as they watched her. Hatred? Or could it be fear?

As the crowd cleared, backing to the edges of the room, Memory saw something far worse.

Eloryn. Roen. Erec.

Memory went cold and stiff all over, as though she'd died many hours ago and rigor mortis had suddenly set in.

Her friends were all bound in heavy webbing that wrapped around them and held them in place, dangling from the branches of the throne tree like living piñatas. Live sport for the amusement of Finvarra and the wider audience.

Memory knew better than to look at them for too long but she couldn't look away. Eloryn's body shuddered with small, sharp breaths, her skin a ghostly gray. Roen had blood crusted along his upper lip and chin, matching the dull red of the Brand on his forehead, and Erec sagged toward the ground, apparently lifeless. All of them had anguish written large in their expressions.

Is it the Brand torturing them, or has it been Finvarra and his court?

Memory wasn't sure, but she could see Finvarra was using them as an amusement, hung there on display. The crooked smirk as he watched her approach built hatred inside her she almost couldn't contain. Every terrible thing he had done to her, to her friends, to the people of Avall, made the magic inside her burn like a white-hot star. The magic he had put inside her. The scar he, as Providence, had cut into her chest as a baby itched and stung. She felt the pain she could see on her sister's face.

The ground trembled beneath her at each step she took. The room fell into total silence and for a moment, the smirk fell from Finvarra's face. She wanted to run at him, screaming and clawing and slicing with the iron blade she no longer had.

Will slipped his hand into Memory's and squeezed tight.

"Deep breaths. Stay in control."

"Thank you," Memory whispered to Will.

Side by side, they reached the base of Finvarra's throne. Nyneve, who had escorted them in, broke off from them and stood on the dais at her father's feet.

Memory swallowed, trying to wet her dry mouth, then spoke. "Finvarra, as queen of the humans, I come to seek the release of my people and the removal of their Brands."

"Hrm, only a small request then?" he grumbled, half a smile on his lips, baring the sharp teeth behind. A few unseelie fae around the room chuckled along with him. "These humans were a surprise gift to me from my people. They were found wandering uninvited in my lands, and attacked my men with iron."

Surprise gift? Your men ambushed us!

Finvarra continued, his words mixed with a mad chortling sound. "The Brand on their faces is proof of their crimes. I have every right to do with them what I will. Why would I ever release them?"

Memory fumed, but she also knew they had walked into the fae's homelands carrying iron. There was too much violence and it was only leading to more. There had to be another way.

"Because I am pleading with you to do so. I'm pleading with you to show kindness." Memory held so much hope within her at that moment, hope that there was any kindness within

Finvarra that she could reason with, that maybe if he could show kindness in that one moment, she could work with him, help him and his people, maybe even forgive him.

But the look in his eyes told her it would not be. He hated her, she could see it. He hated all humans, hated the magic that resided within them, that he thought they stole from the fae.

"Kindness? You ask for kindness?" He spat a huge glob of smoky gray liquid down at Memory's feet. "I will relish watching the Brand leach the life from these few humans as small compensation for the crimes of all your kind against the unseelie race."

"You are not innocent either, Finvarra. I know your crimes." Memory glared harshly at the unseelie king, telling him with her expression that she knew exactly who he was and what he'd done.

Finvarra rose to his feet, back hunched from age. "You dare offend me so in my own court? Crimes? I have committed no crimes!"

The anger Memory had kept contained was seeping out like a poison. "I do dare because I have seen the damage your crimes have done. I've seen the pain on children's faces and the bodies drained of blood. I feel the fire of your crimes inside me every day!"

Whispers ran through the court. Prickles ran up and down Memory's spine.

Finvarra's black eyes held contempt and he steepled his long fingers together, tapping them on his chin. "I think you have gone insane. If you think I have committed crimes against you, then speak the Branding words. Try to Brand me, and the magic will prove my innocence."

"You know I can't! You know I'm forbidden to speak behests. You're trying to trick me into breaking my oath." Rage seized Memory. She was unable to stop seeing the faces of her friends, distorted and distended with agony. Things had spun totally out of control. Finvarra talked her round in circles, confusing her, and getting her no closer to freeing her friends. She didn't want to have to challenge him, but she was running out of ideas.

"I just want my friends back," she sighed, more to herself than as a plea to the monster before her.

Finvarra took his seat again on the throne. He lowered himself slowly, shakily, like an old man. It was an almost human movement, apart from the mad, scary grin on his face. "That is the problem with you humans. You *want* and you believe that your wanting entitles you to taking."

"Says the king who wanted Avall for the fae and lied to every human there about the rest of the world becoming a hell."

"The iron hell is just that," Finvarra snapped. "It is killing my people as we speak. Are we to just sit around and wait for the people in that world to finish destroying it? We have to protect ourselves!"

"By sucking the life from people, blood drinker?"

Finvarra seemed confused. He glanced over at Memory's three friends, hanging beside him.

Scowling at Memory he flicked his hand at her. "You disgusting creature, I've not touched the filthy blood of your companions. Queen of the humans, if you were not who you are, you would be mounted on my walls right alongside the others! I'll take no more offense from you. Get out of my court before I change my mind."

Memory frowned. There was something wrong. She couldn't put her finger on it but it was there, right under the surface. If bringing her friends here was Finvarra's trap for Memory, then why was he telling her to leave?

Memory looked across at Eloryn, who was watching with dull, hooded eyes. Her blonde hair was a straggly mess across her face and she was gagged, unable to speak or use behests.

"I won't leave without my friends. Finvarra, I challenge you to a trial by combat for their freedom."

A wave of gasps spread throughout the chamber. Finvarra shifted in his chair, twitching upright and eyeing Memory. Then he laughed, small at first, then building, growing more maniacal and chaotic in its tones. "Little human girl challenges the King Under the Hill to combat? Do you even know what it is you challenge?"

Memory glanced across at Nyneve, who dipped her head in a small, encouraging nod. That gesture was familiar and more prickles ran along her scalp and skin. "If I win, the Brand will be removed from my friends. I'm also asking that if I win, you release us all from your court."

"Sweetening the gamble for yourself? What for me then, if I win?" Finvarra asked, then answered for himself. "Yes, if I win, I keep you all. What a fine trophy a human queen will be! Let the humans see the proof of unseelie dominance in this world. You will be my toy for eternity, or whatever is left of it for us."

And there it is. Memory sneered. He did want her after all. This must have been his plan, trying to lure her into this challenge so he could claim her legitimately. But did he really think he could beat her? He was a fae, so she knew he would be

faster and stronger than her, but he seemed so fragile and old, and at least partly mad. Memory had her fair share of fights, and could now remember many times she'd taken on more than a few larger bullies at a time. With the extra sword training she'd had from Roen, maybe she could take Finvarra in a fair fight. If that was what this would be.

"There can be no magic," Memory said. She had seen the magic Providence possessed, using behests as freely and powerfully as Eloryn. She couldn't allow Finvarra to turn that on her now, while she had no magic of her own she could use.

"Of course not!" Finvarra growled. "I know the laws of the challenge. Do you?"

Well, no, actually.

Nyneve stepped forward then, speaking up before Memory had to embarrass herself. "The trial by combat to prove the innocence of the Branded is a duel to first blood. One on one armed combat with no magic."

Will squeezed Memory's hand. "Let me take your place."

Finvarra snarled. "I will only fight the queen. I am being *kind* to even give her this chance."

"It's all right Will, I can do this." Memory squeezed his hand again in return then let go, stepping up onto the dais.

Finvarra bent forward off his throne again, walking to meet Memory at the front of the raised floor. His smile was sinister and her scalp prickled again, a warning that something was still off—things were falling into place a little too neatly. He reached out an arm, and within moments a guard rushed forward, knelt, and presented Finvarra with a grand sword of fairy gold, almost as long as Memory was tall.

Holy fuuuuuuuuuuuuu… Whoa, just keep it together. You only have to nick the old goat.

"You've taken away my weapon," Memory said. "I need something to fight with."

"You fight with what you have," Finvarra scoffed.

Memory held up her fingers, showing off the blunt, chewed on nails. "I don't have the same manicurist as you. How am I meant to draw blood?"

"You were the fool to challenge me without a weapon so that is how you will fight. Unless anyone here would lend you theirs?" Finvarra cast a glance out over the sea of unseelie fae, and Memory knew by the look on their faces that no one would help her. Even Nyneve looked away, unable to risk helping her openly.

Will came to her side. "It's not much, but we have this." He handed her the fairy gold dagger he had taken from Mina. It was barely bigger than her own knife, and she looked from it to the sword Finvarra held.

"I guess it will have to do," Memory said, letting her hands close around Will's as she took the blade, hoping it wouldn't be the last time she felt his touch.

"You and your toothpick ready?" Finvarra chuckled, showing rows of gleaming, pointed teeth. He wanted to humiliate her, take away the magic he'd filled her with. He wanted everyone to watch her being beaten and her friends dying. The unfairness, the utter cruelty of it made her stomach churn. Still, she didn't want to fight him. He was weak, dying from the absence of magic, and it showed. He hated her, and she was disgusted by him and his ways, but did it have to come to this?

It was too late though, it *had* come to this. Memory gave him a tight smile. "Bring it, old man."

Any confidence in her cocky statement fell apart as Finvarra's sword swung at her with ferocious speed. A shriek escaped from Memory as she jumped backwards.

The fairy gold knife felt heavy and slippery in her hand. It was hard to hold onto, and its unfamiliar weight and curve made it difficult for her to concentrate, although it became clear at once that she needed to.

Finvarra moved like a different creature. No longer crippled and slow, though still with an arched back, he dashed and spun. His hands were a blur as he came after Memory, twisting the sword like a propeller. His laughter hung around the room as she back-stepped, skirting and circling around the dais. She tried to get a grip on her knife and fight back, but could barely regain her footing as she stumbled away from Finvarra's onslaught.

Why did I think I could do this? It's all I can do to stay alive.

Memory gasped again as the sword slashed the air in front of her face, and she felt the rush of air over her cheeks.

He wanted to cut her face! That made her angrier. He not only wanted to beat her, he wanted to scar her and give her an eternal reminder of what she had lost. She heard Roen groan in pain and her resolve hardened, wiping away the fear taking over her.

Think, think.

Finvarra thrust and feinted. The sharp edge cut through Memory's jacket but missed her flesh. She slipped to the right, her feet sliding on the cool floor.

He's fast, but the sword is still big, and heavy. It's taking him a while to swing it, and he seems to be tiring.

The pale gold blade swung to her left, lifted again, swung to her right.

It's also fragile. My knife is small, but maybe being more compact will mean it's stronger.

Memory stepped toward him, ducking under his arms as they came down so she could get behind him. His elbow clipped her shoulder, crushing hard against her skin and knocking her across to the throne.

To her side, Memory could see Shonae pleading with Will and trying to hold him in place. Memory knew if Will stepped in, the fight would be over, and she could see in the pain on his face that he knew it to. He stayed where he was, every muscle in his body visibly taut and strained. Memory tightened her grip on her fairy gold dagger.

Finvarra grunted with anger, turning around and coming after her again.

As he raised his sword to strike, Memory widened her stance, steadying herself, then met his blade with hers.

The sound of their weapons meeting clashed through the air, a high pitched jangle of breaking glass, and Memory's arms ached from wrist to shoulder. Shards of sword rained down around her, barely missing her as they fell. The impact knocked her own knife from her hand and it spun away, out of sight under the throne.

Finvarra roared and Memory looked up wildly. She'd been only half successful, with the bottom third of Finvarra's sword still intact and dangerously jagged. And she'd lost her own weapon.

I've lost.

Finvarra lunged, and Memory moved close, blocking his arm with hers. Memory gritted her teeth and grabbed the throne for support, but as she pushed Finvarra's arm away her feet went

out from under her and she could not prevent the fall.

Her head hit one of the crystal tree roots with a neck jarring crack. She managed to flip over on her belly and away from his next blow, which would have cut her deeply from shoulder to hip.

Memory scrambled to her feet, blindly stumbling across the dais and crashing into Nyneve where she had remained, watching the combat.

Nyneve clutched at her arm, painfully hard, steadying her. "Take it," she whispered, and held a knife between them, obscured by the sleeve of her dress.

Memory snatched it instantly, and Nyneve let her go, pushing her back into the fray. A warmth and strength of adrenaline filled Memory. Maybe she still had a chance.

She spun faster than she ever had before, trying to catch Finvarra off guard before he realized she had her knife back. She swung her arm in a wide arc and the blade in her hand sang through the air.

She felt it meet his flesh.

The barest of cuts, but that was all she needed.

I did it. Memory's heartbeat pounded through her, ringing in her ears as she finally stilled.

Finvarra froze in place, arms still lifted, broken sword in the air. A deep howl built in his throat, echoing across the room.

The line near his neck where Memory had cut him smoked and fizzed. Black blood gushed out from his flesh and his face went the color of dead ashes.

"What's wrong?" Memory gasped.

Finvarra crumpled, his knees cracking onto the floor, face twisted in pain. He screeched and groaned, clawing at the floor as the life poured out of him.

"What have you done?" Around the room, the unseelie fae cried and wailed.

The blade felt warm in Memory's hand, and her heart turned cold. In the midst of combat, she thought it was just the adrenaline, just the ache in her beaten hand, that made it feel warm. She thought the blade she held, the blade Nyneve gave her, was the fairy gold knife she'd dropped on the floor.

Memory looked at the blade in her hand, feeling dazed.

It was her own iron flick knife.

Memory pleaded, "I didn't know…"

Her words were lost in the furor.

CHAPTER TWENTY-THREE

Finvarra began to thrash about, his face growing grayer and his body shriveling. Horror filled Memory. A black cloud rose from the fallen unseelie king, twisting and writhing.

The fae around the room closed in, jostling against each other as they crowded the dais.

Where they hung from their webbed bonds, her friends also watched. Roen struggled weakly to free himself, and Memory could see the glint of a small blade working. He spoke to Eloryn, but she only looked at Memory, heartbreak all over her pale face.

Memory looked to Nyneve for help, hoping she would come to her defense, or do something to save her dying father. Nyneve crouched over the body of the king that now lay still.

"He is dead!"

"Murderer!"

"She used iron on our king!"

The unseelie turned toward Memory, Will, and Shonae.

"I did not help her. I was forced," Shonae bleated, being pulled away from Will and into the crowd. The fae battered at her body with their fists and claws, shoving her further into the enraged mass.

Memory jumped off the dais, wading into the fray, dodging as many blows as she could and warding fae away with her blade. Will fought his way through too and together they managed to drag Shonae out from under the bodies piling up on her. They bolted back to the throne, keeping their backs to the grand tree structure. Memory looked across to Eloryn again, separated from her by a sea of enraged black-eyed monsters.

The white faun's hair had been torn and her lip bloodied. Her eyes were wide with terror and she hobbled, clutching at Will for support. A harsh, gasping sound rasped through her lips and Memory realized she was crying.

And with good reason. She had brought them there, brought the humans into her kind's court, and now Finvarra was dead, by iron.

Memory's eyes went back to her weapon in her hand. How was this even possible?

Nyneve…

Nyneve had handed her the knife, the knife she'd left on the table at the entrance to the castle. Nyneve held it, and hadn't been burned. How? A slow comprehension began to dawn, tingling in Memory's bones like frostbite.

All she had wanted to do was save her friends and she had

done exactly what Nyneve had told her to do.

She had been tricked. Every step of the way.

Nyneve was looking at her with hatred on her beautiful face and she was smiling too, a hard and terrifying smile as she bent to her father and seized the crown from his head.

Her cry echoed throughout the room. "I am queen now! Be still, my people!"

Memory knew Nyneve wasn't calming her people for the humans' safety, that she wouldn't help Memory in any way again. Her tone was too triumphant. That was the only word to describe her. Nyneve was triumphant, reveling in her father's demise, in the way she had used Memory.

The creatures of the Unseelie Court quieted to a muffled level of hostility. They looked up at their new queen, waiting.

"The human queen has come into our lands-"

Lured here, Memory thought.

"And used the forbidden iron-"

You gave to me.

"To murder my father, the king!"

Your plan all along. But why?

"They have committed an act of war against the unseelie fae!" Nyneve cried, her deep, regal voice echoing through the crystalline chamber. Clamors of assent rose and Will moved closer to Memory, his body trying to shield hers while Shonae ducked below her arm, hiding her face.

An act of war. Memory almost buckled over to be sick on the ground. The final pieces of the puzzle were fitting in, and what had just happened, what she had done, and what that meant nearly ruined her. Only the knowledge that her friends were still in grave danger kept her on her feet. There had to be a way to fix this, but how? She could not bring Finvarra back to life… It was too late.

"You must pay for what you have done. All humans must pay for what they have done. We are tired of being treated as monsters when it is humans who deserve that title. When humans rule our world—OUR world!—and dare to rise above their original stations! Humans were meant to be slaves and slaves is exactly what they shall be!"

Nyneve's voice dropped to a quiet and deadly tone, and silence filled the room as all strained to hear her. "As monarch of the unseelie fae, as a response to the human's act of war against us, I declare the Pact null."

A pulse of magic burst through the room. The Pact was broken. They all felt it. There was a lurch and the world actually moved below their feet. The Pact, which separated Avall from the rest of the world it had been plucked from, the Pact that protected race against race, that allowed Branding, that put the Spark of Connection inside humans, had ended.

A faint cry came from Eloryn's gagged mouth. It was weak, and quickly lost as the unseelie fae roared, cheering their queen. Still, not all cheered. Some looked up in fear, and a few even fled. Shonae wept silvery tears down her white cheeks.

Memory stood muted by shock.

Will's fingers twisted on her arm as Nyneve advanced upon them.

Memory stuttered, "Why? Nyneve, without Avall, your people will die. All fae will die without an iron free sanctuary."

Nyneve smiled. "I won't die, and neither will those loyal to me. There is a way to save ourselves. You should know that by now."

She held my iron knife without being burned… Memory's thoughts raced.

Nyneve spoke just for Memory's ears. "If only you had followed my little clues and gone after Finvarra when I let you find my blood farm. Maybe then I wouldn't have had to capture your friends to lure you here. But you always did make things difficult, and now you can watch them be the first to die."

Memory spun to see her friends. Roen had managed to slip his bonds, and cut the webbing from Eloryn's mouth. But Memory knew it was no good. The Pact had ended, and with it, so had ended any connection to magic within Eloryn. Within all humans. The ending of the Pact had also cleared the Brands from her friends. She could already see the life returning to them, but it barely mattered since Nyneve was screaming for the fae to kill all of them, and to make it painful.

Roen sliced desperately into Eloryn's bonds with a tiny blade, but it was too slow. Erec was beginning to regain consciousness, but was still completely bound. Memory heard Roen cry out as the first of the fae to reach them, a ghastly bird-like woman, slashed down his shoulder with its talons.

There was only one way to save them. Memory did not need the Pact to connect to magic. It was within her—a vast and undiminishing store. All bets were off. The Pact was gone. It was time to break all the rules.

Memory reached deep down inside herself, feeling that furnace of magic within. She opened a Veil door, across the room, right beside her friends. Bellowing at the rush of magic flaming through her that she hadn't felt for so long, she hurled that magic at the fae, clearing them away as she flung her friends, webbing and all, through the Veil door.

"Memory!" Eloryn screamed but Memory's magic carried her along with it on a tide that couldn't be fought.

Memory closed the portal behind them, then prepared to create an escape for herself, Will, and Shonae.

But another door opened, spilling Veil smoke into the room along with golden sparks and amber light. All stopped and stared as Aine appeared.

Her regal figure was surrounded by the guards and followers of her own court, all armed and in a defensive array around their queen.

"What is this?" Aine demanded. "The Pact is broken, we felt it!"

Nyneve met her fellow queen with a mocking bow. "The human queen committed an act of war against us, and as a result I have ended that damnable Pact as I had every right to."

Aine's fury made the wildflowers in her auburn hair burn to crisp ash as she faced Memory.

Memory shrank back, scrambling for the answers and courage to face the chaos before her. "I was set up. I never meant to kill him. I was handed iron, I did not go into the fight with it!"

Nyneve laughed. "Handed iron? By whom? No fae could touch it, so it could only be the fault of a human. Don't believe this child. She is a liar, as all humans are."

Aine turned a distasteful glance to Nyneve. "So pleased, aren't you? You never did agree with the Pact, angered that your lover chose the humans over you."

Nyneve bristled. "Myrddin allowed the humans to include Branding into our Pact, and what did he get for it? Branded and killed by the very humans he loved too much! It's time to put

all humans in their place, starting with her." Nyneve crooked a finger, pointing at Memory. "She broke her oath, and she must be punished."

Aine nodded, turning on Memory. She seemed almost sad, too tired for her usual arrogance. "You used magic when you swore an unbreakable oath not to. For this act alone, the penalty is death. For all else you've done, may the stars forgive you."

Memory shook her head, the unfairness of it all making her feel like a helpless child. "I had to save my friends."

Aine's beautiful face pulled into a grimace. "You chose to use your magic to save your friends. There is a difference. Every action you've taken, you chose, for your own selfish means. You came into our lands, fighting and taking what you please, and look where it has brought us. It will be the end of us all."

Aine drew a long, fine sword from the decorative scabbard at her waist. The sword, however, didn't seem decorative. It looked deadly.

"Kneel and I will make this quick. Fight, and you fight against every fae creature both seelie and unseelie."

It would have been easy then, to drop to her knees and have it end. There would be nowhere safe in Tearnan Ogh or Avall for her anymore. There would be nowhere safe for anyone soon.

But there was still one way out.

Staring into the seelie queen's eyes, Memory said, "I will fix this."

Then she punched a hole straight through the Veil.

Wind whipped, bringing the smell of exhaust and the sound of car horns and sirens. And iron; the wind reeked of its bloodlike scent. The fae screamed, many of them shielded their faces and ran to hide behind the throne.

Not Nyneve though. She stood there smiling that nasty smile and holding her father's crown firmly in her crooked fingers.

Memory took a deep breath, grabbed Shonae by one hand and Will by the other and jumped back into the other world.

The last thing she saw was Nyneve's gloating smile.

CHAPTER TWENTY-FOUR

The tunnel through the Veil was dark, roiling with clouds. It was rougher than Memory recalled, tossing and tumbling her like a wild surf. Memory could see again the golden flow of magic, rushing out like a tide, drawn from Avall and Tearnan Ogh into the rest of the world.

The wind rose, slow but intense. Memory could feel herself being pulled along with it and the urge to fight it was strong, but she did not.

In a huff of air, she landed hard on asphalt. Will and Shonae thudded down beside her, and the Veil door closed.

"Where have you brought me?" Shonae coughed.

Memory looked around to be sure. They'd been dumped

out into an alley. The same alleyway near the children's home where she'd first been confronted by Thayl. Where she'd first fallen through into Avall.

Will stared around him, his jaw set. "We're home."

A rough whimper came from Shonae and she buckled over. She curled in a heap beside a torn trash bag, unable to move. Her entire body shook and Memory knew it was more than just the injuries she had received in the Unseelie Court. It was the world full of iron she had been dragged into.

Shonae looked up at Memory, her black eyes turning milky and gray and her white fur charring to ash. Blood dripped from her soft muzzle. "I don't want to die in this place."

Memory knelt beside her. "I know, I'm sorry."

"You should have left me behind."

"You would have been killed. I couldn't leave you there to die. And you are not going to die now. Don't worry. I have a plan. Well, an idea, at least. A theory. Shut up. Let's just try it." Memory still had her iron knife clutched tight in one hand, and pressed the blade against her palm of the other. It trembled there right on her flesh, the point pressing in but not cutting. It was harder than she thought it would be, cutting her own skin.

"This is seriously giving me the squeams. Ew, ew, ew!" Memory shrieked, then squinted her eyes and pierced the skin. Blood rushed up from the wound.

"Ugh. Done. Right, you. Drink," Memory said, thrusting her bleeding palm at the faun's mouth.

Shonae turned her head weakly, disgust twisting her furry features.

"Drink it, Shonae. It will keep you alive." *Or at least I hope it will. Otherwise things will be pretty awkward.*

Shonae let out a soft sigh that sounded so sad it made tears prickle in Memory's eyes. Then the young dark fae put her tongue out and licked the blood away. Her eyes closed and she began to drink faster, her mouth pulling at the thin flesh there on Memory's palm.

Pain lanced into Memory but she ignored it. She could see and feel Shonae growing stronger.

The faun broke away, gasping for air and staring up at Memory with glossy black eyes.

"I feel… better. Still weak, but I do not think now I will die," Shonae said, her voice hushed and husky.

"How?" Will asked as he helped the unseelie fae to her feet. "How did you know that would work?"

"It was Nyneve that handed me my iron knife. And it was her that was behind the blood lair after all. Her that was behind everything after all. I thought that maybe the real reason she was drinking human blood was as an antidote against iron."

"And now we know it's true." Will looked at Shonae, worry furrowing his brow. "Why did she need so many people, so much blood? Shonae got better so fast."

"I think that's because I have a lot magic inside me, so Shonae got better faster. I am not sure how many normal people Nyneve would have to drink to stay immune but it could be a lot. How she could stand to do that is beyond me."

"She could do it," Shonae said. "Nyneve has harbored her hatred for centuries. The only thing that kept her in check was Finvarra and the Pact, and now he's dead and the Pact is broken."

A low rumble shivered up Memory's legs from the pavement.

"Was that you?" Will asked.

"No. I think that was Avall." Memory groaned.

Shonae shook her head and her wooly hair jiggled around her goat ears. "With the Pact broken, the magic that held Avall within the Veil is ending. It will come back into this world."

Will raised an eyebrow. "Reasonably large land mass, just showing back up in an ocean somewhere… that is going to be bad."

The ground grumbled again in agreement.

Memory ran both hands through her purple hair, tugging at it in frustration. She slouched against the wall. "This is what Nyneve wanted. Think about it, with no haven free of iron, any fae who are against her will be dead soon. If she is immune—think how powerful she would be. Think how much damage she could do over here. Humans wouldn't have a chance against her, her magic, and the other fae that would follow her. She would enslave everyone and use their blood as an antidote against the iron. She wasn't lying when she said she thought humans should be slaves, but she didn't mean just the ones in Avall, she meant *all* humans."

There was a shout from the mouth of the alley and they turned to see a woman standing there.

"You kids! What are you doing down there?"

"Ham biscuits," Memory whispered. "Shonae, time to glamour yourself up, girl."

Shonae nodded, and her figure started fading and blurring. Memory and Will blocked the fae from view as she shifted form.

When they didn't reply, the woman took a few steps closer to them.

Memory squinted. "Doesn't she work at the group home?"

"Hope? Hope, is that you?"

"Time to go," Memory said.

Shonae finished taking on a human form, and the three of them broke into a run, ducking down the rubbished lane and through a maze-like path of graffiti covered alleyways. They quickly left the woman behind, and came out onto a wider street. Memory looked around, getting her bearings. The area was so familiar to her, yet at the same time felt so foreign. They stood right beside the twenty-four hour convenience store she and Will regularly raided for cherry gum. Down the street was their favorite coffee shop and internet café. The group home was only three blocks south of here. It was hard to reconcile the fact it had only been a few months that she'd first been lost from this world. For Will it had been much longer. She looked up at him, but his expression was closed as he took in his surroundings.

Shonae stared openly, her jaw slack. Memory took in the fae's appearance, checking she was passable to be in public. Her clothes, like Memory's and Wills, were like something from a period drama, but she was so beautiful Memory doubted people would care much what she wore. Her body was proportioned like a supermodel, but petite in stature, and her wooly hair was now glossy blonde with streaks of pure white running through it right at the front, as though she weren't able to fully glamour color into herself. Her black eyes were now a brilliant blue, one Memory suspected was inspired by Will's and her mouth was as ripe and red as a berry. Memory had hoped for something a little less conspicuous, but despite her looking like a Hollywood starlet just off a historical romance shoot, most people weren't paying attention to her. Or Memory and Will in their shredded, bloodstained clothes. The continuing earth tremors kept everyone busy and distracted. Everyone was on their cellphones, dashing this way or that, cowering each time

the ground shook. A larger quake hit, lurching the ground, and a few people screamed. One woman grabbed a baby from a stroller and sprinted down the street.

This could be the end. Of everything. And it's my fault.

Memory was too shell-shocked, nearly hysterical, to cry. She wondered whether Eloryn and Roen and the rest of her friends back at Caermaellan were safe— at least for now. She wondered how Eloryn must be feeling, her magic stripped away for good. The same as everyone else in Avall. *Helpless. They must feel so helpless.*

The smell of noodles and fish hung over everything, wafting in from the small Chinatown down the road, and Memory's stomach gave out a loud gurgle.

It's not over yet. I'm still here. I still have my magic.

"The Net Nest is just down the road. We need to regroup, refuel, and re-plan."

The sky above them darkened, the light of early morning shifting unnaturally into a blue twilight haze.

Memory shook off a shiver that tried to take control. "If I'm going to save the worlds, I'm going to do it on a full stomach."

CHAPTER TWENTY-FIVE

Eloryn landed hard.

Her back hit the ground and air expelled from her lungs with a giant whooshing sound. She clutched at her chest and gasped small breaths. She felt so empty inside.

She had experienced this before, when she'd been hit by the wizard hunter's anti-magic darts, but this time she knew her Spark of Connection would never come back.

Roen had landed right beside her. He grabbed her and pulled her to him across the floor, his eyes dark with concern. "Are you still in pain?"

"No." She blinked back tears. Watching him suffer the Brand had hurt her far worse than the pain her own Brand had inflicted. She knew he had felt the same. Finvarra had been amused by that, and had laughed at their anguish, as had the other members of his court. But now he was gone, and with him the Pact.

Eloryn knew that her sister hated Finvarra for all he had done, but to kill him, when the consequences were so great, was an action she couldn't understand.

Watching through pain blurred eyes, the whole ordeal felt like a bad dream and Eloryn was patchy on the details, but she knew the Pact was ended. She felt it inside.

"I feel so empty," she whispered into Roen's hair as he cradled her. "How do you bear it? Having no spark within you?"

"I've never known any different. I am too full of love for you to ever feel empty," Roen whispered back, planting a soft kiss on her cheek.

Eloryn warmed, her own love for him spreading through the emptiness.

"I love you, too," she sobbed.

Erec groaned from nearby. "Lovebirds, would one of you be kind enough to come and untie me shortly?"

Eloryn sighed and rolled away from Roen. Getting to her feet, she saw that they were back in Memory's chambers.

"Memory didn't make it through," Eloryn said, a harsh shiver making her hug herself.

"Not Will or Shonae either," Roen said, as he crouched down beside Erec and started cutting him free with his slim electrum blade. They had all lost their iron during their fighting and capture. "She used her magic to send us back here, to save us. She's broken her oath and there will be no safe place for her from the fae now."

“There is one,” Eloryn said. “She could go home.”

Eloryn hoped her sister had escaped the chaos of the Unseelie Court, but there was nothing she could do now to find out, or to help her. Besides, she had other work to do here in Avall.

The world trembled, and through the window the sky was a thick gray, blocking the sun. Jagged streaks of electricity webbed through the clouds and smote the ground, setting trees alight and crisping the fields and grasses around the castle.

The day was darkened like night, and Eloryn could see the Veil, ripped and torn, fluttering like ragged mist across the sky. The lightning turned red, green and violently purple before going back to silver as it arched across the sky.

Roen cut the last of the webbing off Erec and helped him to his feet. For a moment, they all stood in silence and watched the destructive light show through the window.

“Come now. We must hurry,” Eloryn said.

Candles flickered here and there through the palace, but a bitter wind blew windows open and rushed through the corridors, putting them out quickly. Servants and guards ran by, as other guests of the castle called for assistance. A maid recognized Eloryn amongst the crowds and ran to her, asking for help, but she could not give it. There was no magic left for her, or anyone. Even when Thayl was in power, banning all but the most basic of magic, the people still had light, and warmth. Now, the land felt dead and flat, missing its very heart, and Eloryn knew time was running terribly short. War was coming, and with it death.

“Where is the Council?” Eloryn asked.

“The Round Room, Your Highness,” the maid replied, her

eyes wide and voice shaking.

"Keep calm, and head to the throne room," Eloryn said, and sped up her pace. "Erec, I need you back on duty. I need information about what is happening out in the city, and I need the guards organized and helping the civilians. I need them moving everyone into the throne room and old keep."

Erec nodded, and split off from them. Eloryn and Roen reached the Round Room and found all of the Wizards' Council there, for once in silence. They stood in a circle, faces grave and gray as their hair, bodies bent like a ring of ancient stones.

Bedevere was the first to see Eloryn, and his back straightened. "Your Highness, by the fae, you are safe. But what of your sister?"

Eloryn shook her head. "I don't know."

"What happened?" Madoc spluttered, coming to life as well. "The Pact has ended, we all feel it, as we can feel Avall tumbling back through the Veil into the world of hell we left behind."

"It's true," Eloryn said. "Finvarra is dead. Nyneve has taken the unseelie crown, ended the Pact, and declared war upon humans." She stopped there. Memory's actions, all of their actions that had led to this point poisoned her with guilt.

"What can we do? We are powerless," Madoc sighed, dropping into a seat beside him.

The room brightened slightly, and out from the darkness, Yvainne appeared. The sprite princess's face was as solemn as the humans around her. Her normal glowing presence was dulled, her gossamer dress more like rags, and her hair hanging lifeless.

"Maellan Princess," she said, turning to Eloryn. "You should have remained the one to rule the humans. Now we all

face destruction."

"Is this Memory's doing?" one of the Wizards' Council blustered, and a murmur of gossip spread through the group.

"She played a part," Eloryn admitted.

Yvainne hissed, "She killed Finvarra with iron! And broke her oath not to use her magic, then fled to the human hell to avoid her punishment."

So she did escape. Eloryn took a shaking breath, trying to inhale hope back into her. "Yvainne, will the seelie fae stand beside humans for what is to come?"

For a moment, Eloryn thought she saw a look of sympathy on the normally aloof face of the sprite princess. "We will not. I was sent here to tell you as much."

"We have no magic left," Madoc cried, standing up and grasping for Yvainne. "If the unseelie fae come for us, we will be slaughtered!"

The sprite shook him off in a shower of fairy dust. "We shall all die if Avall smashes back into the human world unchecked. The seelie fae will be doing what we can to stabilize our refuge as it returns through the Veil. That is all we can do, for the humans and for ourselves."

"Can you not stop it returning?" Eloryn asked.

"It took the combined power of the seelie and unseelie fae together to draw Avall into the Veil when the Pact began. Without the help of the unseelie monarch, without Nyneve, all we can do is stem the damage as we prepare for the end of the fae." Yvainne turned away. "I am sorry."

Eloryn lowered her head as the sprite faded away. "Me too."

"We are to face the unseelie armies alone then," Roen said, his voice empty of emotion.

A dramatic gasp broke the deathlike silence, and Clara ran into the room, her face covered with tears and her red hair loose and streaming across her shoulders.

She huffed and pounded softly on Eloryn's arm with a fist. "The pastries went cold and none of you came back and I've been so scared for you all and I've been hearing all sorts of terrible things through the speaking mirror and NOT ONE OF YOU SPOKE THROUGH THE MIRROR AND TOLD ME WHAT WAS HAPPENING!"

"Oh Clara, I'm sorry," Eloryn said, and pulled her in for a hug.

"I… I couldn't do anything. I know I am not a hero but I wish there was something I could have done. Now the Pact is gone and everyone is totally freaking out."

"Totally freaking out? You have been spending far too much time with Mem," Eloryn's smile felt false and wobbly. "I think you will be able to help Clara. Tell me, are you still hearing anything through your piece of mirror?"

CHAPTER TWENTY-SIX

The Net Nest was jam packed. People were staring down at their laptops, tablets and the few desktop computers around the room, glued to the news as it came in from around the world. Another small tremor shook the ground. A few people shrieked or stared white faced at the shuddering walls of the internet café then turned back to their screens to type in new search codes or status updates.

Memory spotted a table where some empty coffee mugs hadn't been cleared away. The staff seemed too busy gossiping and looking at their own screens to be servicing the tables. Walking past, Memory swiped two cups in a casual movement, and took them to where a dripolator sat beside a sign reading

"Free Refills." She poured herself and Will a healthy dose of coffee that she liberally doctored with milk and sugar.

A desktop PC became free as a man took a call on his cellphone and left in a rush. Memory indicated to Will across the room, and met him and Shonae there, handing him his coffee.

"Sorry Shonae, only two hands. Also I figured you wouldn't be interested."

Shonae sniffed. "Quite right."

Memory and Will each took a sip and sighed deeply.

"Oh, bad internet café coffee, I've missed you so much," Memory said to her mug, stroking it tenderly. That first sip helped steady Memory, but her stomach still ached. A sandwich lying on a table, uneaten while its owner stared at his laptop, drew her eye. She looked from it to Will and nodded, hoping he'd remember their old tricks.

Stretching his arms in a wide yawn, Will shielded Memory with his body while her hand snaked out and grabbed the sandwich. She split it, handing Will his share of the booty. She offered some to Shonae who turned up her now human nose at it. By the time the owner of the sandwich looked at the plate again, Memory and Will had bellies filled with rare roast beef, mayo, and rye bread.

"Remind me I hate rye," Memory said tilting her cup toward her mouth.

"Shame there are no cakes unguarded." Will grunted.

Memory looked at the glassed in display counter with a twinge of greedy regret. "I know, that pumpkin cheesecake looks good."

"I was thinking the scone."

"Go get it then," Memory challenged. "Bring me back the

cheesecake."

Will surveyed the room and ducked his head, muttering something about not being a cake commando. That made Memory laugh and she squeezed his hand. The warmth of his flesh below hers strengthened her more than the coffee and food ever could.

Memory poked the keyboard in front of her but the screen only showed a login gate. "Forget the cakes. What we need is cash. I want to check on something online, but we have to buy the minutes."

"The usual way?" Will asked, dark eyebrows lowered. Memory frowned back. He never was happy about her thieving ways, but he always went along with her, even when he was so much younger. *Wow, I really took that kid's innocence didn't I?*

"Don't worry, I won't make you do it this time." Even Memory wasn't too happy anymore about stealing. It used to be a rush, the thrill of the risk and the joy of new possessions drove her to fill her pockets in every store. She didn't need those thrills and superficial joys anymore. She'd found true happiness, and known true danger, and somehow developed a conscience amongst it all. If they weren't in real need of food and information, she wouldn't be up to her old tricks.

Squeezing through the crowd to the counter, Memory smiled to the assistant there who glanced up at her from his own screen.

"If you're after more coffee you're out of luck. The water is off," he mumbled.

"Can I get the bathroom key?" she asked.

"I said the water is off." The scrawny young man looked at her over his thick brimmed glasses.

Of course it has to be difficult, Memory grumbled in her head.

"That's okay, I just need a private place for a moment, you know, for lady things," she said.

With a small humph, the man turned to grab the key off the wall. While he did, Memory leaned over the counter, her hands a blur as she plucked a few bills from the shallow tip jar. By the time the key had been handed to her she had almost twenty bucks up her jacket sleeve. The assistant went straight back to his screen before Memory could say thank you.

A noise distracted Memory as she turned away from the counter. A sound like her own voice, calling out quietly amongst the chatter and clamor of the busy room.

"No way," Memory said under her breath. She plunged her hand into her pocket so fast she sliced her finger on the mirror shard there. Swearing softly, she pulled the mirror out and held it up to see what looked like her own eye, but shadowed by thick ivory bangs.

Her heart thudded. The speaking mirror was still connected to Avall, and her sister was there.

Speeding back across the room, Memory slapped the money on the desk beside Will.

"Get online, I'll be right back. Gotta take a call," she said, angling the mirror so Will could see the tiny view of Eloryn there.

Memory's hands shook as she tried to fit the key in the lock and get into the customers only bathroom. On the third try, the key slipped in and she pushed the heavy door open.

The bathroom was tiny, and a strong smell of lemon disinfectant overpowered the room. Memory put her hands on the cold sink and took a deep breath to steady herself, then

looked at the speaking mirror. She could see only the ornate ceiling of Caermaellan palace now.

Her heart sank, and with it her body. She slouched against the tiled wall, sliding down to sit on the floor, wedged between the toilet door and basin pipes.

"Eloryn?" Memory called out, holding the mirror close to her face.

Her voice caught and tears prickled under her eyelids. Part of her almost hoped Eloryn wouldn't answer. As though talking to her sister would somehow make the grand weight of her failure more real. *I've screwed up everything.*

Nyneve's betrayal stung and confused Memory. It was all so obvious now, too obvious. She should have been smarter, she should have wondered why Nyneve was trying to help her, instead she had simply assumed she had a kind heart and wanted to see peace restored to the lands. But it was clear now Nyneve had no love for humans. Something in her past, something to do with her relationship with Myrddin, Memory thought, had twisted her into a creature of hate and vengeance.

"Mem! Please, Memory is that you?"

"Lory?" Seeing her sister looking back through the mirror at her made the fresh tears building in Memory's eyes spill out. "I'm so sorry. I've really pooched things."

Eloryn was silent for a moment. "Are you well? Are you safe?"

"For now. How bad is it? Over there?"

Memory heard Roen and Erec's voices in the background, then Eloryn spoke. "There is a lot of panic. The Spark of Connection has left every human in Avall. It is dark, and everyone is scared."

"Lory, listen. Nyneve was Providence all along, not Finvarra. It was her that gave me my iron knife."

"How—?"

Memory kept talking. "She's resistant to iron. It was her drinking human blood and that was why. And I think she will use the people of Avall as a blood farm to make her unseelie fae army also resistant to iron as Avall shifts back into the rest of the world."

Memory heard Eloryn draw a long breath. "We always knew Providence wanted a human monarch with great power in her debt, and this was why. She wanted to use them to kill Finvarra, bringing her into power and letting her break the Pact and start a war."

"When Hope couldn't get a deal out of me, Nyneve started messing with my head, working me into killing Finvarra in a different way, making me think he was Providence, was the one who had done everything bad to me." Memory leaned her head back against the cold tiles. "She knew I would be angry. She counted on it. She had to make me angry enough to want to kill him. Nyneve let us find the blood lair and set it up to make us think Finvarra ran it."

Eloryn followed on, the two of them thinking in harmony. "As Princess of the Unseelie Court she had control over the knights who captured and branded us, to drive you to Finvarra."

"She told me to challenge him then slipped me the iron knife mid-fight so that Finvarra would die in front of the entire court at my hand."

They both fell silent.

From outside the door, Memory heard sirens wailing and a thick scent of blood was building in the air, overpowering even

the lemon disinfectant around her.

"You have to come home. You can explain to the seelie fae what happened. There has to be a way we can repair this."

"I did this, so I will fix it. I just have to work out how. Until I do, just please try to keep everything from… from…" She squeezed her eyes shut. What could she say? Everything had already fallen apart.

Eloryn's voice was small. "I don't have my magic anymore. I don't know what I can do."

"You can kick ass is what you can do. Sis, you're the smartest person I know. Trust yourself, believe in yourself. I know you will work something out."

The mirror shifted and Memory saw the hint of a smile on her sister's lips. "Okay. I'll do what I can here in Caermaellan to keep everyone safe while you save the world."

"No pressure," Memory giggled.

"Dear sister, I hope you know how much I love you."

"I love you too," Memory said, wiping tears from her cheeks. "See you soon."

The mirror went dark.

CHAPTER TWENTY-SEVEN

Eloryn tucked the shard of speaking mirror away into a pocket. Her clothes were still stained with the black ichor of the vines they had fought through in Tearnan Ogh, and with her own blood. Her hair was loose, tumbling down to her hips in long tangled falls, and her scalp tingled as though the air was filled with static. She picked up the ends of her locks and rolled them into a knot at the back of her head, pushing damp strands clear of her face. *Memory is right. I can do this.* There were people who needed help, and she knew she could offer it.

Erec had returned a while ago and brought her news from the city. Unseelie fae were already in the streets, and there were reports that they were snatching any human they could find.

Eloryn shivered. *The people must be so scared, without light, without magic, being hunted in the dark.*

Erec remained in the room, silent and at attention with a small group of guards. Awaiting orders, but also there to protect her, Eloryn knew. Without Memory here, Eloryn was the only Maellan blood left to protect, not that she had any magic to show for it anymore.

Eloryn called order in the room and had the Council members take seats. Placing her hands on the repaired round table there hardened her resolve. She knew she had done that, repaired the ancient table from the splinters it had become after the explosion. If it could be fixed, maybe the shattered Pact, the breaking worlds, could also.

Eloryn sent Clara to fetch a book for her, then addressed the aged men. "I think you all heard what Memory said. I trust that she has a way to save us, but we must protect ourselves in the meantime however we can."

One of the wizards cleared his throat. "We are helpless without magic. We know what happened, and we know it was not Memory's fault, but what can we do against the fae? We're nothing but old men now."

"It is hopeless," another muttered.

"You are not defined by your magic alone," Eloryn said. "I am sure you have wisdom that can help us. When in hiding, Providence, or Nyneve rather, was sending unseelie fae to hunt down wizards as well, and yet you remained hidden from them for years. The fae see through glamour more easily than humans. How did you remain unfound?"

Bedevere's eyes sparkled despite the dull expression on his face. "Clever child. You're right, we used some of the old ways

to ward against the fae, methods from before the Pact, methods that don't require magic."

Another councillor perked up, straightening his crumpled black and purple suit. "They were indeed effective. Kenth was chosen because there were only few fae there already but it was our wards that cleared them from the area entirely."

"Could they work again here? Do we have what we need to create them?"

"I'm sure," Bedevere said. "All we need is refined salt, and common herbs and branches wreathed into the right patterns."

Roen called a guard beside the door over to them. "Get down to the kitchens and stores and see what we have on hand. Madoc, please go with him to provide a list."

The wizard left, shuffling along at a hurry with the guard. Roen nodded at Eloryn again to continue, confidence in his eyes. It was contagious, and Eloryn felt it straighten her back and strengthen her voice.

"With these wards, we could make some safe areas, or even perhaps force the fae in the direction we wish," she said.

Eloryn closed her eyes, trying to think tactically. If she were Nyneve, she would be using small armies across Avall to herd people up and imprison them in the long term, but would hit the city of Caermaellan first, it being the largest city and the largest concentration of people. They already knew that attack had begun.

Eloryn called Erec over. "Put out the word to arrange for all civilians in the city to either flee into the countryside or come here to the palace. Anyone who can fight, we want here. Every horse and carriage in the castle, send it out to help. We're not going to let it be easy for Nyneve, just snatching up people off the streets. If she wants human blood, she will have to come to us. And we will fight her for it."

Roen stood up beside them. "The militia that Hayes instituted could actually do some good. Send them a call to arms, too."

Bedevere scratched the corner of his eye, his ever dour face solemn. "Even if we find many to fight with us, we have little hope against the fae without magic. Our weapons are but nuisances to them."

Eloryn, however, was on a roll, enthusiasm building as she developed her strategy. "We have iron."

Bedevere merely raised a bushy eyebrow.

"Quite a reasonable amount, which strangely enough you can thank Thayl for." Eloryn raised her voice over the shocked whispers around the table. "We are facing a war against the unseelie fae, with no Pact and no Brandings. Iron is one of our only defenses. Erec, take some men to retrieve it. Roen can show you the way."

Bedevere's eyes were wide, a crooked smile on his mouth. "Full of surprises, you and your sister are. Just how much iron is there?"

"Not enough. Thirty, forty pieces at most but not any more than that. We might be able to split some larger pieces to spread it around more."

"Forty pieces of iron is at least forty dead fae," Erec replied, then turned to gather his men, delegating a range of orders through the group.

While he waited, Roen grinned largely up at Eloryn from his chair.

"What?" she asked.

"Just you. Don't mind me, keep going, you're doing splendidly."

Eloryn grinned back, and Clara trotted into the room, holding a thick tome cradled against her chest.

"I hope this is the right book," she said, and placed it on the table in front of Eloryn.

Eloryn ran her fingers over the worn blue-gray fabric of the spine and the embossed gold letters on the cover.

The Principles and History of Infantry Warfare.

The pages riffled below her fingers and her heart ached as she thought about the times that Alward had read this and other books with her. She spoke a silent thank you in her heart for all that Alward taught her.

The pages were a blur, the dim lighting too weak to see any detail on them.

Eloryn blinked and muttered, "Àlaich las."

The words came to her from habit but her behest fell on deaf ears. Eloryn winced. It was so easy to forget her magic was gone, so natural to try and call light to her with a behest.

Roen chuckled. "Now you know what my life has been like. Still, I got by. Perhaps everyone might have to learn some tricks from me."

Extending an arm, Roen flourished his fingers toward an unlit candle in front of him. The harsh whisper of them rubbing against his palm was followed by a loud burst of flame appearing and setting the wick quickly alight.

Eloryn gasped in surprise and delight, and then her eyes narrowed. "I don't suppose you could reproduce that effect on a larger scale?"

"Planning to hire me as the official palace candle lighter?

Because you should know my rates are costly."

"Actually, I was thinking of something much bigger." Eloryn smiled, and pulled the newly lit candle close to her book.

Finding the section she'd been seeking, she spun the book sideways so Bedevere could see the diagrams there. "Here. This is the strategy I think we should use."

"Look at this," Will said as Memory made it back to the computer.

Shonae's eyes were wide, leaning back in her chair away from the screen as though it were a poisonous snake. The café was now almost deserted. Everyone had gone out on the sidewalks, staring up at the tumultuous skies. Some were openly weeping, holding onto their loved ones. The air was filled with the scent of blood and tingle of static, as if the air was charged with iron magic.

A few people snapped pictures on their digital devices, or just stood there, staring, faces caught in an expression of complete confusion.

Shonae said in a frightened whisper, "This is bad magic."

Memory snorted. "A centuries old agreement between the humans and the fae being torn apart? Yeah. It's bad magic all right… Oh, wait... You mean the computers, don't you?"

Memory snorted and rolled another chair over, straddling it backwards. She looked over Will's shoulder at the screen which showed current news. Half the world seemed to be experiencing

the tremors, which were increasing in frequency and strength. Wild electrical storms, tornadoes and rising tides were striking all over, all apparently caused by a strange landmass appearing and disappearing in the middle of the Atlantic Ocean. Avall.

"I saw Nyneve talk to Mina at the palace. I bet she had something to do with persuading Mina to take me away to Tearnan Ogh. I was just a distraction for you, a tool to lure you there. I'm so sorry," Will said. "We have to get back to Avall and stop Nyneve."

"You mean kill her," Shonae said. "The only way to stop this is to kill her and hope her successor will want to restore the Pact and Avall's place in the Veil."

"I don't want to kill her," Memory said. "Killing can't be the only option. I want peace and you don't get to peace by walking over the bodies of people you kill."

"Good luck with that," Shonae said, sounding as human as she looked. "We are all going to die."

Memory stared at the people on the street. What could she do to fix this? The flicker of an idea kept taunting her, but nothing was locking into place. She needed to know more.

Memory rolled her office style chair forward, bumping into Will. "Squidge over. I've got to check something."

He slid across and she took control of the keyboard, tapping in her search string.

She talked as she typed and skimmed text on the pages that came up. "We already know that legends of King Arthur tie into Avall. Well, I've been thinking a lot about Caliburn, or Excalibur. I think it could help us."

Memory pointed at the screen to an image of a man throwing a sword into a lake. "And I think I know where it is."

Will only frowned. "Isn't that a bit like saying you know where to find a talking harp based on reading *Jack and the Beanstalk*? I mean, how did the stories of Arthur continue on over here after Avall was separated off? How would anyone know?"

"Because some people crossed over. The fae kept doing their little import and export thing until the amount of iron over here became too much for them, and some wizards toying with Veil door magic tried to come through as well. People like…." Memory rolled the scroll button on the mouse, scanning her eyes over the words on the screen. "This guy. Galfridus Arturus. I know his name from my Avall history book. He's a wizard who went missing maybe a century or two after Avall was pocketed away into the Veil."

"And he stayed here, in this horrible place? Why didn't he return to Avall?" Shonae asked.

"Unlike Thayl, nobody kept a door open for him," Memory said.

"We don't have anyone keeping a door open for us either," Will pointed out. "And if I'm thinking what you're thinking, Caliburn is back in Avall."

"Yeah, it would have been almost impossible to get back before. With all the magic running out of Avall to here, trying to go back to Avall is like swimming against the tide. But since Avall is shifting through the Veil back into this world already, I don't have to punch all the way through the Veil by myself. We might be able to just slip through."

"Then we get Caliburn, and then what?"

"I… don't know," Memory admitted.

Memory turned back to the screen, but the words were

blurring in her eyes. She turned away, staring down the city street as she took deep breaths.

Will took over on the computer again. She could hear his fingers gingerly pressing the keys, one slowly after another. Sixteen years was a long time away from technology after all.

I owe him so much. Now I owe everyone so much. What can I do?

The thought of the dire hatred Nyneve must hold against humans made Memory's stomach contract into a tight ball. Memory couldn't stop asking *why*. Why was she doing all of this? Did she hate humans so much she would do something so destructive, or was she truly insane? Inside her mind, Memory laughed wryly. No, Nyneve wasn't insane. She had planned so carefully and so cleverly for so long. She never seemed insane. If anything she just seemed deeply sad, and hurt.

Memory closed her eyes to the chaos around her, trying to think.

"I know how horrible it feels," said Hope. "The pain of having someone choose somebody else over you."

"You never did agree with the Pact, angered that your lover chose the humans over you."

"Myrddin allowed the humans to include Branding into our Pact, and what did he get for it? Branded and killed by the very humans he loved too much!"

Myrddin. His name was different here, and so was Nyneve's. Merlin and Nimue, she'd seen these names reading over the Arthurian legends just now.

In those legends, Merlin disappeared, and from the play she saw in the pub on her night out with Clara, as far as those in Avall knew he'd just disappeared as well. But Nyneve had definitely said Branded and killed. She loved him, but he chose Arthur and

the humans over her, and then was Branded and killed. It hurt in Memory's heart just thinking about it. That could be the kind of pain to twist someone forever.

Across the street, a man stood on top of a truck whose bed held a round tank. A water reservoir. People lined up down the side walk, holding metal cooking pots, buckets, and jugs. One woman came out of her house holding a tall glass vase.

The water is off, Memory recalled. Such a simple thing, but something humans couldn't live without. Memory wondered if living without magic for the fae was like humans living without water.

The man on the truck took a long hose and dipped it into the tank, filling the length of the hose with water. Keeping one end twisted closed in a tight grip, he pulled the hose back out of the water, with the other end still in the tank and lowered the closed end down to the waiting vessels.

When he released his grip and opened the hose, the water started to flow, rushing through the hose, starting a syphon, bringing more water with it.

This world, filled with iron, is draining away all the magic from Avall. I've seen it in the Veil, rushing out like a tide, taking with it the life of all the fae. Without that magic, without the spark of connection within humans they need to defend themselves against the unseelie fae, they will all die. And yet I have so much magic inside me, so much it burns me up.

"I can be the hose," Memory said in a whisper.

"What? Mem, are you okay?" Will asked.

Memory just nodded silently. A plan was forming in her mind and with it, peace was settling on her. The feeling was like what she'd experienced when she'd once decided to end her own life, that same sense of calm and closure, but this one came

with a sense of determination. She would fix this, no matter the cost.

Memory turned around and looked at Will and Shonae. Shonae still had her human appearance, but her eyes had shifted back to all black, her glamour fading along with her strength in this world of iron. "It's okay. We're going back to Avall," Memory told her, and then looked into Will's eyes, her newfound calm almost breaking under their cool blue gaze.

"I have a plan," she said.

Will looked back at her for a long moment, a frown growing deeper as the moment dragged on. "Your mouth is saying you have a plan, so why am I hearing you say goodbye?"

Memory's mouth smiled, but her eyes were sad. Will always did know her too well. She didn't want to say it, but everything told her that it was goodbye. Goodbye to everything good she had found in her life, in herself. Goodbye to Will and their love for each other. Goodbye to her sister, and Roen, and all her new friends. Goodbye to everything she knew.

I don't want to go, not again, a tiny voice cried inside her.

Memory closed the voice away. She didn't have the luxury of selfishness or weakness anymore. "I have a plan," she said again, studying Will's features, the earthy shade of his tangled hair and the way his dark brows made his blue eyes flash like lightning, trying to capture and lock them in her mind forever. "And I know you won't like it. I know it might be goodbye. But I have the power to do this so I have to do it. I can save the humans, the fae, and Avall."

Will reached for her and held both of her hands in his. He spoke slowly, his voice crackly with emotion. "I don't want to lose you, but I understand. You've always been my hero, but as much as I want to, I can't keep you for myself. I know it's time for you to be a hero to the whole world."

Memory leaned forward in her chair, wrapping her arms up around Will's neck and shoulders, holding him tight.

He kissed her once on the space between her cheek and ear, then whispered, "Just know, no matter what happens, you'll never lose me. I'll always be there for you. I'll always wait for you. Always."

The lights began to flicker off and on and more tremors hit. The floor buckled, splitting the linoleum, and every computer screen went black.

"I think that's our cue to go," Memory said. "If my plan doesn't work we'll need a backup. Plan B is using Caliburn to stop Nyneve. The sword should be powerful enough to work against her even with her iron resistance, since it's made of magically dense iron. Fingers crossed, anyway."

Memory cast the man on top of the water tank one last glance. Her fingers tingled with adrenaline as she stood up and said, "It's time this vessel spilled."

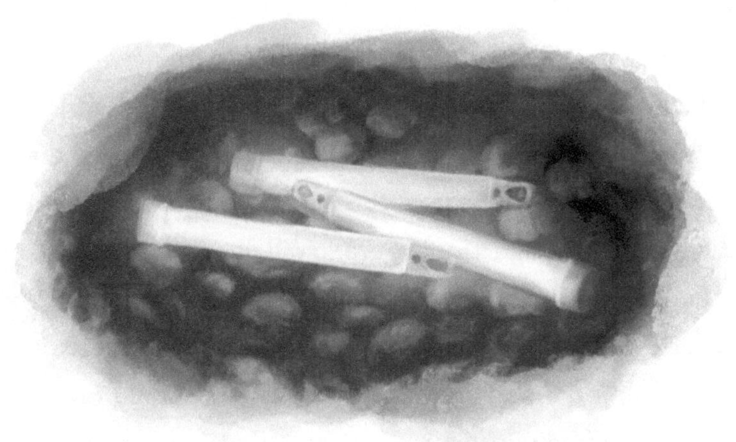

CHAPTER TWENTY-EIGHT

Only half of the horses and carriages sent out into the city to bring back civilians returned. The last horse that returned, returned without a rider, followed by a sea of monsters. Unseelie knights led them, mounted on their huge black griffons.

Eloryn watched from the grand balcony that fronted the palace, her hands clutching at the icy marble balustrade, a cold wind blowing in her face.

The plan was simple, force the larger unseelie numbers into a small space so that their best fighters could take them on armed with iron. Alward's book had spoken of three hundred men holding off an army of thousands by doing that and she was hoping to make that work for them too. It had to work. If it did not they were lost and Eloryn knew it.

Even if it did work, it was only a short term solution.

The throne room would be their battle ground. The balcony stood at the front of it and Eloryn looked behind her, assessing the preparations. The space was part of the old inner keep, directly below the Round Room, built of solid stone that had lasted a millennium. The two back entrances had been blocked off, hiding and protecting the people of Caermaellan where they sheltered in the servant quarters within the ancient fortified walls. Wards against the fae had been carefully placed out of sight through the large entry hall in a way to channel the fae without being too obvious. The wards would not hold forever, and once the fae worked out what they were doing, the wards could be found and destroyed. The fae could only move in a certain direction thanks to those wards, blocking all other entries and leading them straight to the fighters with iron. Erec stood there, shoulder to shoulder with his best men. Behind the first row of fighters stood more soldiers, prepared to take up the iron of any who fell, and keep fighting. Behind that were doctors and wizards, ready to care for the injured.

Roen placed his hand over Eloryn's. "It's ready. We only had time for one, but it is ready to go when you are."

Eloryn nodded. She looked down at the people in the hall. They were all ready and willing, but could she really give the order that would send so many of them to their deaths? Eloryn exhaled slowly, feeling the breath warm her cold lips. She had to.

She faced the army of unseelie fae before her. A mix of twisted creatures filled the palace courtyard, giants standing out between them, looming over the rest. Higher still, those that could fly hovered and swooped in the air, ready to attack. Eloryn

glanced at the window beside her, double checking the glazing of salt that had been applied.

The unseelie knight that had captured them in the lands of Tearnan Ogh came to a stop just below the balcony and looked up at Eloryn. His lion-like steed roared through its sharp beak.

"Leave here now," Eloryn called down, making her voice as strong as she could over the wind and thunder and shuffling of the monstrous army. "We still have our magic and will defend ourselves with it!"

"Human lies!" the fae knight roared to his troops.

Eloryn nodded to Roen. As she lifted her arms to the sky, Roen set off the flash bomb he'd created above the balcony. A huge fireball swirled through the air above Eloryn's fingertips, lighting the courtyard and raining orange sparks over all of them.

The unseelie fae shrank back, but the knight in command reared his steed. "Magic or none, we will fight! Our queen commands it."

Eloryn's hope that her ruse might turn the army back without any more deaths dissipated into the air along with the smell of black powder. Her hearing was already humming with the sound of her pounding heart when the knight called the order to attack.

She stood still, numbed. A fairy gold tipped arrow streaked past Eloryn's face. Roen grabbed her arm, shocking her back into action.

Together they ran down the stairs and through the entry hall to the first line of fighters.

The fae crashed through the front doors, crowding into the hall behind them.

A semicircle of steps led up from the hall to the throne room. Eloryn's legs pumped and her breath came in hard gasps as she ran up them. She had never been so frightened. Everything seemed sharper, clearer. Every breath was one she drew purposefully, nothing was unconscious. She might die, and every breath seemed incredibly precious.

When she and Roen reached Erec, he nodded to one of his men beside him. The man was huge, and when he grabbed Eloryn around her shoulders and lifted her from her feet, she knew there was nothing she could do. She raged against him anyway. "What are you doing? Stop this!"

Roen's face twisted in on itself, anger and sadness and guilt all there as he looked at Eloryn and did nothing. "I'm sorry. Without your magic you can't be on the front line, and we knew you would insist anyway."

Tears filled Eloryn's eyes like hot acid. "Of course I insist! I can't leave you here. How dare you do this to me?"

Roen stood by Erec and drew the iron bar he'd been armed with, facing the oncoming horde. "Take her to safety, quickly," he told the large man. The soldier did as he said, carrying Eloryn swiftly through a cleared path between the human army to the back of the throne room.

Eloryn sobbed and screamed, betrayal firing off every emotion in her. And even then, she knew Roen was right. She could do nothing at the front line. She could not fight with a sword or blade as Roen or Erec could. She would only get in the way. Her own uselessness hurt her even deeper than the fact that Roen and Erec had to force her to accept it.

But if that was the last time she ever saw Roen, she wasn't sure she could take the pain.

Reaching the back wall of the throne room, the large soldier put her feet back on the ground, but kept her wrists held tightly in his. Around them, the wizards of the Council had laid out blankets and cots, pots of boiling water, liquor, bandages, every non-magical healing supply they could collect from around the palace. Bedevere and Bors flicked through the pages of an ancient book on herbalism. They stood there ready, looking in understanding at Eloryn and the man who held her.

"You can let me go," Eloryn said, trying to calm her ragged voice. "I will stay here, but I need to help tend to the wounded as they come back to us. It's something I can do. Please let me."

The crash of metal sounded from behind them as the first unseelie fae met the front line. Some tried to fly through to get behind them, but the wards blocked them midway along the room, holding them back like an invisible barrier.

One harpy got brave and tried to fly low through the front line of soldiers. She swooped, and Eloryn saw an iron blade clip her as she tumbled past the soldiers. She continued to tumble through into the back of the room, not far from Eloryn. The fae died screaming on the floor, writhing and twisting, her feathered wings burning crisply and sending the scent of burning flesh into the air.

The soldier let go of Eloryn's wrists, running back up to the front line to fight. Eloryn took out the iron button Clara had handed over, and for a moment thought to join him. Then the first of the injured came back to her, dragged out of the fray by one of the supporting guards. Every nerve ending in her body cried out as she forced herself to calm her breathing, and knelt by the injured soldier. Bedevere met her there, and together they worked to bandage the large gashes in the man's neck, trying to save his life. Everywhere hung the stink of battle, the sizzle and smoke of iron meeting fae flesh, the sweat and fear and blood of humans.

She would not be useless in this fight. While others took lives, she would do everything she could to save them.

Opening the Veil door back to Avall was easier than Memory hoped. Stepping back through the Veil was harder. Shonae went first, eager to leave the iron filled human "hell", and Memory and Will followed hand in hand. Memory could feel the strength in his hand, and knew he wouldn't let go.

They stepped out of the Veil into the darkness of the underground lake, deep beneath the palace of Caermaellan.

"Can you just imagine if I had been able to use Veil doors when we were younger? The trouble we could have gotten out of, or into." Memory sighed as she cracked some super-sized glow sticks they stole from a sporting goods shop before leaving the other world. Will had also grabbed a fitted black t-shirt from the store, discarded the last shreds of the old shirt he wore and put it on. By the time they left, they weren't the only people looting shops, but having the Veil door escape plan still made it easier.

Memory shook the glow stick, and the bright radioactive-yellow color it shed gave the cavern an eerie feeling. It sparkled over the black water in front of them, and the white fur of Shonae's natural form.

"There is iron here," the faun said.

Memory looked at the now empty crates left scattered on the loose sand and rocks. All the iron Thayl had hoarded there was gone, so her theory about Caliburn must be right. "Will, do you remember how you told me that the fae never came down here, for a long time, even before the other iron was here? The legends of King Arthur have these vague references to Excalibur coming from a lake, and being returned to a lake after Arthur's death."

Will said, "I thought the sword came from the stone."

"For something that is in the realm of myth and hearsay, passed down by word of mouth from the original source and changing every time, we have to work with what we've got. And what we've got, is this lake."

"Definitely worth a shot," Will agreed.

They unwrapped the rest of the glow sticks, and the sound of them cracking echoed in the quiet cave.

Memory stripped off her top layer of clothes, dropping her mostly shredded jacket on the ground beside her boots.

"Shonae, I need you to be our sensor."

The fae looked her up and down, mouth open in offence. "Your what?"

"I need you to come with us and feel out where Caliburn is."

The faun blinked, shivered, and stepped back. "Do you know what you are asking of me?"

"Yes," Memory said. "And I'm sorry. But there is more at stake here than just us."

"I am free of my debt to you now. I would leave, but the strength of the iron here saps my magic." Shonae sighed. The dark water whispered over the pebbled shoreline like hushed words, and Shonae's black eyes held Memory's in a level gaze. "If I had not been so afraid to die in your trap, none of this would have happened to me. I will accept my fate now. So be it."

Shonae began to walk out through the water. Her cloven hooves clacked and slipped on the pebbles, and Memory extended a hand to help her.

The water was so cold it burned Memory's toes as she stepped in. She gasped, trying to get her balance and keep both of them up. Will had left his new t-shirt on the shore and waded into the lake in front of them as though he didn't feel the cold at all.

They left a few glow sticks on the shore, and each held a couple as they moved with hurried caution into the vast black body of water.

Shonae clutched tight to Memory's arm, leaning heavier and heavier to support herself. It was obvious that the fae was weakening fast. Caliburn had to be near. Just how near was the question. Would Shonae die before they even got close?

The water became too deep to walk. The three swam together, marking a rough grid pattern through the lake, Will and Memory working together to keep the faun afloat.

Shonae went limp and cried softly. Her head went under the water and Memory grabbed for her, holding her up.

The faun's eyelids hung heavy over her black eyes, water beading over her furred muzzle. "It's here… very near. I cannot go farther."

"No, you can't," Memory agreed.

Memory dropped her glow sticks into the water, watching then float down until they were like a small, pale stars in the

depths. Will nodded, and with a deep breath, he dived down.

Shonae fell again, her body sliding under the water and her eyes slipping closed. Memory grabbed the faun, pulling her close and forcing her face to the air. She leaned back, floating with the faun on top of her, kicking slowly to the shore. Shonae was a dead weight in her arms and almost pulled her under as well, but Memory held tight, handfuls of the fae's soft white fur held tight in her fists.

Arms and lungs aching, Memory's feet finally touched ground again, and she walked the fae out of the water until the two of them fell with a splash in the shallows.

Panting and choking, Shonae looked up at Memory from where she lay in the water, her white woolly hair floating around her face like a halo. "Why did you save me? Before in the other world, and again now? Why bring me back away from Caliburn? I thought you would leave me to drift away alone in the water. I'm just a monster after all, aren't I?"

Memory blinked the water from her eyes and gave the faun a sharp look. "You really think I would have just left you there to die? No. You're not a monster. I get it now, really. Things aren't just black and white, seelie and unseelie, human and monster. That's why what I'm going to do is to stop all the fae from dying. Save all the fae from the lack of magic that is killing them. All of them, seelie *and* unseelie."

"You would really save us all?"

Memory sat on the pebbles and watched as Will's head emerged from the water to take a breath, then dive down again.

"That's my plan," Memory said, almost a whisper. "I just hope that will be enough to stop a war."

Shonae pushed herself out of the water, sitting on her

knees. She reached out, placing her palm against Memory's chest for a short moment in a gesture that seemed strange to Memory. *Must be a fae thing.*

"If that is truly your plan, if you think you can save us all, I want to help you. I will stay with you."

Memory saw the glint of something beneath the water.

"Thanks, Shonae, but it looks like you will have to stay at least a few steps away from me."

Will's face came up from under the black water again, close to shore. He stood up out of the water, rivulets running down his hair and over his chest. In one hand he clutched a bright steel sword, shining with the yellow of the glow stick in his other hand.

He strode into the shallows and knelt in the water before Memory, his chest panting with the effort of diving deep in the lake. He placed the sword across her lap.

"I believe this is yours," he said. "The sword of King Arthur."

He shook his head, staring at it with a small smile on his mouth. The sword was beautiful, just as it had been illustrated in Memory's history books. A huge amethyst was embedded in the hilt and the blade still sharp and untarnished, no rust or damage from its centuries underwater.

Shonae skittered backwards quickly until she reached what must have been a comfortable distance, about three body lengths away.

Memory wrapped her hand carefully around the hilt and stood up, lifting the sword with her. It felt perfect in her hand, made for her. It made the magic inside her *sing.*

"We have to get back to the castle, get Caliburn to Eloryn

and the human army," Memory said.

Memory held up the sword, staring at her reflection in the shining metal. "I just hope we don't have to use it."

CHAPTER TWENTY-NINE

Memory's breath hitched in and out, and there was stitch stabbing at her ribcage. The sprint up the narrow stairs into the palace left her dizzy. Her adrenaline was up and her nerves were stretched thin. But she had to keep moving.

Will followed close behind, and Shonae a little behind that, as Memory led them through the old keep section of the castle, trying to follow the sounds of battle that seemed to echo from every direction. The tunnel from the lake emerged behind a wall on the second floor and the halls were devoid of life, not a human or fae to be seen.

Following the sounds of fighting, Memory took a shortcut into the Round Room to find an entrance down to the front of the palace.

Memory was first through the door. Momentum carried her forward even after she saw Nyneve appear before her. She was simply going too fast to stop.

Memory's bare feet skidded on the slick marble floor, wet from her dripping clothes. She slid straight toward the unseelie queen. Nyneve laughed a husky chuckle that sent shivers down Memory's spine.

Nyneve's fairy gold sword flashed in the dimness.

Pain shot through Mem's entire body.

The clang of dropped metal battered her eardrums.

She went hot, then cold. Something was wrong. Very wrong.

She tried to raise Caliburn but the sword was on the floor, skidding away from her, still clutched in her fingers.

Her mind spun.

My hand is on the floor. She couldn't comprehend. *My hand is on the floor.*

Memory screamed, clutching at where Nyneve's blade had severed her at the wrist. She fell, her legs sprawling underneath her.

Everyone was screaming around her, for her. Nyneve was laughing still, louder now.

"Thought you could come back and kill me with damned Arthur's sword?" she said.

"That's not why I came back." Memory gasped the words out, pain making everything difficult. Blood oozed from her wrist in small spurts timed to the beat of her heart.

She couldn't even move as Nyneve swung for her again.

Will had gone after Caliburn. He ran back to her, sword in hand, but was too far away.

The sword meant for Memory struck into something soft in front of her eyes. The soft white body of Shonae.

Nyneve's sword took her in the chest, slicing right through. Dark blood sprayed across the unseelie queen's diamond gown as she wrenched her weapon out of the faun. Her gaze was cold and distant, as though the young faun was nothing but a nuisance to her.

Shonae slumped to the floor, her dark eyes going pale.

"No!" Memory cried out.

Shonae had jumped in to save Memory, had died for her. Memory could still hear in her head the fae's desperate cries from when they had first trapped her, so scared for her life. Now that life was gone. An animalistic scream of pain and rage sounded from her lips.

Nyneve didn't even hesitate to thrust her sword again. This time, Will stepped between Nyneve and Memory, blocking with Caliburn. The fairy queen scowled, adjusting her swing and sweeping her sword away before it made contact with the iron.

"You don't have to do this," Memory said. "There's another way, a way to save all the fae."

"Do you really think I would agree to a new pact with humans?"

"No, that's not—" Mem protested but Nyneve was not finished, her venomous words continued to tumble out in a calm, calculating tone.

"You've treated the unseelie fae as monsters for too long. The humans will be my slaves. The blood of the people of Avall will save the fae. It will protect me and my followers as I take over the rest of the world too, destroying every last human. Then, then the fae will be saved."

"No... Work with me. Can save everyone. Humans, fae, don't have to die." Memory's eyes were losing focus and she was struggling to stay conscious. Her own blood formed a growing pool on the ground around her, mixing with the blood of the faun. She managed to get her belt off and used it to tourniquet her wrist.

Nyneve kept her eyes on Caliburn, where Will held it steady in front of her face. She swayed slightly, sidestepping casually, testing him, but he kept the point aimed strong. The unseelie queen's own sword wavered close by, threatening, but not daring to meet the iron.

"You do have to die, every one of you. Humans have always been a scourge. It's past time you were finally removed for good."

Memory tried to reason. "Myrddin was half human, you loved him."

Fire flashed in Nyneve's eyes at the mention of that name. "And he betrayed me. He chose humans over his dominant unseelie side, chose Arthur instead of me. Even though Arthur never loved him in the same way." Nyneve's deep voice was low, the hurt in it clear. She edged forward as she spat the words, but Will kept her in check, forcing her away until she backed up into the wall. "I still loved him anyway, and when he went missing it took a millennium of study and sacrifices to find he'd lost himself in the Veil. When I finally found him, and pulled him out, I discovered he'd gone into the Veil to save himself from a Branding. A Branding from his precious humans, a Branding he got defending Arthur from his own poisonous family."

The words floated around Memory, her mind drifting in a haze of pain. She stared from Shonae's crumpled body, to her hand where it lay, just an inanimate object, nothing but dead flesh.

Poetic justice perhaps, Memory thought. *To lose the hand that once cut off the hand of another.*

"Once I'd found him, we barely had time to say goodbye before the Brand took Myrddin. He let humans sway his heart and he is forever gone because of it. I made sure Maellans have paid for their treachery over and over again throughout the years and now I will finish the last of them."

Will growled, a ferocity in him bringing out his animal side. He had backed Nyneve into a corner, and he was going to kill her, Memory knew it. Part of her wanted him to kill her, to cut her as deeply as possible, to claim vengeance for Shonae and so many others. The rest of her never wanted to see death again.

Will chanced a glance back at Memory, and the fury and worry in his eyes scared her. He placed the tip of Caliburn against Nyneve's neck. Memory saw a small bead of blood well up there, dark against her silver flesh. She heard Nyneve's hiss of pain as the wound sizzled. She transformed right in front of their eyes, becoming Hope.

"Go on, little boy," she taunted, looking just like Memory, wearing the black broken-heart t-shirt. "Where's your guts, you little pet? You animal."

The glamour flickered and faded, the strength of the iron in Caliburn too strong for Nyneve to hold onto her magic. She frowned at that, a scowl that twisted her serpentine skin. Her dark hair flew out behind her as she roared.

Her sword flashed in her hand, moving faster than a normal human could dodge.

She struck out at Will's chest, but he was no normal human, Memory knew. Not anymore. His time with the fae had changed

him, made him stronger. He jumped backwards, twirling and striking back. Nyneve cried furiously at him, dodging away around the round table, holding her weapon away from Will's.

"Beirsinn fair nalldomh!" she yelled, reaching her arm toward Memory. Memory knew those words, but the realization came too late as her own iron knife weakly wriggled free and clattered across the floor toward Nyneve. She scooped it up, angered by the weakness of her magic. She faced Will again, fairy gold sword in one hand and iron blade in the other.

Will's next swing was met with iron against iron. Nyneve swept the smaller blade upwards, channeling the motion of Will's strength away in a smooth movement. Sparks flew.

Will grunted with effort and Nyneve faded back into her form as Hope, taunting him as he followed her across the floor, their eyes locked on one another's as the battle between them began in earnest.

Memory knew that Nyneve was taunting him on purpose, baiting him into anger so he would not think, only react.

Memory knew that was what she had to do now. She had no time left to think. She was unsteady on her feet, her reflexes were slowing and she could barely see past the thin gray darkness seeping in at the edges of her vision.

Kneeling there on the floor in the sticky blood, she knew she had to act now, before she fell, and all was lost.

CHAPTER THIRTY

Memory's entire body ached with the strain of raising her magic. She fumbled, trying at first to use the hand that was no longer there, and the pain of that injury and loss almost broke her. Gritting her teeth, she changed her posture, working only with her remaining hand. She pinched the Veil, tearing it the way she had learned from the dragon, then created a larger hole, punching a Veil door that led from right there in Avall back to the rest of the human world. She brought herself to her feet and stepped within it, half in and half out, feeling the magic trickling from the Veil into her, drawn there by the store of magic inside her, like calling to like.

Memory hesitated. In the periphery of her consciousness

she knew that Will was still fighting Nyneve, but she didn't know where they were. She knew she could not wait for the outcome. The whole world felt like it was tilting on its ear, and she could barely stay on her feet. She had to do this now. If it worked, she might be able to level the battlefield for the humans, and save the fae too. She did believe that they needed saving, they all needed saving, and she was the only one who could do it. She had hoped to sway Nyneve to her side, that if she knew there was another way, she would stop her war and help keep Avall in the Veil, but Memory knew now that wouldn't happen.

Memory summoned together all of the magic within her. The vast stores of magic that had been drawn into her through her years within the Veil, that felt like a fire in her chest. She said a silent goodbye to Will, to Eloryn, to Roen, to Avall, and to herself, and then expelled all of that magic out into the world.

The magic flowed out of her like a river, churning smoothly and spreading, rippling like water. She felt it going. It was like letting go of a rope she had been holding for too long, a rope that had a huge weight hanging at the other end.

She sent some of her magic into every human of the land, re-creating their Sparks of Connection. The rest of the magic went out into Avall, filling it again with the magic that had been drained away, saving the fae who had been starving without it.

Her expulsion of magic created a movement, a flow through her. It was like creating a siphon, a two-sided funnel which would bring the magic through from the rest of the world into Avall. As the iron in the rest of the world drew magic away, her siphon would draw it back in, never leaving Avall or the fae without magic, as long as she remained the hose through which it could travel.

The magic throbbed and flowed through her, coming in from the other world and out into Avall. The flow was intense, golden-edged and flaming. It lifted her from her feet, holding her in the air, burning out of her skin.

The first burst of energy ended and when it went there was blankness. A darkness in her mind came through, burning through her memories, taking them away and her with them. Panic built within her as her identity fled her body. All the moments and memories that made her were so tied and tangled with the magic she cast out, that they all went with it.

I chose this. I accept this. It's what had to be done.

She repeated it over and over, reminding herself while the emptiness built inside her and the fear came with it.

There was a white static in her head. Sleepiness overtook her even as she was more awake than she had ever been in her life. A man and a strange woman blurred through her vision. Who were they? Why were they fighting?

Remember who you are. You chose this… She tried to hold onto just one memory, just the one that told her what she was doing, and why she was doing it, but soon it too was gone.

There was only pain and confusion.

What's happening? Where am I?

Everything hurts.

She tried to break free, to see, to understand. Her vision was a blur of golden light.

I can't move.

She couldn't feel the ground, could feel nothing but pain. Nothing made sense.

She was nowhere. She was nobody. There was nothing to hold onto to. She had nothing left. All she knew was nothingness.

Who am I?

She didn't know. She was stuck, trapped in this vortex of pain and confusion. Trapped forever.

Magic slammed into Eloryn like a wave. It flowed over her, leaving a small spark behind, warming her, filling the empty place inside.

She gasped, straightening up from where she bent over tending an injured soldier. She saw the effects of the invisible wave ripple through the chaotic room. Wizards rose from their patients, gasping as she had gasped, clutching their chests.

Eloryn's sleeves were rolled up and her hands bloody. There was barely enough floor space to hold the dead and injured being pulled back from the front line. Eloryn had desperately tended one after another, doing whatever she could for them. There hadn't even been enough time for Eloryn to see whether one of those dead or injured was Roen.

But now things had changed. Now she had her magic again.

Eloryn knew that this was Memory's doing. The magic, it tasted of her, of her consciousness, just as she had known it once before. Somehow, her sister had returned the Spark of Connection to her, and for what she could see and guess, to all humans in Avall.

Eloryn didn't know how. But she was determined to use it.

Getting to her feet, she cried, "Briseadh cassahn deannil dom es."

In a line from where she stood to the front line of the battle, the floor began to buckle. It split, breaking a pathway between the melee as it went, pushing away standing or fallen bodies. Eloryn strode down it in long steps, drawing her iron button into her hand as she went.

She could see the heart of the fighting now. Some of the soldiers had also realized their Spark of Connection was returned, and cast minor offensive spells into the fray to blind or stun their enemies. The unseelie fae seemed even more intent on killing the humans now that they had their magic returned to them. The magic their queen had told them was stolen from the fae. They were in the madness of rage and bloodlust and fear, driven by the lies of their hateful queen.

Eloryn spoke to the iron in her hand, and it shattered, turning into small deadly drops like fine mist. She reached the front line and stopped there.

Bellowing out her words of behest in a way to make herself known to all around her, she held out her small, white hand, and let those droplets of iron spray out into the oncoming fae.

The effect was instant and devastating. Unseelie fae fell screaming, twisting in pain from the iron raining upon them, burrowing and burning into their skin. Five or six creatures deep from the front line were hit, falling like wet autumn leaves to the ground. The creatures behind them cowered, unsure.

"Stop now!" Eloryn yelled. "Stop fighting now. Please do not force me to do that again."

She grabbed an iron spearhead from a bloodied soldier beside her. She turned it into deadly droplets as well, letting them float in a threatening cloud above her hands.

CHAPTER THIRTY-ONE

Nyneve's fairy gold sword sliced a shallow streak diagonally from Will's ribcage to shoulder. Blood spilled out, sticking the fabric of the t-shirt to his skin.

His arm ached with every thrust of the magical sword he wielded and his mind burned with fury.

No matter what he was feeling, he knew Memory was suffering more.

Her hand. His lips curled in a snarl.

It was too late to save her hand. No healing magic available. Maybe, maybe if he could stop Nyneve soon enough, they could get back to the other world and get to a hospital. If Memory was still conscious, still strong enough to get them there. Either way, he had to stop Nyneve now or there would be no rest of the world to go to. He had to stop Nyneve, and keep Memory safe until then.

Will struck fast and fiercely at the unseelie queen, driving her around the large circular table and away from where Memory had fallen. His pants were still wet and tugged at his skin, restricting his movement. Strangely, Nyneve in her long shimmering gown seemed to have no such trouble. She feinted and parried, slipping the crystalline sword always out of reach of Caliburn, brushing the iron away with Memory's small steel knife instead. Will knew if he could only get the angle right, that small knife would also break under the strength of Caliburn, but Nyneve's movements were fluid, redirecting each blow. She spun her arms and torso like a dancer, always in movement, a blur of dark hair and sparkling blades.

Will had still managed to land a few blows, small nicks and slashes. The stomach of Nyneve's gown was sliced open, black blood oozing around the diamond encrusted fabric, smoking slightly.

But no matter how often he struck, Nyneve didn't slow. Her dark magic healed her far too quickly. Will started to wonder whether her iron immunity was enough to protect her even from Caliburn.

Nyneve's sword swiped right in front of his eyes and he back-flipped to escape the blade. His vision blurred and the muscles of his calves tightened, burned and itched as he fought to keep his footing on the slick, bloodied floor.

A strong wind filled the room, swirling in the round space like a vortex. In the corner of his eye he saw a flurry of mist spill into the room as Memory opened a Veil door and stepped

within it. Was she leaving him? He wished he knew what her plan was, all of it, any of it. All he had now was trust.

But he knew he could not spare more thought for Memory if he were going to help her. He had to keep Nyneve from getting to her, and to do that he had to concentrate, forget what Memory was doing, might be suffering, or sacrificing.

The room filled with a golden glow, and Nyneve's eyes widened.

Will didn't miss his chance, and lunged at the distracted fae. He grunted, yelling strength into his swing, and Caliburn struck Nyneve's shoulder, cutting in the width of the blade itself. For a moment she swayed, her eyes losing some of their dark sparkle.

Will hesitated. He drew Caliburn back away, and could see strength already returning to Nyneve. He could swing again, and end it now. But he knew that wasn't what Memory wanted. She was doing something, something that she hoped would end the killing. He just had to buy her more time.

Will chanced a glance behind him and saw Memory suspended in the air, radiating amber light. He didn't know what it meant, but the expression on Nyneve's face suggested she did, as did the renewed vigor in which she turned again on Will, trying to slice through him to get to Memory. He knew then he shouldn't have hesitated. Everything on Nyneve's face said that she would not stop, she would never stop.

Will worked fast to readjust, but Nyneve's new fury had him on the back-foot. She threw a chair into his path, and when he twisted to dodge it, she kicked him hard in the chest, her gown swirling up past his face in a spray of stars.

The force of the blow knocked him onto his back, sliding across the room until he hit a column.

His skull met the marble and pain shot down the length of his body. Caliburn was no longer in his hand.

In his swaying vision he saw Nyneve standing over him, her sword raised high.

Her gold weapon flashed in the air, aimed at his vulnerable neck and Will knew, in that tiny split second of time; he knew he was going to die.

He had let Memory down. He wanted to spend the rest of his life with her, and in a way he had, but it was too short.

Nyneve's sword sang a high, thin song made by the air being cut into halves by the razor edge, but just before it came down on his throat it met another weapon.

A shattering sound filled the room, as though the world had been made of glass and been hit by a sledgehammer.

Will blinked, sure he was dead, sure his head was bouncing along the bloodied ground somewhere, but instead Mina stood in front of him. Her glittering wings hung like broken cobwebs and her face and hair had gone the color of spoiling milk, white with a greenish tinge.

Her lips were set in a determined expression as she held Caliburn pointed at the unseelie queen. The hilt was wrapped in a thick layer of fabric, protecting her hands, but she clearly suffered to be that close to the magical iron.

Nyneve's fairy gold sword lay all around them, a spread of broken, glittering shards. Her composure also broke. This sprite's presence clearly wasn't part of her plans. "What are you doing?"

Mina hissed. "I won't let you hurt my boy."

The words echoed through Will's ears. *My boy.* The fear the sprite could take him away again got him scrambling to his feet, using the column as support.

"I lost him and it is your fault. You told me to steal him away! You promised if I took him to Tearnan Ogh he would be mine forever and you lied!" The tip of Caliburn sank from where it threatened Nyneve, down to touch the floor, and Mina's shoulders slumped. She was weakening too fast. The sword dropped from her grip.

Will acted fast, scooping the sword into his hands.

Mina cried out as Nyneve sliced her across the cheek with Memory's knife. She fell to the ground, a crumpled heap of fairy dust and long trailing hair.

Before Nyneve had even finished swinging at the sprite, Will drove Caliburn up and through the unseelie queen's rib cage.

Nyneve looked down at the blade protruding from her chest, dull confusion marring her brow. All of her glamour twitched around her, shifting between Hope, Providence, and her true, midnight-haired form. Memory's knife fell from her hand and clinked on the floor.

Will pushed forward again, driving Caliburn in deep, running the fae through. A thin ooze of blood swelled, crystalizing and crackling across the dress's fine fabric. Nyneve's face went still, her mouth open but silent.

The blood around Caliburn sizzled and dried, crumbling. Dark veins ran from the wound outward across Nyneve's body. A low grinding sound began, and her chest changed, turning from silver to a mix of dull gray and rust red, hardening and disintegrating at the same time. The rusty tide spread through her, down her legs and along her arms before encasing her face and hair. She stood there still, like a tarnished, powdery statue.

Will grimaced as he stared at the where the sword he held

entered Nyneve's body.

He jerked Caliburn back, and the iron ore that had been the unseelie queen crumbled into bits, and blew away in the wind that rushed around the room.

Will exhaled slowly, letting his sword arm relax. The wind in the room blew his dark hair around his face and smelled of blood. He heard a whimper at his feet.

Mina lay crumpled there, ill from even the presence of the magical sword clenched in his fist. Adrenaline still rushed through Will. He knew he could kill her so quickly, so easily. Part of him wanted to. She had tried to kill him. She had kept him as a pet for so long, and the fear she could somehow claim him again made his sword arm twitch. He could finish it now and never fear being owned again.

It's not what Memory would do.

The girl he loved believed in second chances, in finding another way, in trusting people to learn and do better. Will knew he had to do the same.

"Mina," he said. He knelt beside the sprite where she curled in a tight ball. She shuddered.

Will placed Caliburn on the ground and pushed it across the room, away from the fae girl. She turned slowly to look up at him, a long gash still sizzling across her cheek.

She was losing some of the blue tint to her face but she was weak and it showed. He helped her to sit up, his hands lingering on her shoulders.

He remembered then how she had first found him, alone, cold, and starving. Weak and dying. She had done him a great wrong, but she had cared about him in her own way too. She risked everything to hold Caliburn and fight Nyneve.

Will bent his head and looked her in the eyes. "You saved my life, again. Thank you."

Mina pouted. "Does that mean you aren't mad at me, that you will be mine again?"

He dropped his forehead onto hers. "You saved me when I was too lost and hungry to survive. You have shown me wonders greater than I could have ever imagined. You are the most beautiful thing I've ever seen."

He felt Mina shiver. She whispered, "Who do you love above all else, even your short mortal life?"

"Memory."

Mina pushed Will away. She stood up, swaying slightly, but her color returned with her stubbornness. She humphed, and Will sighed, a small smile stealing onto his lips at the childish behavior he knew so well.

"I do care about you," he said. "But I am not your pet. I will never be a pet again. Not anyone's. But maybe, one day, we could be friends."

She looked at her feet. "You do not need or want me any longer, Will. I know it. A pet that is determined to roam will, and if you keep it chained all you will get is bitten."

"Still not a pet." Will rolled his eyes.

"But maybe friends?" Mina fluttered her eyelids as she looked up at him again.

Will nodded shallowly. His gaze was already back on Memory, still held in the glowing rush of magic within the Veil door, suspended in the light, a heartbreaking expression of pain and confusion on her face. "Friends help each other. Will you help me now?"

Mina shrugged one shoulder in a non-committal way.

"Go to Eloryn. Bring her back here for me. For Memory. Please," he asked.

The look Mina gave him was a sad one, but with a small nod she vanished before his eyes.

An eerie stillness had fallen.

Inside the throne room, the unseelie fae army had halted their attack. Outside the throne room, Eloryn could hear the storm still raging through the sky and the Veil, a sky that swirled from blue to red to black to a low hanging indigo-purple. Whatever Memory had done had given the humans back their magic, had stopped the war, but hadn't stopped Avall from crashing back through to the rest of the world.

There were murmurs through the unseelie fae, a change to the emotion in the room. Just as the humans had been given back their Spark of Connection, Eloryn sensed something was now different for the fae as well.

Still, she held her cloud of iron at the ready, a warning to the enemy who were paused in confusion.

At her feet, the dead lay in piles. Bodies sprawled with open eyes staring up, both human and the fading black of lifeless unseelie fae.

Eloryn squinted her eyes closed away from the sight, terrified then that she might see the caramel eyes of Roen there.

There was a light touch on her waist and she opened her eyes. There he was, standing – leaning – beside her. Alive. Roen

was alive.

"You're hurt," Eloryn choked out, her words crushed under mixing relief and sadness.

"I'm so sorry. I'm sorry I sent you away. Can you forgive me?" he said, looking up at her from under a mess of tawny hair and blood splatter. He held a broken flagpole tucked under one arm, supporting his weight on it like a crutch.

"I would not have forgiven you if you had died," Eloryn sniffed. "Is Erec—?"

Roen lifted his chin, and through a small crowd of soldiers, she saw Erec sitting on the steps, catching his breath.

She smiled and swallowed away a sob.

In the small gap of space between the recovering humans and unseelie fae, a darkness roiled up from the ground. Eloryn readied her iron, her nerves taut and her mouth moving as she began the spell to release that iron, but she stopped as the thick fog of the Veil took shape.

The unseelie fae staring at her was a regal looking woman she had never seen before. Long, slender hands of smooth silver-white were held up in a human gesture of surrender. Her black hair hung almost to the ground, and her resemblance to Nyneve was unsettling. Unnaturally tall and thin with a smooth, almost featureless face, she turned to the unlight forces gathered behind her and it was clear they all knew who she was.

Her voice echoed as she said, "Nyneve is dead. I am Oonah, wife to Finvarra, and I claim the unseelie throne."

There was a shuffle of movement as the unseelie fae bowed before her. Oonah lowered her arms, her silver and gray robes drifting in the powerful gales of wind. "We have been saved. Magic is returned to us, and to Avall. This war is over, leave this place!"

The unseelie fae were quick to act. Some fled on foot, others vanished through the Veil. Each movement caused a wary reaction from the human soldiers, their eyes wild from the strain and carnage. The short silence in the room became noisy turmoil again, men running to aid others, bring them to the wizards once again able to use healing behests. A blur of movement surrounded Eloryn and the new unseelie queen. Eloryn let her arm down. It shook from the effort of holding the iron cloud in check. The iron spearhead reformed, falling to the ground.

Oonah turned to Eloryn. She peered down at her from twice the height. Her black eyes were large and wide, no eyelashes or brows. An intricate wreath-like silver circlet created a boundary between her nebulous ebony hair and her moon-like face.

"Human queen, we will speak soon. I must leave now for the seelie court and work with Aine to keep Avall from leaving the Veil."

"Thank you." Eloryn nodded slowly, then shook her head, confused. "I'm not the queen."

"Are you not the next in line? You are the last of Maellan blood."

A chill spread slowly across Eloryn's body. "What do you mean? What's happened to Memory?"

The ground shifted under her feet and she wondered if it was real, or her own grief making the world seem to tumble. Roen grabbed for her, steadying her, and Oonah looked out the front of the palace at the violent sky, urgent concern on her thin lips. She left without another word.

Eloryn's mind raced. *What happened to Memory? Where is my*

sister?

There was confusion everywhere. Eloryn stared about at the snarl of bodies and living and waved for Erec. He finished giving commands to the men around him then began walking over.

Bedevere and the Council were hard at work on the injured, and Eloryn could see Clara, face white and looking away from the bodies, picking through the crowd toward her as well. Eloryn waved to her. Maybe Clara had news from Memory. *I hope she does.*

Eloryn turned her back away from where the battle had been and faced Roen "We need to find Memory. Do you need me to heal you now, or will you—"

"For Nyneve!" A harsh voice cried over Eloryn's words.

"El! Roen screamed.

Something hard hit her, knocking her to the ground. A strange and almost inarticulate scream split the air and hot red fluid seeped along her back. She could feel it sinking into her shirt. A soft weight pressed her down onto the floor. A freckled hand and strands of bright red hair flopped down in front of Eloryn's eyes. Everyone screamed around her and she heard the clashing of blades again. She tried to scramble out from under the weight. Roen knelt beside her and helped.

Rolling free, Eloryn saw with horror what the weight was. Clara lay there, her eyes open and lifeless as blood still spread from the fairy gold dagger in her heart.

Beside her on the ground was the body of the unseelie knight that had led Nyneve's army. Erec stood over him, his eyes wild.

"Clara?" Eloryn called, but it was too late. Too late for

words or tears or magic to bring back the life that was gone.

Roen placed his hands on her cheeks and turned her face away from the body of their friend. “Don’t look.”

Tears burned tracks down Eloryn’s face and Roen’s fingers. “How? How did this happen?”

“She saved you,” Erec said, kneeling on the ground beside her. “That wasn’t her job. It should have been mine. She shouldn’t have—” His voice broke and he looked away.

Clara had always said she felt like a coward compared to the rest of them. But this shouldn’t have been the way she proved she wasn’t. It was all too much. The only thing holding Eloryn together was Roen’s hands on her face, his gaze holding hers.

“Memory will be devastated,” Eloryn said in a hush. “If she’s… If…”

In a sparkle of fairy dust, Mina appeared beside Eloryn. She looked around the room, her normally mischievous face solemn. “Your sister needs you.” Her expression changed quickly to impatient. “Are you coming then?”

Eloryn looked to Clara again. Erec brushed her red hair from her face and closed her eyelids. Eloryn wanted to stay, to cry hot tears for Clara and all the dead around her until the earth was soaked in that salt water.

But grieving had to wait.

“Erec, stay with Clara for me,” she said.

He nodded, face hard and closed.

Roen took Eloryn’s hand and she wiped her face.

Her voice was commanding when she told the sprite, “Take me to my sister.”

CHAPTER THIRTY-TWO

Rushing air from the Veil door tore like claws at Memory's purple hair and tattered clothes.

Will stood before her, terrified and helpless, staring at her vacant eyes.

He wanted to pull her free, use brute force to save the girl he loved, but he was too scared he might do more harm. So he stood there, where Memory could see him, and hoped his presence was a small comfort to her, if nothing else.

Memory's blank face gave no indication she knew he was there at all.

In a flash of light, Mina returned, bringing Eloryn and Roen with her.

That they were exhausted and wounded was clear. Eloryn's hair was hanging around her wan face and her hands were stained with drying blood. Roen's shirtfront was liberally smattered with gore, and he leaned heavily into a makeshift crutch.

Eloryn ran straight to Memory and raised a hand that hovered tentatively just away from the golden glow of magic.

"Oh, Mem," she gasped. "You stupid, clever girl."

"What's happening? What did she do?" Roen asked.

"This is how she gave us all back the Spark of Connection, how she brought magic back for the fae. She turned herself into a doorway. The flow of magic she started, she's part of it now, tied into it."

"For how long?" Will growled.

"Forever," Eloryn whispered.

Will clenched his teeth and spoke through them. "No. I don't accept that."

I can't. I can't lose her now.

Roen hobbled over. "Can't we just pull her out?"

Eloryn's head shook. Her voice caught. "You don't understand. She's not stuck in the doorway. She *is* the doorway. She *is* the flow."

Roen wobbled slightly, then slumped to the ground, covering his eyes with his hand.

Will's breath came in ragged gasps. Memory really had been saying goodbye. She knew this would happen, that once she started this, she would be giving herself to her plan forever.

Why did she have to sacrifice herself? Will knew why, he knew the hero Memory was, but it still hurt. Too much. It just didn't seem fair.

Will picked up a chair from beside the round table and flung it at a wall.

Eloryn's watery eyes followed the flying furniture, flinching when it smashed and clattered to the ground. Will saw her expression change from hopeless to curious.

"Is that…?"

She strode across the room to where Caliburn lay discarded beside a column.

She crouched down, brushing a fingertip along the blade.

Her head shot back up fast and she spoke breathlessly. "Caliburn."

Roen looked up, his eyes red-rimmed. He struggled back to his feet, supporting himself on his crutch. "You're thinking something. What are you thinking? Please, if anyone can save Memory, it's you."

Eloryn grinned wryly. She ran her hands into her hair, holding her head as her eyes looked about as if seeking answers. "Maybe we could… It might… We might be able to swap them. We might be able to exchange Caliburn for Memory."

"We can save her?" Will asked in a whisper. Whether they heard or not, no one replied.

Eloryn clutched the sword and strode back to the Veil door and Memory. "If anything were ever a stronger channel for magic than Memory, it is Caliburn."

She thrust the hilt into Roen's hands. "You will put Caliburn into the flow."

Looking Will in the eye, she said, "You will pull Memory out. I will be doing what I can with my magic to redirect the flow and bind Caliburn into Memory's place as the doorway."

"What about me?" Mina's voice was small. She stood away from them, arms cuddling herself and face confused.

Will tilted his head. Maybe she really was trying to change.

Eloryn said, "Go back to the seelie court. Oonah said she is going to work with Aine to stop Avall breaking back through to the rest of the world. Keep us updated on their progress."

Mina cast a sidelong glance to Will, then nodded and left.

"We have to time this just right," Eloryn said breathlessly. "On my mark."

The three of them stood in a semi-circle before Memory and the Veil door she had merged with. Magic blasted their faces as they drew closer.

Eloryn began chanting, speaking her behest words, talking with the earth and the Veil and the very magic of life. The glow surrounding Memory built, crackling like electricity.

Without a break in her words, Eloryn flung her arms out, gesturing to Roen and Will.

With both hands, Roen lifted Caliburn high, then plunged it downwards into the Veil door beside Memory. The point sliced into the marble there. Digging deep, it held, propped up in the stone.

Will stepped into the gushing stream of magic, shielding his face and eyes to the brightness. He pushed through, each step a battle against the tide.

With one final grunt of effort he reached Memory and wrapped his arms around her waist. Her purple hair whipped in his face. He cried out as it took all of his strength to pull her free.

They tumbled out of the Veil door together, rolling across the floor, with Memory cradled in Will's arms.

Will could hear Eloryn continue to cast, binding Caliburn into the doorway, allowing the flow of magic through, keeping

all the fae renewed and the magic life force circulating properly the way Memory had sacrificed herself to achieve.

But all Will cared about then was the tiny, limp body in his arms.

"Memory," he said, brushing his hand down her cheek.

Her eyes were still open but unaware. He laid her carefully flat on the floor.

"Eloryn, I need you here now. I need you to heal her. Something is still wrong."

She was there immediately, Roen by her side.

Memory moved slightly, her eyes blinking, looking all around, blinking again.

Roen grinned wide. "There, she's okay. You're okay," he said, smiling down at Memory.

She shied away. "Who are you?"

At those words, Will's hand tightened into a fist and he almost broke.

A dismal gasp came from Eloryn. "No, please no."

Memory brought herself up into a sitting position, becoming frantic as she looked around the room. She tried to put down her hand that wasn't there anymore and cried out in pain as the stump scraped the ground and she slipped back down to her back. She brought the limb in front of her face and screamed.

"What have you done to me?" she sobbed. "Why can't I remember anything? Not anything!"

That sentence broke Will's heart. Memory had accomplished what she had set out to do but she had paid a high price. Her mind was gone again, all of her memories wiped clean. How could that be fair? How could that be fair at all? For what she had given she deserved so much more.

He wrapped his arms around her, bringing her up onto his lap. At first she struggled, but then she curled into him, weeping.

"There is nothing to be scared of. You're safe now. I'm Will," he whispered to her. "This is Eloryn, and Roen. We're here for you. We're your family."

CHAPTER THIRTY-THREE

They tell me my name is Memory.

They tell me that I did amazing things.

They tell me all about this land I'm in and the changes that are happening here.

Avall was experiencing a wary peace.

Oonah was proving to be a kind and intelligent ruler of the unseelie fae. She was Finvarra's wife, Nyneve's mother, whom Nyneve had exiled for being too sympathetic to humans. She and Aine worked together with the forces of seelie and unseelie fae to stop Avall shifting back to the rest of the world, stabilizing it within the Veil, separated again from the world it had once been part of. But the doorway that Memory had opened between the worlds, whose opening was smack in the middle of the Round Room of the palace of Caermaellan, remained open. At least, on Avall's end.

The Wizards' Council had used their magic to hide the opening at the other end. They did not think Avall was ready to be rediscovered by the rest of the world yet. Most were afraid of that world and its technology, but some were excited by it, thrilled at the prospect of being able to share again, to import new things and to allow Avall to move forward. It had been stuck in its time rut long enough, and it had outlived the antiquated ideals and principles that had once ruled the land. Bedevere had already made a number of trips into the other world.

The world they told Memory she was also part of.

I try to understand, but the hole inside me feels so big that it could never be filled.

Will looked across at Memory, his face the normal mix of small smile and small frown she had grown to know. He was always by her side, as long as she wanted him to be. There were times when she needed to be alone and he would let her be, but mostly she appreciated his presence, and his answers. They sat together on the balcony of her bedroom, staring out at the springtime flowers in the courtyard below, legs dangling over the balustrade, feet tickled by the ivy leaves that grew there. Memory smiled back at Will. He had become a good friend.

She had a sister here, too. Eloryn. And Eloryn's boyfriend, Roen, seemed to treat Memory like family as well. They were around often, but also had responsibilities that kept them busy. And there were many other friends she was learning the names of. There were also a lot of names that were spoken of friends who were gone.

Alward, Thayl, Waylan, Peirs, Edele, Shonae, Clara. Memory recited the names often, although she couldn't remember the people themselves. It hurt her, to know that maybe she would never remember them, that these people had died and she would never now have a chance to know them.

Eloryn had tried to explain Memory's complicated relationship with Thayl. At times it made Memory too sad and she had to stop her sister, taking the story in small installments only.

A warm breeze blew past the balcony and Memory sighed. "So many terrible things," she whispered quietly to herself.

Will's normally small frown deepened and Memory had to remind herself again how good his hearing was.

"Lots of terrible thing have happened. To this world, to you, and to me," he said, staring over the courtyard to the forest beyond. He turned back and met her gaze. The icy blue of his eyes made her heart jump. "But know you're the best thing to happen to me, and to this world."

Memory looked down at her right hand, or what used to be her right hand, and sighed. A finely crafted silver prosthetic hand was now attached there. Eloryn had spent days planning an intricate behest which imbued the replica hand with a sort of life. It responded to Memory's thoughts and moved just as a real hand would, however while it could touch, it could not feel. Sometimes she could have sworn she still felt the tingle of real flesh, then when she looked down and saw the cold metal at the end of her arm it confused and scared her beyond anything she wanted to admit.

Losing her hand, losing her memories and herself, were the sacrifices she had apparently chosen to make. Everyone said she had changed everything, and talked about the differences, but she did not remember what it had been like before.

There was no Pact anymore, no forced peace treaty, and no threat of Branding. There was just an implicit agreement to treat everyone, seelie and unseelie and human alike, as equals. So far everyone had managed to behave. Nobody knew if that would or could last, though they all hoped that it did. The fae had been given life again due to Memory's actions, and there was a grand sense of gratitude for that. The numbers of fae spending more time in Avall had grown and it was rare to spend a day without seeing a fae of one kind or another. And with the return of the fae, the weather had also improved. The bitter snows ended and a mild sun shone across a flourishing land.

The Kingdom of Avall was being managed by the people Memory had put in place, but they had yet to crown a new ruler. Memory was still queen, at least in name, and everyone seemed to be waiting for her, hoping that she would regain her memories or learn enough again to step back into that role. In the meantime Eloryn was acting in her place.

There was a quiet knock on the door, and Eloryn and Roen came in together. The happiness Memory could see in them always made her happy as well, and somehow sad.

They didn't say a word, just came over and joined Will and Memory on the balcony. The sun had just begun to dip toward the horizon, warming the clouds around it to a blazing gold.

Eloryn rested her head on Memory's shoulder, and Roen put a hand on hers, and together they watched the sunset.

Memory found the whole thing strange, the way people treated her, and talked about what she did. She felt like they were talking about someone else. In a way, they were. She didn't

recall doing those things, didn't know the people who spoke to her, and she never knew what was exaggerated. It all sounded like an exaggeration to her. Could anyone really have had that much magic? How had she have survived it? It seemed like she would have just exploded, or imploded, something oded, just to get rid of it at some point. It had to have hurt.

When things became too confusing, Will was always there for her, always ready to comfort her and to talk to her and to tell her about their shared past. Guilt swamped her on a daily basis. He loved her. It was obvious, despite how he tried to hide it, how he tried to put no pressure on her to feel the same. Her heart was as empty and hollow as the spot in her head where her memories had once resided. She apologised daily that she wasn't the person he remembered. He said he could wait, and that he would wait forever for her if he had to. She believed him. He treated her with nothing but the utmost patience and love.

Everyone treated her like a hero even though she remembered nothing of what she had done. But she knew one thing— that person they all saw in her, that was who she wanted to be.

EPILOGUE

The wedding between Eloryn and Roen was a sumptuous affair.

It was a celebration of their love, but also a celebration of the new peace and prosperity Avall and all its inhabitants had found. Seelie and unseelie fae and people of all walks of life were in attendance. The ballroom was filled with sprites dancing, their wings shedding bright colors onto the fur of black-eyed fauns and satyrs around them. People in rich velvets and homespun cottons, women in tightly laced corsets and fae in wispy gossamer gowns filled the chamber and overflowed into the gardens and grounds of the palace.

The feast was huge and many of the people who had been

going hungry in the land were at the groaning tables, stuffing intricately iced cakes into their mouths and laughing joyfully. There was plenty for everyone. The fae were no longer in danger of leaving the world forever and so Avall was no longer at risk of becoming a barren wasteland again. The land was healing, and the races along with it.

Music swirled and the dancers clapped their hands. Gaiety was everywhere, or almost everywhere. Some people remained still, looking around with the sad expression of a person searching for someone who will never come in the door again.

Memory leaned against a pillar, watching Eloryn dance with Roen. It was tradition in Avall for the bride to receive a gift of some form from a fae, and so Eloryn's gown was a gift from the seelie queen. It was a blend of gauzy, lighter than air fabric and gems like dewdrops that fell in smooth lines from her waist, spilling onto the floor like a shining pool at her feet. The golden tones mirrored her hair, which was pinned up in a mass of curls, highlighting her delicate face, made more beautiful by the flush of happiness it held. Roen wrapped his finger around one loose curl of hair, his eyes only for Eloryn's as they spun in slow circles around the room.

Leaning on the other side of the pillar, Will asked, "Do you want to know how they fell in love?"

"No," Memory answered. "It's enough to see that they are."

Memory swallowed, mustering up the courage to ask something she hadn't yet been able to. She'd pieced some of it together herself, from how Will and her other friends behaved and talked, and at first it made her only feel sad. But something had been stirring inside her, and she felt she was ready. "If you could though, if it's not too hard… maybe sometime could you tell me about how we fell in love?"

Will had a guilty look of being caught out. "You know?"

Memory grinned mockingly. "Sheesh, give a girl some credit! You can't look at me with those eyes without me seeing all the feels."

Will looked at his feet. "I didn't want to force anything by having you know."

"I know. Thank you. But I want to know. I'm not saying I'm ready to be in a relationship with you again or whatever it was we were. I'm not sure that is the path I want for myself now. Not that I don't like you, I mean, I do like you, I mean…" Memory took a deep breath and looked away from Will's blue eyes and mess of dark hair and strong shoulders. "Yeah, so. Ahem. Maybe we can have that chat sometime."

Will nodded and looked away, sparing Memory from him seeing the growing redness in her cheeks.

Across the room, Memory saw Oonah giving Eloryn a gift, some kind of large book. The two turned in unison and looked straight at Memory. She felt strange under the Unseelie Queen's inhuman stare, and the mix of emotions on her sister's face confused her. She didn't know either of them well enough to understand what it meant.

But she didn't have to think about it for long.

"Dance with me?" Will asked, his voice so slightly shaky.

"I don't know how to dance," Memory said.

Will chuckled. "Do you think I do?"

Memory grinned, and took his extended hand. They shuffled out into the crowd, awkwardly trying to copy the moves of those around them. Soon they let joy and silliness and the beat of the music take over, moving any which way they liked, laughing and panting and swinging about the room.

As one lively song ended and a slow waltz began, Memory found herself in Will's arms. They stood mostly still, swaying together on the spot.

Will bent down, tentatively, and gave her a soft kiss on her forehead. She smiled at him and her heart swelled, as though growing to love him again was the most natural thing in the world.

"It's late," Roen said, silhouetted in the doorway.

Eloryn looked up at him from where she was hunched over the desk in the queen's office. "Is it?"

Then she frowned at him, seeing him standing there in the darkness. "Where is your wisp light? You've been getting good at that behest, but you do still need practice."

"Thanks, teacher," he said, and Eloryn imagined the grin on his face despite not being able to see it. She did see him shrug. "I guess I'm just not used to being able to do that yet. I've always been comfortable in the dark. Àlaich las." A small glow appeared in his hand, shining up and making his caramel features turn to gold.

Eloryn smiled. He had been getting much better. When Memory replaced the Spark of Connection in the humans of Avall, it entered everyone. Even Roen. Even Will. Eloryn had been teaching them how to use their new connection to magic. Just one of her current projects.

Roen walked in and sat on the arm of her chair, putting his hands to work on the tight muscles at her neck. She closed her eyes, enjoying his touch.

His words were quiet. "I know what you are trying to do, and I want it as much as you do, but please don't lose yourself to this."

Eloryn looked back at the desk where Nyneve's journal lay open. Oonah had proved a kind ruler in many ways, and this wedding gift to Eloryn had been just one. Somewhere in these pages they hoped would be a way to help Memory.

The book was bound in leather that still held a stickiness like wet blood. The pages had been created out of thin linen and the ink was clear and legible even when the hand that had written the words within had shaken from grief or rage or jealousy.

The book felt wrong. The cover and pages had a weight to them that made Eloryn want to wipe her fingers on her skirts after each leaf turned.

"There are things in here I would be better off not seeing or knowing. Nyneve was beyond the darkness, she was headed into lightless territory," Eloryn said.

"I will try to keep you in the light," Roen replied.

A smile took the shadows from Eloryn's face.

She had to admit it, reading Nyneve's journal had taken a toll on her.

It started out innocent enough. Then Myrddin began to appear often in the text, and soon Nyneve's love turned to poison, to hatred. She refused to see what she was doing to him and their relationship, with her jealousy over Arthur and the humans that Myrddin loved so much.

The emotions in those words were so raw and powerful that

Eloryn could feel them tangle her insides. They battered at her heart and she had to stop reading those passages. But the next passages, once Myrddin had gone missing, were worse. Dark spells, sacrifices, and blood pacts, anything to bring Myrddin back to her. Her first body sacrificed was Myrddin's father, using his blood to make like call to like, drawing Myrddin free of the Veil. It was much as Alward's failed Veil door and Eloryn had accidentally drawn Memory back out of the Veil when she had been lost.

Once Nyneve learned that Myrddin had attacked Mordred, seeking revenge on the man for killing Arthur and was then Branded by the human, things really turned dark.

That's when the blood drinking began.

Eloryn learned that while Nyneve had been building her resistance to iron by drinking human blood, she had also been testing her resistance to iron by being in contact with it. When Memory's past was freed into the world after beating Thayl, Nyneve had been able to experience some of Memory's past, filtering the memories into her through the iron.

Nyneve could not possess Memory's past, but she could learn enough from it to act as Hope. But there was something there, something in her methods that started connections firing in Eloryn's mind. Eloryn knew that holding iron had returned some memories to her sister in the past, but magic came with it, and she didn't want her sister suffering from an overflow of that again. The Wizards' Council had collected and locked away all remaining iron artifacts after the battle, understanding now its connection to magic and what too much contact with it could do. They did small and highly monitored tests, and in their own way were trying to help Memory too. But they hadn't yet discovered a way to return Memory to herself.

The rest of the pages of Nyneve's journal were filled with darker magic than any before. Blood sacrifices, runes cut into flesh, and spells with hearts the color of coal. The journal needed to be destroyed, or taken somewhere and hidden for all time so that nobody else could use the evil magic and spells inside. The lure of that power was too tempting, even to Eloryn.

"No, I won't lose myself." Eloryn shuddered and closed the book, no longer wanting to see those words, to feel the residual magic, twisted and sickening, that lingered there.

She moved out of Roen's grasp and turned to look at him face to face.

"I found something, in Nyneve's mad words. The way she returned Memory's past to her the first time, it might be a way to bring our Memory back to us."

"But without any sort of sacrifice, of course?" Roen asked, one eyebrow raised.

Eloryn frowned. It was a sacrifice of sorts, for Memory. Eloryn closed her eyes, picturing how she saw her sister earlier that day. She was laughing, rough-housing with Maeve on the palace lawn, green grass clinging to her dress and a daisy tucked behind her ear. She seemed so happy. None of the weight and pain of a terrible past, the suffering she had lived through. Would it be better if she remained free of that suffering forever?

It's not your decision.

The words bounced around in her head and she wished they were not true, but they were. It was up to Memory whether or not she wanted them back.

Roen's eyebrow rose further. "You're worrying me here."

"No, no sacrifices," Eloryn said.

"Do you think she will be okay?" Roen asked, echoing Eloryn's fears. "The last time she got her memories back, she tried to kill herself."

Eloryn stood up and put her arms around Roen. "I know. I'm scared too. But this time, we'll be there for her."

Memory, Eloryn, Roen and Will, stood staring at the open Veil door that sat in the center of the Round Room. Wispy gray smoke circled the blurry window to the rest of the world, and in the middle stood Caliburn, wedged into the floor and glowing golden, spilling light and magic out into Avall.

The room had been cleared of everything except the round table itself, and a crystal display case holding Memory's iron knife. A mural had been painted on the wall that wrapped the space. On one side it showed Arthur and his knights, riding through flowered fields. Fae of all shapes and sizes fluttered around them or spied from the surrounding trees. On the other side of the room was an artist's impression of the Veil door they stood before. Caliburn was shown illustrated within, stylized curling flames surrounding it, and behind that, a small, feminine silhouette, aglow with magic.

Memory wondered if it was meant to be her. She looked down at her silver hand and the stump it concealed. "Will I remember… everything?"

Eloryn tilted her head. "Yes."

"But you don't really remember pain, do you? I mean, I'll

see what happened, but I won't feel it?" Memory grunted and stuck her tongue out. "Gah, I sound like such a coward. But seriously guys. Hand cut off. I don't want to feel that again. Or anything… else."

"The memories may be painful in themselves. But this time it will be just the memories returned, not the magic. Caliburn is the key, using it as a filter as it channels magic through the worlds. We can filter just your memories back to you." Eloryn held her sister's remaining hand. "Mem, I made a promise to you long ago that I would restore your memories to you. It's a promise long overdue in its keeping. I think it's time."

"Yeah." Memory exhaled the word. "You're right. Let's do this. I know I am going to see and remember stuff I don't want to, but I do want to remember you, all of you. I want to remember me. I want to be whole again."

They all clasped hands as they gathered around the doorway and the magical sword within. Memory took a long moment to look at each of her friends' faces, the faces she didn't really know anymore, but had and would, she hoped, know again soon.

"See you on the other side guys." Her voice faded as Eloryn spoke her magic to the Veil door and the wind began to howl out a mournful tune. The flow of magic from Caliburn was directed through Memory, filtering through her, rushing through like burning ice.

"We should wake her up."

Everything was warm, slow, and dark. The words drifted around Memory in her haze of sleep.

"No, we can't. She has to recover on her own. Getting her memories back is going to be traumatic."

"It's been days. What if… what if she doesn't wake up?"

"She has already relived her memories once, now she has to start all over and what is more, now there are new horrible memories. What if you had to recall every single detail about your life? The bad stuff, the stuff you don't want to talk about, the things that cut you the most? What if she doesn't want to wake up?"

"She wants to."

"Then why doesn't she?"

It's okay. I'm here.

Her mouth and eyes didn't want to work yet. But her mind was waking up. It was giving names to the voices. And faces. And pasts. The exact shade of Will's eyes and the bad haircut he got when he was eight. The color Eloryn's cheeks turned at regular intervals. The corner of Roen's mouth that twitched up when he was doing something charming. Erec's sandy complexion that was so much like his brother, Peirs's. Peirs, who died to save her. Clara, who died to save her sister, and had lived to flirt with every soldier in the palace.

"If I had to live the worst again, I might never get out of bed," she heard Erec say, and she knew he was thinking about Clara. It had only become clear after Clara was gone, the love he'd been harboring for her. Only clear to Memory now, now she remembered everything again.

Will spoke, his voice low and hoarse. "There used to be a

story about a prince who kisses the sleeping princess and brings her back to life. Just a fairy tale, but I wish I had that magic, some way to help her."

"Maybe I've been waiting for you to give it a try?" Memory croaked, her voice rough from sleep. She peeled dry eyes open and looked up at Will and her friends, standing around her bed. Daylight streamed through the window, making dust motes spark like pixies in the air.

"Memory?"

"Yes. It's me. All of me."

Will fell on top of her on the bed, scooping her up.

She could feel his heartbeat against her chest, then more arms wrapped them, and she heard the small, squeaking sobs of her sister and Roen's relieved laughter.

She took a moment to know them, really know them, to recall exactly who they were. Some of her memories were awful. She had done things and suffered things she almost couldn't live with, but there were so many good moments too, memories of these people, her family.

"I love my cuddle fests," she sighed, nuzzling against her friends. Then she pushed them away. "But I smell food. Get me to the food, I'm starving! How long have I been sleeping here, a hundred years?"

"Felt like it to me," Will said.

"It was barely two days," Roen scoffed. "How you ever waited those sixteen years I'll never know. This fellow is the most impatient person I've ever known."

"I'm so happy you're home," Eloryn said.

She helped Memory out of bed, holding her hand and supporting her by the elbow on the other side. Memory noticed she was wearing her old broken heart t-shirt, and what seemed to be brand new sweat pants. She quirked an eyebrow, wondering where they came from, but was happy to be in their fleecy embrace regardless.

In Memory's living room, every surface was filled with bouquets and garlands of flowers, and mountains of cakes and pastries. Rainbow colored roses from Loredanna's rose garden filled the room with a sweet scent, and… was that a cake shaped like a hamburger? *No way.*

The thought of Clara, missing this, being gone from their lives, drilled a deep hole of pain in Memory's heart. *Alward, Thayl, Waylan, Peirs, Edele, Shonae, Clara.* She remembered them all. She would never forget them again.

Memory swiped the first delicacy that was within reach and bit through the flakey crust to the custard cream inside.

Maeve entered the room, wearing a palace maid's uniform and balancing another tray of food. Her wild mass of brown hair was bundled neatly atop her head and she looked stronger and healthier than ever. She stopped abruptly when she saw Memory awake and eating.

"It is you!" she yelled, dropping the tray onto a table, and running in.

Memory was enveloped in a huge and almost smothering hug and she laughed, "Yes, it is me. Sorry I was gone for so long. How are the kids?"

"They are amazing, thanks to you and your friends. Some of them still have nightmares though, and might for a while yet."

"I'm sorry I didn't ask about them sooner."

"How could you have?" Maeve said. She held up a fist,

and Memory punched it three times then they both mimed an explosion.

Memory laughed. "You were totally just testing if I really remembered, weren't you?"

"Maybe," Maeve grinned. With Clara gone, Maeve had fought other servants off almost physically to be the one to take over her position as Memory's only assistant. Maeve had known, even when Memory couldn't, that it was what she would have wanted. Memory pulled the feisty girl back into a hug again as a silent thank you for that.

They all sat down together, relaxing on the floor and chairs. Not talking, just eating in silence, knowing they were all together again and that that was enough.

The friends that were missing weren't completely gone. Memory closed her eyes for a moment, feeling the weight of them, their loss, their lives, in her chest. Holding onto every precious memory.

She still felt fragile, brittle like fairy gold, from the return of her old memories. But she also felt stronger from the return of her newer ones.

She no longer burned inside with all the excess magic she had felt her whole life. All that was left was just the normal, small Spark of Connection. No missing soul, no missing past, no longing for a family she didn't know.

She had everything she always wanted.

She finally felt whole and complete.

The rest of the day was spent much the same, just enjoying each other's company within the small space of Memory's chambers. After a while Erec and Maeve left together, and then Roen and Eloryn as well.

Will hugged Memory close, and she leaned up to kiss him. His lips were warm and soft and she let herself melt into him. Memory closed her eyes, a smile blooming on her face.

Finally, she was home.

MEMORY'S WAKE
SELINA A FENECH

HOPE'S REIGN
SELINA A FENECH

PROVIDENCE UNVEILED
SELINA A FENECH

SELINA A FENECH
BESHADOWED
DARKNESS UNKNOWN

SELINA A FENECH
BESHADOWED
BLOOD BOUND

SELINA A FENECH
BESHADOWED
SHADOWS AWOKEN

SELINA A FENECH
BESHADOWED
EVERDARK CURSED

EMOTIONALLY CHARGED
1
SELINA A FENECH

EMOTIONALLY UNSTABLE
2
SELINA A FENECH

EMOTIONALLY POWERFUL
3
SELINA A FENECH

ABOUT SELINA A. FENECH

Whether it's painting artworks or writing novels, creating fantasy works is Selina's biggest passion. She lives in Australia with her husband and daughter and loves food, gardening, geekery, and all things fantasy.

Find out more about Selina at her official website-

www.selinafenech.com

www.ingramcontent.com/pod-product-compliance
Lightning Source LLC
Chambersburg PA
CBHW020915310726
48980CB00011B/893/J
9780648708087